Ernie leaned in close and said, "So, they really messed up this time letting a prick like you go." Then he slapped Pace twice, very hard and fast.

Pace's ears rang. He took another step back and Ernie grabbed him by the collar, pulled him closer, and hissed in his ear, "Listen to this, killer."

"What?"

"If I ever see you again, I'm going to hurt you so badly you'll never walk again. Do you understand?"

"Yes, Ernie," Pace said.

"Do you?" Ernie slapped him again. "Do you got it good?"

"Yes."

"Right, because there's nothing else I'd like better than to—"

Pace blinked and saw Ernie's eyes roll up into his head and blood begin to rim his nostrils. Ernie's sharply angled features fell in on themselves like wet clay drooping. Pace watched as a hand came up and thumbed two small wads of cloth up Ernie's nose.

Pace cocked his head, puzzled. The hand pressed against Ernie's sternum and kept him propped against the side of the booth.

It took another second before he realized he'd just broken Ernie's nose without actually seeing it happen.

Cover illustration by Caniglia
Design by Aaron Rosenberg
ISBN 978-1-937530-28-0 — ISBN 978-1-937530-27-3 (pbk.)
 For information address Crossroad Press at 141 Brayden Dr., Hertford, NC 27944
www.crossroadpress.com

First edition

NIGHTJACK

TOM PICCIRILLI

Crossroad Press

For Michelle

and Byron and Edgar
my two pals who were there with me through it all

and Criswell
who we lost along the way
Miss you, my boy

and Jack Barbera
more Jack than you can handle!

and in memory of Jack Cady
Jack of All Trades, Master of Each

Part One

Persona Non Grata

one

Are you cured?

They actually ask you that right before you step back into the world. While you're standing there in the corridor, twenty feet from the front door, holding tightly to your little bag of belongings. You've got a change of clothing, five or six prescriptions, the address and phone number of a halfway house. A few items they let you make in shop, what they called the Work Activities Center. Maybe a birdhouse. A pair of gloves that didn't fit.

Pace had an ashtray and a folded-up pair of pajamas that he'd stitched together himself on an old-fashioned sewing machine. It reminded him of the one William Pacella's grandmother had in her bedroom. She used to make clothes for the whole family, had this big sewing basket with two thousand miles of multi-colored threads and yarn. She'd crochet sweaters for him every year for Christmas. Always in the hairnet, wearing black, she'd say, *Non strappi questi, mie mani sono vecchio.* Don't rip these, my hands are old. Pacella would hug her and hear the click of her poorly-fitted dentures as she pressed her wrinkled lips to his cheek.

Are you cured?

A final test to see if you're really on your toes. Like you might suddenly drop, fling the pajamas aside, and thump your chest with your fists. Cry out, No, I'm still insane, you've found me out, seen through my thin charade, damn your eyes.

But then again, you could never tell, it had probably happened before.

So they escort you back to your room, unfold your pajamas, put the ashtray back on the nightstand, and get your slippers ready for your feet again. You step into the lounge area and all the other headcases look at you like the prize screw-up you are. Sort of laughing while they say, You botched the question, didn't you. We practiced and rehearsed but you went and told them the truth, that you were still nuts. The hell's the matter with you?

his voice either. It said, almost buoyantly, "Fine."

Dr. Brandt smiled at Pace, the condescension mixed with something else. Fear maybe, or disappointment. Like she missed the man he was before she got her hands on him.

Her face was one of those sculptures that looked too perfect to be real. So beautiful it had a kind of awful magnificence that had enthralled him from the beginning. It didn't have so much to do with her looks as it did with what lurked beneath. A kind of force he connected with even though he couldn't see it and didn't know what it was.

It made him ache. Her prim gait, the angle and curve of her thigh beneath the plaited skirt. The thrust of her breasts under the suit jacket. If her hair was in a bun he'd be living out a porn movie scenario—they hit the music and she pulls the ribbon. The hair comes loose and with a casual flinch the jacket and skirt fall to the floor. Except her hair was never in a bun.

The first time he'd seen her he was just waking up in the hyper-white hospital room, strapped into this funky straitjacket that was tied to stainless steel railings surrounding the bed.

It was supposed to induce calm, revert you to the pre-natal lull of the womb. Give you the feeling that you were weightless, hanging there in mid-air. Like you might wake up unable to move and actually feel good about it. Just turn your chin aside and smile at the three doctors and two burly attendants standing around waiting to pummel the shit out of you if you got out of line.

Dr. Maureen Brandt introducing herself by name while she flicked a fingernail against a syringe, making sure there were no air bubbles. Pace looked down and saw he was completely covered by the straitjacket, even his feet. The only place she could push the plunger was into his neck.

Unless your mother had a significantly fucked-up pregnancy, this was not the pre-natal lull of the womb.

The biggest irony here: He'd voluntarily committed himself.

"Are you sure you're all right, Will?" she asked as they hit the front door. He was back in the present. He had some trouble keeping himself focused on the here and now.

She carried her briefcase with a sort of haughty air, swinging it a little. Five pounds of notes, files, charts, digital video, and transcribed interviews. Two years of his life distilled into the most boring reading anybody would ever have to suffer through. Every third word something you'd have to run to the Psychiatrist's Dictionary to look up. His life, all his many lives, all the many *hims*, laid out like tacked Luna moths.

"Yes," Pace answered. "I'm fine."

It was drizzling. They headed down the cement walkway to the guard station. The guy in the tiny booth perked up when he saw Pace coming. He stood with a hand on his taser, hoping he'd get to yank it and fire some current into an escapee's ass.

Pace wondered if it would affect him, the way he felt. Maybe it would wake him up some.

They entered the booth. Dr. Brandt still had to sign reams of release forms. Every piece of paper saying that Pace was sane, or if he wasn't, she'd take responsibility for it.

Talk about ego.

Smiling like she was thinking, Sure, if this guy goes Ginsu crazy, I'm responsible, you come slap me around for it when someone else winds up dead.

"You want an escort to the train station, Doctor Brandt?" the guard asked.

"That won't be necessary, Ernie."

Thunder murmured. The rain began to pelt down a little harder, in spurts. Ernie glared at Pace because the secret was out. There really was somebody named Ernie who hadn't climbed Kilimanjaro or lived with a banana-head in a basement apartment on Sesame Street.

This was the Ernie you got. The guy glowering like he wanted to beat you to death with a ball-peen hammer. That was all right, it was easy to understand why. Pace's room on the ward was three times bigger than this little booth Ernie practically lived in all year round. Made you wonder who was the lunatic.

While Dr. Brandt went through the paperwork, Ernie pressed a hand to Pace's chest and shoved him out of the booth and into the rain. Pace dropped his bag of belongings at his feet. He heard the ashtray he made in Work Activities break against the cement.

Ernie leaned in close and said, "So, they really messed up this time letting a prick like you go." Then he slapped Pace twice, very hard and fast.

Pace's ears rang. He took another step back and Ernie grabbed him by the collar, pulled him closer, and hissed in his ear, "Listen to this, killer."

"What?"

"If I ever see you again, I'm going to hurt you so badly you'll never walk again. Do you understand?"

"Yes, Ernie," Pace said.

"Do you?" Ernie slapped him again. "Do you got it good?"

"Yes."

"Right, because there's nothing else I'd like better than to—"

Pace blinked and saw Ernie's eyes roll up into his head and blood begin to rim his nostrils. Ernie's sharply angled features fell in on themselves like wet clay drooping. Pace watched as a hand came up and thumbed two small wads of cloth up Ernie's nose.

Pace cocked his head, puzzled. The hand pressed against Ernie's sternum and kept him propped against the side of the booth.

It took another second before he realized he'd just broken Ernie's nose without actually seeing it happen.

Sometimes you were idle even when you were moving—like falling inside a dream. Sometimes you were in motion when you thought yourself immobile, like now. It got confusing.

Pace stuck his hands in his jacket pockets and felt that the lining had been torn out. That's what he'd crumpled and jammed up Ernie's nose.

Ernie started to slump but the hand came back and braced him again.

Dr. Brandt exited the security booth and said, "Thanks, Ernie," without looking too closely at him. She had her head down against the rain. Pace picked up his bag with his pajamas and broken ashtray and stepped in line beside her as they proceeded down the block in the direction of the train station. Ernie slid down the wall.

She said, "Will, is anything wrong?"

"No."

The sound of Ernie hitting the ground and falling over into the mud was muffled by the rising wind. Pace thought, I should be laughing. Why aren't I laughing?

"You're sure?"

"I am."

"Okay then. I don't want to push."

"You're not pushing."

"You have parameters. You have your safety zone. If I'm encroaching, simply inform me."

"You're not encroaching on my safety zones," he said. The fuck are safety zones?

Maybe he wasn't laughing because the rain reminded Pace of Jane,

William Pacella's murdered wife. He held his palm out and watched it fill up and spill over. Pacella and his wife had spent a lot of time together in the rain, out east on Long Island, down at the south shore sailing and walking on the beach. He caught a glimpse of the wife's face wreathed in flame, her lips melting off. She was trying to say his name, but the flesh ran into her mouth and she had to spit it free.

Another moment passed before Pace noticed he'd stopped and Dr. Brandt had continued walking and was way ahead of him standing at the corner, staring back.

There were always eyes on you, and then they went and wrote on your chart that you were paranoid.

He caught up and said, "Sorry, shoelace was untied."

"Let's go."

They continued on and the subtle tension between them grew thicker. Maybe it was sexual in nature. Perhaps he hated her for what she'd done to him, the things he couldn't fully remember. Worse things than the needle in the neck. His mind seemed to be made of flitting images, clips of a history that warned him not to delve too deep. Funny how your head tried to protect you, to keep you outside your own skull.

Three blocks away, the train station loomed through the gray afternoon. It was so close to the hospital because back in the early forties they used to route thousands of shell-shocked vets to Garden Falls from all across the country. There were plaques and photos all over the hospital showing guys fighting in the Pacific Theater, holding up American flags, getting decorated by Eisenhower.

She was going to hit him with a trick question soon.

She carried an umbrella but hadn't opened it yet. What the hell did that tell you about her? What symbol did you take away from it? That she thought she was dirty and needed to wash herself clean? Water is a birth sign—did she want children? He could imagine what the psych books would say. If it was Pace standing there with the folded umbrella in a downpour, you could bet your disability check the doctors would have something to say about it, happy as hell to see such a display. Like spotting the pervert who keeps forgetting to zip his fly.

She kept talking and he answered by nodding and uhm hmming. She explained to him what would be necessary for him to stay healthy. How often he needed to take his pills, how the halfway house would be run. He would have to be in by seven p.m. every night, before dark. He couldn't drink. The job they'd found him was some kind of factory work in a fish cannery.

She talked non-stop the whole way to the station. She kept looking back over her shoulder, checking all around, and he started doing the same thing. Now what was the matter? The streets were empty. Nothing but a couple of colorless motels and closed shops lining the road. Just enough of a burg for the families of the patients to buy the necessities for their ill children, schizophrenic wives, bipolar husbands, over-tranqed parents. You had to wonder about a town whose main source of income was the import of psychotics.

Dr. Brandt made a joke about the factory where he'd can the fish. It wasn't funny. He heard himself responding to her animatedly, and even with some sardonic humor. It struck him as funny and he hacked out a guffaw. A low, flat sound almost evil in its implication. She turned her head and looked at him, and he smiled pleasantly.

The trick question, here it was.

"Will, what's the first thing you're going to do when you get to the halfway house?"

This one you had to be careful with.

You couldn't say get laid, get drunk, get high, take a shit, call some friends from the time before you were sick. You couldn't tell her you wanted to lie in bed and stare at the ceiling until the roof peeled back and you saw a hundred faces peering down at you. You couldn't admit to your rage. You couldn't go chat with the other lunatics and plan the revolution. Couldn't mention Jane, say how he wanted to see her grave, wail and rip out chunks of weeds from around her headstone. Come back and teach Ernie a few manners. Kill anybody in the Ganooch syndicate he'd missed before.

"Will?"

"Yes?"

"Tell me what you're going to do."

Her voice had a shrill, anxious quality to it, but he sensed it had nothing to do with him. She was nervous all right, but about what? A flicker of fear filled her eyes and then dispersed. Her smile was rigid and sexless. He got the feeling she was asking questions that didn't matter to her.

He said, "Introduce myself to the administrator of the house, have an early dinner, read the newspaper and catch up on the sports scores"—sports were okay, current events weren't—"and get a good night's sleep before work in the fish cannery tomorrow. I've got to be there nine a.m. sharp."

It was a good answer. You couldn't say you were going to sit on the bed and read the Bible all night, even if you really were. There was too much of a chance that they'd think you might start hearing the voice of God coming out of the paperboy's ass, run around shooting people in their naughty bits.

Again, the flash of disappointment in Dr. Brandt's expression even though he knew he'd given her what she wanted. She nodded sadly, her wet hair flapping around her shoulders.

Christ, if they didn't beat you with the meds then they went and did it with this vague look of shame. He was obviously doing something wrong here, but he couldn't figure out what it was.

"Do you miss teaching?" she asked.

"Teaching?"

"You remember. We've talked about this. You used to be a high school teacher. You taught twelfth-grade English literature."

"Yes, I know. And no, I don't miss it. Not much."

When they got to the train station, the place was empty. Water puddled around them on the tile floor as she visibly relaxed and even allowed herself a relieved smile.

He grinned back at her feeling very stupid. What the hell, let's stand around and be happy, tomorrow I start canning fish for the rest of my life. The joy can't be contained.

She took his hand and squeezed. He tightened his fingers around hers and thought about how weak he'd become, even if he had broken Ernie's nose and hadn't quite seen it. Once his hands had been strong, he thought. Almost unbelievably so.

Perhaps it was true. These fists weren't entirely his anymore. Maybe they never had been.

Dr. Brandt led him over to the automatic ticket booth and she started punching numbers and feeding bills into the machine. He wondered if he should pay, but he didn't know if he had a wallet or any money on him. He stuck a hand in his pants pocket and pulled free a folded piece of paper.

The note, written in a ornate cursive handwriting, read:

Don't take any more of your medication, no matter what they tell you. Protect Doctor Brandt, she's in danger. They all are. Remember Cassandra and Kaltzas and Pythos. The dead will follow.

Dr. Brandt couldn't get one of the bills to work in the machine. It kept spitting the dollar back out at her. Her fingers trembled. "Oh, damn."

"Flatten it."

"It is."

"Uncurl the edges," he said.

"They are."

Pace shrugged. That was about it so far as his ability to help went. He wasn't sure where they were going, which button she intended to push for the tickets.

Where did they can fish? He'd never seen a fish cannery before.

The things you had to worry about, one second to the next. Didn't they have robot slaves to do that sort of shit yet?

A scraping sound drew his attention to the left.

He turned and, shoving his hair from his eyes, watched as three figures rose from the corners of the waiting area. A girl scuttling out from beneath a distant bench, two men unfolding from behind the ATM across the station. Even muggers would never lower themselves to hide in such spots. Nobody in their right minds would.

He tapped Dr. Brandt on the shoulder and she said, "The edges are uncurled!"

"Don't worry about that now."

"I hate these stupid things."

"Forget that."

For a moment the station seemed filled with people. A cacophony of voices and noise erupted around him. Pace bit back a yelp and steadied himself against the side of the ticket machine.

The benches and aisles suddenly overflowed with people and animals. Wings flapped past, brushing his neck. A dog howled forlornly. A woman with blue skin and obsidian eyes began writing flaming runes in the air. A nun was running around with a yardstick screaming, "Don't eat paste!" Kids laughed. An Indian with lengthy braids twirled a pair of six-shooters and aimed here and there, practicing taking the tops of skulls off. There were others Pace couldn't focus on, who moved in and out of his vision, shifting and fluctuating. Blurred colors and activity swept across the station, through his head, and appeared to reach some kind of a peak as he went to one knee, then stopped altogether.

Dr. Brandt couldn't handle wrestling with her dollar bills anymore and started checking the bottom of her purse for coins. "Maybe I have enough change."

"Really, that doesn't matter anymore."

The three figures that had climbed from their hidden corners continued forward, faces unclear as they approached. His eyes were focused, everything else was distinct, except for their faces. They came at him sort of frolicking, what they used to call gamboling when people would do that sort of thing. Silently easing nearer. Features dim and clouded, but their names somehow known to him.

Pia.

Faust.

Hayden.

The closer they got, the more obscured their features became. Pace stepped out in front of Dr. Brandt. Change fell to the floor and she said, "Will?"

"I think we should leave."

"What?"

"The fish cannery is going to have to do without me."

She turned and the three figures slid past him and were on her. Pace thought, This is why she was afraid, she must've been expecting this. He shook his head. But if that were true, then why didn't she let Ernie escort her? Why didn't she just give me a train ticket to the halfway house and drop me off at the curb?

Dr. Brandt let out a shout—a strangely feminine sound that was part annoyance, part indignation. He threw a wild punch and missed all three of the intruders, no easy achievement considering how close they were to him. Somebody took one of his wrists and somebody else took the other.

"My God," Pia said. "He's so slow."

"He's not going to be any good to us in this state," Faust said. "Our father who art inhibited."

"He can hear you just fine though," Pace told them.

Hayden twisted Pace's arm. "There was a time when nobody could put a hand on you, if you didn't want it there."

"When was that?" Pace asked, genuinely curious.

"You were stupid to let them do this to you."

"I think I might have to agree."

He looked at where the guy's nose would probably be, waiting for his hands to snap out and break it, but they didn't. He expected Dr. Brandt to scream or start speaking in that cold, indifferent way, but she didn't. He couldn't figure out what was going on and kept hoping something else would happen that he wouldn't be responsible for. Something that might reveal a truer nature.

Faust almost came into view for a moment before fading again. The faceless figure approached, inch by inch. Without features it managed to peer into Pace's eyes and say, "Ah, our father who art indifferent. I think they may have cured him."

two

His first week in Garden Falls he spent mostly in the straitjacket, tied to the bed for twelve to fourteen hours at a clip. Dr. Brandt kept shooting him in the neck with something that calmed him enough so they could let him loose most of the evening.

Pace would wander the corridors of the ward wearing a blue bathrobe Jane had bought William Pacella for Christmas four years earlier. There were matching slippers somewhere at the back of his closet at home. He kept wanting somebody to bring them to him, but he couldn't form the words. Whenever he tried to speak he would drool on himself, and the crystalline fury within him would continue to grow beneath the docile exterior. Some outrages can never be forgiven.

Garden Falls had hallways so bright that they made you flinch, like you were dying and starting to head into the light. All you wanted to do was scream it wasn't your time yet.

That first week, the cops kept stopping in and questioning him. They'd come in pairs, detectives with gold shields, mostly older guys, from some kind of special mob-related task force. Six in total. Each team asking him the same questions. Pace answered everything the same way.

They asked about some guy named Big Joe Ganucci, called himself the Ganooch. Pace said he'd heard the name before, in the papers, but that was all. Inside himself something shuddered with a crazy glee.

The detectives had a prescribed way of interviewing him. All three pairs asked the same questions in the same fashion. First about the Ganooch, then what they called the Ganucci crime family. Then they mentioned the fire at the restaurant and Jane's death, and then they talked about his burns. As soon as he started discussing his scars they asked him if he knew how to use a serrated Trident field knife with a stacked micarta handle.

Pace said he didn't even know what a serrated Trident field knife with a stacked micarta handle was or how to use one or where he might get one. The cops always leaned in when he said that, searching his eyes. He stared back at them, complacent, bearing his truth, and again there would be that tremor within himself, somebody giggling.

The detectives would thank him for his time and shake his hand. All six of them eventually. It seemed very important that they each make some kind of contact and squeeze his hand as hard as they could, trying to crush it. Every time he let out a pained gasp and flinched away. The cops would try to hide their smug smiles, but they couldn't keep the arrogance out of their faces.

Once he woke up in his room seated at the table with these strong plastic cuffs tying his ankles to the legs of the metal chair. Dr. Brandt sat on the other side of the table watching him, jotting notes, already involved with a conversation that Pace was only now coming in on. She said, "You don't remember?"

"What don't I remember?"

"Why you're here."

"No."

"We think you've...hurt several people."

"You think so? You don't know?"

"At this point the police aren't certain. That's why they've been interviewing you so frequently."

"Isn't it a violation of my civil rights to be held here then?"

Dr. Brandt smiled at Pace, that same condescension mixed with that same something else. Jesus, she must've really practiced it. Her face, so lovely it had become a kind of devastation. Between moments of falling in love with her he thought, this lady is going to destroy me, or I'm going to snuff her. He looked over the side of the table at the curve of her thigh beneath the plaited skirt. The pulse in his ankles throbbed against the plastic cuffs. "You're under extreme emotional duress. And you signed a voluntary committal."

"I did? When?"

"When you were brought in."

"While I was under extreme emotional duress? Wouldn't that nullify the 'by choice' quotient of the word 'voluntary'?"

Dr. Brandt said nothing, but her smile reached her eyes and grew more authentic.

"I think you folks are definitely exploiting the situation and abusing my civil rights," Pace said.

"Do you feel persecuted?"

"Only to the extent that I'm currently tied to a chair."

"That's for your own protection as well as our staff and the other patients."

He touched his throat and felt the bruises and needle pricks there. He thought if Jane were here right now, she'd probably break Dr. Brandt's jaw. It was a soothing image for a second, until the stink of burning flesh filled his nostrils. He turned his head aside and closed his eyes. When he opened them again, Dr. Brandt was in a different position. Time had clearly passed. He couldn't tell how much. He wondered if it was the same day, the same conversation. The drugs they were pumping into him were fouling up his sense of time. It was called *aphasia*, and they were giving it to him.

He took the chance that only a minute had passed by. "Who am I supposed to have hurt?"

"I'm not at liberty to say."

"Who is?"

She cocked her head. "Pardon?"

"Who is at liberty to say?"

"I'm not at lib—" She cut herself short, caught her bottom lip between her teeth and worked it back and forth A defensive, delaying tactic. It stymied her, being forced to repeat herself. "We'll get to that later."

"So you're not at liberty to tell me who I'm supposed to have hurt which has, consequently, nullified my civil rights?"

If you said the term "civil rights" enough times you can break down anybody working in a state-run facility.

Dr. Brandt shifted in her seat and cleared her throat. Another sign of distress. "You also attacked one of the orderlies."

Using the word "also" to denote a separation of circumstance, community, and situation. So, presumably, he hadn't only injured a member of the staff.

"Why would I hurt one of the orderlies?"

"He said something you didn't like."

"Which was?"

"I won't repeat it."

Pace let out a sigh. It was easy to get the feeling that she liked keeping him in the dark, tied down, powerless.

"Well, if I didn't like what he said, then I'll surmise I was provoked."

"Do you remember doing it?" she asked.

"No."

"You're sure?"

"Yes. Did it have something to do with a knife?"

She couldn't write that down fast enough, hunched over her pad circling and underlining words. "Why would you say that?"

"It was important to the police."

"No, it wasn't about the knife. Not directly."

"Indirectly?"

"In a manner of speaking."

If you weren't already confused before you went into the nuthatch, they sure did everything they could to baffle the shit out of you once you were inside.

Pace concentrated and fought backward through the fog inside his head. Memories surged up, snippets of images and voices, but it was like chasing snowflakes. Every time he got close to one it evaporated or disappeared into the storm. He squinted, screwed his face, and dropped his chin to his chest. Jane whispered in his ear, Will, don't let them do this to you.

Yeah, he remembered it now.

The orderly's name was friggin' Brutus, if you could believe it. He was six-feet-two and went two-forty of muscle going to fat. He demanded that everybody call him Brutus. It was some kind of badge with him, a sign of toughness. Who knew what the hell it meant, but he insisted on it even from the most delusional patients.

There were old women on the ward who would shuffle past, smiling at him like a long-lost grandson, calling him Johnny or Fred or Erasmus. This Brutus, he'd get right into their withered faces and snarl at these righteous elderly ladies, Call me Brutus, you loony old bags.

He had this thing where he'd lean against the wall and actually sniff at a pretty nurse as she went by, get her to giggle, then mock the patients to amuse her. Corner some schizophrenic who thought rats were gnawing at his belly, rats with the face of his father, his daddy chewing through his bellybutton. The nurse going, Tee hee hee.

Brutus grinning while the schizo son of a bitch stared in terror at his own stomach. Brutus pretending his fingers were the mouths of vermin, then running his hands over the schiz's skin. The nurse going, Tee hee hee. Brutus would squeak and hiss like he was a rat, and the patient would suck air deeper and deeper into his lungs getting ready to screech. Then Brutus and the girl would skirt into a corner and the schiz would shriek about his father crawling all over him tearing his guts out.

The nurse going, Tee—

Fed up with it, Pace threw himself at Brutus one day, but he didn't know how to fight. He held his hands up in front of himself and this Brutus, he just laughed and took a step forward and hit Pace five times hard in the guts. Pace threw up on himself and staggered around in a daze. Brutus smashed him in throat, clipped his chin, and threw another punch that would've broken Pace's neck if it had connected.

But it didn't. Pace was already on the ground by then, staring up, knowing that in the next thirty seconds or so he was going to be beaten pretty fucking badly, maybe to death. They hired maniacs to look after the lunatics.

Odd, the way you meet yourself. Pace didn't know it before then, but he had a guy named Jimmy Boyd living inside him, a welterweight born in Dublin in 1883. Jimmy's family moved to Pittsburgh a decade later and by the time Jimmy was twelve he was working the mines alongside his father and two older brothers.

Jimmy Boyd was embarrassed by how poorly Pace fought and how easily he bled and folded up. It was a question of manhood, always struggling to get back onto your feet.

Boyd had fought such Hall of Famers as Joe Blackburn and Harry Greb, and in 1906 he'd lost a fifteen-round decision to John "Honey" Mellody, whose left jab Boyd couldn't weave away from. A year later, at the Portland Athletic Club show, during the ninth round of a feature bout, Boyd killed Douglas Burke with two stiff punches over Burke's heart.

Pace said, How about if you handle this one, Jimmy?

Jimmy said, I been jest waitin' fer the chance, boyo.

Jimmy Boyd rolled over, propped himself up with one hand, and jumped to his feet. His teeth were full of blood as he grinned and raised his fists. He looked at the clumsy orderly and said, "All right, son, would ye like to lay another one to this chin now? I'll wager my dog's ass ye won't be able."

The other wrong answer was when you told them, Yes, I'm fine. Then they knew you were still fucked.

What they really wanted to hear you say was that you were sick and you'd always be sick, and you knew you'd always be sick but that you'd make an effort to stay stable by taking your medication regularly. That you'd attend the outpatient group therapy sessions, keep in touch, and if you had any serious troubles along the way, you'd check yourself right back in for a short-term observation period.

So Pace told them that.

He meant it too, and thanked them for all they'd done. Humbly grinning at the nurses, the guards, the other staffers of Garden Falls Psychiatric Facility. All of them moving off down the hallways, giving him the stink eye that said, Whatever happens, just don't come back here. We have enough trouble.

All right, so he was almost back on the street. He looked left and right down the corridor once more, feeling a little lost. He was alone now. It was a condition he didn't like and couldn't seem to get used to.

He started for the front door and stopped. He was supposed to wait here for somebody. For a minute he couldn't remember who, and then—as she stepped from her office and came at him—he did. His shrink, the assistant Chief of Staff, Dr. Maureen Brandt, was at his side, moving in sync with him as they walked to the exit, shoulder to shoulder.

Dr. Maureen Brandt. The name didn't exactly slide off the tongue. He'd worked it around in his mouth for almost two years now. She often frowned when he said her name because he usually rested on it an extra second, as if he had to remember it all over again. She'd jot notes on her pad and look up at him without raising her chin, her dark gaze burrowing into his head. It wasn't exactly an unpleasant feeling.

"How are you doing, Will?" she asked.

All the nutjobs on the ward always said fine because they didn't have the wit to say anything else. The candor had been burned out of them with primal scream therapy. Three in the morning and these idiots are practicing their prehistoric shrieks, regressing back to cavemen. Hauling ass down the hallways trying to escape the mastodons and saber-toothed tigers. This was supposed to help them with the issues they had with their parents, the oily uncles who took them into the bathroom. Instead, it just started the whole zoo shrieking.

Pace opened his mouth and the word wasn't his word. The voice wasn't

Brutus went, "Wha'?"

Jimmy missed the days of slugging it toe to toe with Honey Melody and all the rest. He wanted to make this last for a while but thought it might just be better to get it over with quick and get on with his day.

All he needed was three jabs and four right crosses before Brutus was unconscious with pulped lips and dislocated jaw.

The nurse going, Yeee ahhh AHH.

Pace opened his eyes. Jane whispered in his ear, Will, hold on, hold on. There's still one more you need to finish.

"You're here because you're ill," Dr. Brandt said.

"Well yeah," Pace said, "I figured that much."

"And you're considered dangerous."

"By you?"

"Yes," she admitted. "You're a threat to yourself and others."

"But I can tell you're not afraid."

"I am, but you're my responsibility."

"What did you want to do before this?" he asked.

"Do? What do you mean?"

"When you were a child. No little girl wants to grow up to be a psychiatrist, right? What did you want to do?"

"Be a veterinarian. I lived on a farm with my aunt and uncle for a short time when I was a child. It made a great impression on me at the time. What did you want to do?"

He knew she'd turn it around, but even so, she'd given up a portion of herself. If he ever asked her a question, the question came back around to him. It limited his curiosity. "I don't remember."

"You told me once you wanted to be a rodeo clown. You could make people laugh and also save lives. The danger also appealed to you."

"A kid doesn't understand," he said, thinking of her on a farm, feeding newborn calves with a baby bottle. Tossing handfuls of chicken feed, tending to wounded animals. It also rang some bells, struck a few deep chords. Why would she go live with her aunt and uncle? He wanted to ask more questions.

If he actually had signed a voluntary committal then maybe he really did need help and had actually recognized the fact. But which him—which of the many *hims*—had done it? "You going to fix me up?"

"That's my intention."

"When?"

“Soon, I hope.”

“Fine,” Pace told her, smiling, his hands flat on the table in front of him. He reached down, grabbed the broken plastic cuffs he’d snapped with his leg muscles, and handed them to her. “Let’s get on with it. I still have someone I need to kill, and I’m sort of in a hurry here.”

Dr. Brandt going pale, making notes, sweat on her brow, dripping.

three

Pia could barely handle the loose steering on the '78 Chevy she was driving. The bald tires squealed every time she shifted lanes or hit an exit ramp, the car shimmying wildly on the wet roads. Faust sat in the passenger seat, reading all the road signs out loud and muttering oddly phrased prayers. He glanced left and right because two angels, one fallen and one not, accompanied him everywhere.

Pace sat in back between Hayden and Dr. Brandt. Hayden turned to him and said, "Jesus Christ, you're breaking my heart. Aren't you glad to see us?"

He still couldn't make out their faces yet, but the back of Pia's head was in perfect focus. Everything was clear until she angled her chin aside, and then her features blurred. He reached out once and stroked her short black hair, noting how it curled slightly at her neck. She said nothing, did nothing. He looked in the rearview trying to make eye contact with her, but there wasn't any reflection, just a watery haze that flowed and eddied.

Dr. Brandt clutched his hand, but not in distress—he'd been mistaken about her being afraid of them. She'd not only been expecting them, but had actually been hoping for them, though she didn't seem to want to admit it to herself. She had plenty of her own barriers. He thought, This lady here, she's got some troubles of her own.

He tightened his grip and said, "I won't let anything happen to you."

"I know that," she told him.

Pace kept flashing in and out, maybe going into a trance state, maybe just napping during the long drive. He awoke to himself once and his heart was hammering and he was clammy all over. His mind felt a little clearer, as if his body was trying to boil off the meds and force them out of his system. Somewhere inside himself there was a lama from Bhutan who could stick a spear through his arm and, without touching it, urge it free inch by inch without bleeding.

Faust turned, leaned over the wide headrest, and asked, "Do you know who I am? Do you recognize me?"

"Not really," Pace said.

"What's that mean 'not really'?"

"I know it's you, Faust, but I can't see you very well. You've got no face."

"I don't have a face?"

"No."

Faust, perhaps smiling, a kind of quelled laughter coming from him.

Hayden said, "So much for them curing him. We're lucky. He's still a wacky son of a bitch."

Dr. Brandt ground her back teeth together, the sound of bone grating on bone filling the car. "It's a byproduct of his treatment."

"A coerced, discriminating hysterical blindness?" Faust said. "Wouldn't that merely be another form of elicited hallucination?"

"It was necessary," she told him.

Pace waited for further explanation but it didn't come. She didn't act aggressive in any way, as if afraid to behave like the family psychologists with their own daytime shows. They were popular on the ward, everybody gathering around the television and tossing empty plastic pill cups around the room. Watching the puffy doctors who'd bellow into crying women's faces and grab abused wives by the shoulders, shaking them like they wanted to smack the shit out of them in front of thirty million viewers. The ward would go bananas, listening to these guys yelling, "You want to be a victim! He beats you because you subconsciously welcome the attacks! Take back your life! You're allowing this tragedy to enter your home!"

Like you could just put a sign on your window, No Trauma Allowed.

Like you could ever control yourself.

"It's important we discuss this situation," Dr. Brandt said.

Pia's hair shook back and forth, curls swirling down over unseen ears. "Not yet."

"Why not?"

"Will isn't here yet. Not all the way."

Pace faded out for a while. When he came back they were in the Bronx heading down into Manhattan. Faust was still reading the signs. "Henry Hudson Parkway South. George Washington Bridge, New Jersey, Bear Right. There's an arrow going to the right. Tollbooth Ahead. Slow Down. Radar in Use."

"Would you please stop that," Pia told him. "Just sit there and be quiet."

"If I don't help, you might drive us into a river."

"I'm not going to drive us into—"

"Off a bridge. Our father who art insatiable. We could pile up on the parkway and kill entire families on vacation, don't you realize that? Is that what you want? Children mutilated, infants—"

"Hey," Hayden said, "Mister Jolly, how about if you shut the hell up for now, huh?"

Pace looked in the rearview again and saw the vague outline of Pia's face in the wavering drift and swell of silver. She turned her head as she changed lanes and he saw a slight tinge of pink that might be her cheek. He reached out and touched it. Her skin was downy and cool. No one said anything, not even Pia.

She made good time easing through the city, tires screeching on occasion. She knew how to drive in bad weather and in city traffic, boxed in by taxis and delivery trucks. The rain tapered off.

It took another forty-five minutes to ease down to the Lower East Side, an area of Alphabet City that hadn't been hit by neighborhood revitalization efforts yet. She parked in front of the kind of block they'd be doing a Broadway musical about in a few years. The quick-witted, lovable pimp and the brazen, courageous methadone addict. The ventriloquist priest who sang about tax exemption and junk bonds with his look-alike puppet.

Dr. Brandt grabbed him by the wrist. "Will?"

"Yeah. I'm all right."

"You look pale."

"My head is sort of spinning."

"Take your medication."

"No!" Hayden shouted. "We need him back."

"Not like that. Not when he gets bad."

"That's exactly what we need. You know that. It's why you're here."

"I've made a mistake," she said.

"Maybe so, but there's nothing you can do about it now." Hayden opened the Chevy door. "Let's go."

The building stood flanked by shooting galleries, meth and heroin addicts leaning against brick walls and bumping into lampposts. Two blocks west were museums, art galleries, and apartments going for the mid-seven figures, but right here was squatters' row.

Walking slowly with determination, Dr. Brandt appeared set in her ways now, as if she'd thrown in with the losing team but wanted to see it through to the end. Pia led them up the front steps of a brownstone with most of its windows boarded.

Dr. Brandt asked, "So is this where you've been staying the last four months?"

"Most of the time," Pia said. "Here or other places like it." A note of pride chimed in her voice. This life had hardened her for a specific purpose. Pace wondered what it might be, and what role he was supposed to play toward fulfilling it.

He stepped up against Dr. Brandt and felt the brush of her breasts, and something in his chest ignited once more. He wondered, Am I in love?

Pia unlocked the front door and Pace saw the hint of pink once more. He couldn't help himself and had to touch it again. Pia remained silent and Dr. Brandt let out a slightly mournful sigh.

Here he was, stuck between two women—one utterly, perfectly beautiful, and the other without a face.

Sometimes the symbols and metaphors of your life grew so large and wide that you couldn't avoid them no matter how nutty you were.

Pia hit the lights and the hideous sound of scurrying erupted all around them. Pace couldn't tell if they were rats or roaches, but his stomach tightened. A cereal box on the kitchen table toppled over. Dr. Brandt let out a gasp and took a small step backward directly into Pace's arms. He held her for a moment and she didn't fight, didn't respond. He let her go.

The furnishings had been appropriated from gutters and alleys. A legless couch propped up on bricks, a scarred kitchen table, and hundreds of water-stained books which Faust must've ferreted out of trash bins. A gorgeous leather chair with a tear directly in the center of its back, as if the guy sitting there had been run through with a cutlass.

On the table were Hayden's pads and pens. For years he'd been composing one long letter to his mother, who'd died when he was three. His father had drank himself to death when Hayden was eight. There were no family members to take him in. He was misdiagnosed with an IQ of 62, considered a moron, became a ward of the state, and placed in a home with the mongoloids and mentally challenged.

The day he turned eighteen he walked into the office of the executive director of the institution where he was living, found the IQ test in the filing cabinet, answered the questions on the spot, and even graded himself. One hundred thirty-five. Pretty frickin' good. He told the director that he wasn't stupid, he just had more important things to worry about when he was a kid.

The executive director decided that pretending to be a simpleton in order to live with the mentally disabled proved he was nuts, and immediately shipped Hayden off to Garden Falls. He'd been there nearly five years when Pace met him.

The compulsive letter-writing was a symptom of *hypergraphia*, the obsessive need to write extensive journal entries or missives. Hayden always left the ongoing letter out in the open so somebody, if not his mother, might read it. Pace never did. After Hayden filled up one pad he destroyed it and proceeded to the next.

Pace sat in the leather chair but couldn't get comfortable. He drew his bottles of medication out of his pockets and looked at them.

Dr. Brandt said, "Do you want to take your meds, Will?"

"I guess you're not too worried about me becoming psychologically dependent on drugs."

"They help you."

"They weaken him, you mean," Pia said.

"Are you prepared for what might happen if he goes off them?"

"No, but we have no choice. I thought it was already decided."

"You know he needs them."

Hayden let out a snicker, part distilled cynicism, part little boy fear. "Not as much as we need him."

So, that's the way it was going to be.

Faust circled the small room, once, twice. He brought a hand to the emptiness where a mouth might be, stroking a bottom lip that wasn't there. "Let him decide."

They all stared at Pace. Terrific. He couldn't figure out if the meds would let him see their faces or blank them out totally—body, voice, and memory. He thought of Ernie slapping him. He thought of Brutus punching him. He thought of Jane, burning, reaching out. Her ghost telling him not to die. He thought of the thing inside him that even now was snickering, thinking about blood and kidney pie made with human kidneys.

It was crazy allowing a crazy person to decide whether he should take his pills or not. He wasn't dealing with stable people.

Pace walked to the window and looked out. The street was full of activity. Men seated on the steps of the building, drinking beer, passing a joint back and forth. The meth-heads lay out across the sidewalk. A Chinese delivery boy riding by on a bicycle. Two whores laughing, two others arguing. Cars rolled past slowly. Someone shouting in Spanish.

Remember Cassandra and Kaltzas and Pythos.

The dead will follow.

He took out his pills. You had to give it to science, packing so much dread and possibility into something so small. 200 mgs of magic that slapped foam across your searing brain.

"What do these damn things do?" he asked.

"They help control your dissociative identity disorder."

It certainly sounded like serious fun. Something inside of him was being willfully obtuse, making him ignorant. It didn't want him to remember. "What the hell is that?"

"A condition in which two or more distinctive identities or personality states alternate in controlling your consciousness and behavior."

"Oh. Multiple personality. Yeah."

"That's an outdated term. MPD has been re-designated DID. Dissociative Identity Disorder. Many doctors think it may be a variation of PTSD. Post-Traumatic Stress Disorder. There are other causes and conditions as well. These include head injuries and brain disease. AIDS dementia complex. Epilepsy or other seizure disorders. Identity disturbances in DID result from the patients having split off entire personality traits or characteristics, as well as memories. When a stressful or traumatic experience triggers the reemergence of these dissociated parts, the patient switches—usually within seconds—into an alternate personality."

Pace liked listening to her. "Oh?"

"Some patients have histories of erratic performance in school or in their jobs caused by the emergence of alternate personalities during examinations or other stressful situations. Patients vary with regard to their alternates' awareness of one another."

It was good to know what you had, and what had you. He wondered if he could keep all the anagrams straight, if they had some kind of trick to help you memorize it Doe-Ray-Me style. "I wondered about all the people inside me."

"You still feel them?"

"Yes."

"All of us suffer from it," Faust said.

Dr. Brandt nodded and looked around, like she was fielding questions from an audience. "Many DID patients sometimes have setbacks in mixed therapy groups because other patients are bothered or frightened by their personality switches. But you four—"

Again, she stopped. Never just giving him the answers he wanted, always forcing him to beg for more. And the thing inside him not wanting to hear.

"Us four what?" Pace asked.

"You four accommodate one another."

"You say that like it's a bad thing."

"It is. You make each other sicker."

The name on the prescription bottles was WILLIAM PACELLA. Pace felt heat rising on the back of his neck and he saw Big Joe Ganucci's elderly face, the Ganooch just sitting in his wheelchair in the middle of the room with the sacred heart of Jesus picture on the wall, overlooking the gutted bodies of his bodyguards.

The guy who was giggling inside Pace started toying with a knife.

four

"Tell me again, please, what do these pills do?" he asked.

"They keep you from killing people," Dr. Brandt said.

There it was, finally. The truth laid out, raw and bleeding. "Who would I kill? Who did I kill?"

"I'd prefer not to go into that right now."

Just like a shrink to fuck with you when you were down. He shook his head. "I'd be in jail, not a psych ward. And if I was found not guilty by reason of insanity, which almost nobody ever is, then I couldn't have gone in voluntarily, and I wouldn't have ever gotten out of the Falls."

"The police didn't have enough evidence to indict you."

"Then maybe I didn't do it."

Hayden, letting out a wild burst of laughter that sounded more animal than human, said, "Oh, believe us, you did it."

He remembered Ernie calling him "killer." Pace was recollecting pieces here and there, retaining more without the meds. "Tell me who Cassandra and Kaltzas and Pythos are."

"You're beginning to remember them?" Pia asked. "It's a long story."

He stared into the void where her eyes should be and said, "Give me an abbreviated version in thirty seconds, okay?"

She let out a deep breath and the scent of her lips, which he knew well, wafted against the back of his throat. "We were on the ward with Cassandra Kaltzas, daughter of a Greek shipping magnate." The anxiety ratcheted her voice up an octave. "Are there any other kinds of magnates? Aren't they all goddamn 'shipping magnates'? What the hell is a magnate anyway?"

"Faster," Pace said.

"Cassandra was beaten and raped on the ward four months ago. Kaltzas thinks one of you did it, and that I helped."

"Helped?"

"I didn't like her very much. I was jealous. Sick, you know? I have mother issues. Sister issues, really. Well, mother and sister issues. I wasn't on the ward for my goddamn health. Anyway, the bastard sent men to visit us. They asked questions like they were our friends, but they had us marked from the beginning. They knew all about us, everything in our files, all about our lives. We think they were planning to kidnap or kill us. That's why we skipped from the Falls."

"You're sure about this? It wasn't just paranoia?"

"It's always paranoia, but yes, we're sure."

"How did you escape?"

"I fucked the guards. We got out."

Pace thought about how many attendants there were between the ward and the front gate. He counted four. "All of them? One after the other?"

"Where's the challenge in that? No. Collectively."

Jesus Christ. "Ernie? You screwed Ernie?"

"I don't know their names."

"I hate Ernie. And Brutus."

"I hated all of them. I have father and brother issues too. And men in general. Well, men and women."

Pace thought about it some more. "What about forensic evidence?"

"From the guards?"

"From the rape."

"There was no ejaculation," Dr. Brandt said. "No sample of semen to test against your DNA."

"Then how do you know it even happened?"

"Severe vaginal bruising. Rectal bleeding. Scratches, welts characteristic to sexual molestation."

"Who did she say raped her?"

"She couldn't say anything. The trauma sent her into a fugue state. Her father immediately had her taken back to Greece."

"How many patients were on the ward?"

"Thirty-five," she said.

"So why were we singled out?"

"We don't know, except that it's likely he considers you four the most likely suspects due to your histories."

"Hey," Hayden said, "I never did any evil shit like that."

"Me neither," Faust said.

"I only fuck men," Pia said.

Rape? Pace wondered. Was he even capable of that?

Hayden said, "You might've been getting it on with Cassandra, we don't know, but if you were it wasn't rape. You had a special relationship with her."

"I did?"

"You'll remember soon enough. But because of that bond you shared with her, Kaltzas thinks you might be responsible for what happened."

Dr. Brandt's lovely face screwed up with anguish. Her shoulder muscles tightened. It had to be tough on her, being surrounded by her greatest failures. "No one on the ward is known for violent tendencies. Since you're the only true cases of DID at Garden Falls, it cast greater doubt on you since one of your alternates may have been responsible for such brutality even if your primary personalities weren't."

"It could've been one of the attendants."

"There were three on duty and two night nurses." A hint of embarrassment crept into her voice. "They were busy playing strip poker together."

"They could be covering for each other."

"They're too selfish to cover for anyone. They've all been summarily fired and have charges still pending."

The laughter was trying to work its way up Pace's throat again. He turned to the faceless Faust and asked, "Why didn't I go with you when you ran?"

"You were supposedly in a straitjacket, shackled to your bed in a secured room. Solitary confinement. It's where they put the *tempestuous* cases."

"He was there," Dr. Brandt said. "He was having a bad reaction to his last medication. It was making him very manic. He struggled with the guards, broke one of their arms."

You had layers to your life, and within those layers were other strata. Levels and planes and tiers. You got a hold of one memory and it slipped away in a torrent. There was the person you were before the madness and then the one you became. The many you became.

The man he was now meant nothing except in relation to the one he was an hour ago, and the one he'd be an hour from now. He felt ephemeral, tenuous as tissue paper.

Pace looked at Dr. Brandt. "Four months ago I was shackled and today I walked out?"

"You're perfectly stable when you take your new medication."

Okay, he wasn't stable, but he was right enough to play their game.

"So one of us might be a rapist."

"Or one of our multiples," Faust said.

Hayden laughed bitterly. "That makes about a hundred and thirty-seven suspects. You want to include yetis, aliens, dinosaurs, robots, demons, dogs, or fallen angels, you gotta add another twenty-five or so."

Pace felt the need for contact again and touched Dr. Brandt's wrist. It electrified him, put him back in his body. "Why have you thrown in with them?"

"Alexander Kaltzas holds me accountable as well. For failing to keep his daughter safe in the hospital. For allowing you and Cassandra to have an association."

"So it's not all paranoia? This man is really after us?"

"Yes. I've met him before. And his...his agents visited me at home. He frightens me."

"Worse than we do?"

"Yes."

"Didn't you go to the police? The FBI?"

"They can't do anything without proof."

"Couldn't you go ask help from your friends? Stay with someone?"

"I don't have many close friends."

Pace thought, She's as nutty as any of us.

"And did you allow Cassandra and me to...associate?"

"You were close friends. You were both notably calmer in each other's presence. You were better off together than apart."

He looked out the window at the prostitutes below. In his depths, somebody opened up a doctor's bag and pulled out scalpels and instruments and a heavy leather apron. Pace wondered if he should run. Steal the Chevy and drive through the tunnel and find himself a fish cannery. Stay the course, start slapping back the meds. Forget this little detour ever happened.

"I need sleep."

"It's only three in the afternoon."

He could sense a burgeoning realm of misery building within him, a growing understanding. Within it, he thought, would be design and purpose. Further blood, maybe redemption, perhaps even the reclamation of Jane.

There were two bedrooms in the apartment, a small one with a door and large one without. He knew the three of them would be sharing the mattresses on the floor of doorless room, afraid to be closed in or spend the night too far away from one another.

He walked to the other bedroom. They'd left it for him. There was an old box spring and mattress, but the sheets looked clean. Maybe they planned on giving him Maureen Brandt too, as a sacrifice. They were scared and wanted to appease him.

five

When he awoke, the orange lace of dusk slipped in through a barred window. They were still shouting in Spanish on the street.

Atop the sheet kneeled the blue woman.

Her gills eased open as she breathed, arching above him on the bed, watching him. As she shifted her chain mail dress jangled, crusted with jewels, seashells, and coral. She drew fiery sigils and spells in the air. Arcane symbols and covenants in a sea language that had been chiseled into rock at the bottom of the deepest trenches and abysses of the ocean.

Her black and lidless eyes, like a shark's, somehow retained a great humanity. He sensed her sorrow.

Princess Eirrin, ten thousand-year-old sorceress and heir to the Atlantean throne, one of Pia's alternates.

"You awaken to this world once more," she said in a voice strong enough to be heard even under the frothing waves of the Aegean. She used to show him treasures taken from centuries-old galleon shipwrecks: gems, Roman coins, doubloons, riches from the fallen empires which she used to decorate her throne floor.

Pace said, "Hello Princess, it's been a while."

Beside her sat a panting pug which she stroked with one webbed hand. The dog cocked his head at Pace, climbed up the blankets, and laid his chin on Pace's forearm. This was Crumble, one of Hayden's personalities.

Eirrin undid Pace's shirt and pressed her palm against his chest: it was cool, a bit clammy, soft and meaty like dolphin skin. She moved her nails against the burn scars, tracing their ridges and contours.

"You remind me of another human male I knew millennia ago. Odysseus. He too suffered because he would not bow to a greater fate. The orders of his commanders were not enough to persuade him. He refused to accompany the Greeks to Troy, feigning madness by sowing his fields with salt."

Even imaginary friends could be a little insulting. "Is that what I'm doing? Feigning madness?"

"He eventually complied and, the greatest of all heroes, was cast out upon the ocean. He spent decades on the water with his men, hurled away from Troy by typhoons. I did what I could to help, but my magic failed. It wasn't possible to alter the thread of his destiny. I fear I cannot amend yours."

"Odysseus wouldn't show proper deference to Poseidon," Pace said. "That's why the gods wouldn't let him return home. I have no home to go back to."

"You would if you set aside your blood oath."

"If I could set it aside, it wouldn't be a blood oath."

Eirrin leaned in closer, and he saw himself reflected in the black, prehistoric eyes. "Your vengeance has already been fulfilled."

"Not entirely, Princess."

Crumble barked and licked Pace's face happily. He petted the dog and said, "Good boy, that's a boy." He knew what was really happening—that Hayden was on the bed with his tongue hanging out, grunting and slobbering. But Pace patted the dog's head and felt only fur, the wet cold nose, the fleshy pug wrinkles.

That was his talent, the real genius of his madness. He not only saw the other alternates, he could interact with them. They were as real to him as anyone else in the world.

The door opened again.

Daedalus, with his wings folded, entered. The father who knew not to fly too close to the sun when wearing wax. What your humanities teacher would call a "masculine solar deity" even though Daedalus wasn't a god. Just a poor architect in ancient Greece trying to pay homage to his mad king who saw treason in every act of grandeur.

He said nothing, only wept for his dead son smashed into the sea. The leather straps crossing his muscular chest creaked as he came closer to the bed, the tears running into his knotted beard. The lost father was an alternate of Faust's.

The three of them ringing Pace on the mattress.

This hallowed ceremony meant solely for lunatics, shared only by the damned.

Dr. Maureen Brandt sat on the couch smoking a cigarette. Pace stepped into the small living room and the three faceless figures followed. He sat in the leather chair. She glanced at him once with shamed eyes.

"I'm sorry, Will."

"Don't be.

"You're my patient. Your health and well-being are paramount to me. At least they should be."

"You just got tangled up with us. You can't straighten out our kind of sick."

"With your meds you'll be—"

"They just hold back the storm for a while. But they can't stop it."

A voice from above said, "Do you remember us?"

Pace looked up.

Stuck to the ceiling were three faces staring down at him.

Pia, only twenty, a pale blue-eyed next-door cutie-pie. You took one look at her and you wanted her to care for your fevers when the rains came, cuddle with you under an afghan while the snow piled high against the windows. Elfin, that might be the right word, and she tugged at every heart. Lower lip cocked in a half-grin. Like she knew something you didn't, and she was never going to tell you.

Hayden, always with that expression you just wanted to smack. Sharp nose, chin, and lips, the thrust of thinning black hair knifing down to a widow's peak, everything on the man like a razor, especially his teeth. Only the eyes were misleading, set about a half-inch too far apart. It was understandable why the doctors thought he might be mentally impaired. He was, just not the way they thought.

Faust with the blazing glare of a holy man who wills himself to see God everywhere. Like somebody who'd gone into the desert and eaten honeyed locusts for forty nights, meeting strangers on empty roads, seeing through lies to the heart of every matter. His blue-black beard was flecked with silver. The thick, raised scar on his forehead stood out like a badge of honor. He'd never told anyone how he got it, but the injury brought on temporal lobe epilepsy.

The faces dislodged from the ceiling and gently floated down as if on a breeze, rocking, swirling. Pace kept staring and wondered, If one lands on me, will I become somebody else? Would they possess me even more than they already do now?

"What is it, Will?" Dr. Brandt asked. "What do you see?"

"A hell of a show."

The three faces swept against each other in a ballet of form and ritual. Mischievously they settled on the wrong bodies momentarily before peeling off, twisting in mid-air, and settling squarely onto the proper heads of the three shadowy figures. They affixed themselves there.

And with those features fastened in place now Pace felt himself returning from the faraway place he'd been.

The sense of unbearable speed and insane distances was incredible. He had to tighten his grip on the arms of the chair and champ his teeth on his tongue to keep from crying out. A rush of disjointed memories flooded back into his head.

Dr. Brandt took a long draw on her cigarette and blew smoke toward the floor. She used to do the same thing when she ate lunch by herself, seated on the canopied patio outside the ward, looking lovely and a little pitiful.

Pace looked and saw the cigarette pack in her purse, alongside a paperback copy of *Psychoneurotic Disorders—The Intrusive Past: The Flexibility of Memory and the Engraving of Trauma.*

He said, "Got another?"

"No, this is the last one."

It was more than a white lie. She was testing him, pushing to see which him was going to respond. Like so many other minor temptations, this one had become a dare. No matter how many hoops you jumped through, there were always more to go.

Something happened so fast then that no one saw anything but a smear of motion. The cigarette was gone from her lips and Pace had it between his own.

Faust walked forward but stopped out of arm's reach. "Our father who art incessant."

Pia stepped up and kneeled at the side of the chair, pressed her cheek to his thigh. She let out a wracked sob.

"So," Hayden said. "You're back."

"Most of me," Pace told him. "There's still a lot absent."

"We've missed you, Will."

"I'm not Will."

The cigarette tasted magnificent. It was the first one he'd had in years. He looked at the fiery tip and thought of Jane again, screaming as flames swarmed and swept over her. He nodded. He'd returned from purgatory, right back into hell.

Kaltzas would be watching and now he would know. His men would have had the hospital staked out. They'd have followed behind the Chevy. They'd have parked on the street with high-powered binoculars. That's what the agents of a furious shipping tycoon would do. You weren't going to hide from a magnate with a mad-on, not even in Alphabet City. Now they'd be in the building. Up the steps. Pace heard footsteps in the hallway.

He jumped out of the chair, pressed Maureen Brandt aside and yanked Pia behind him. He had time enough to say, "Down!" before a shotgun went off and the front door exploded.

six

Some of the memories were still there. He knew that the gunner was a kid named Rollo Carpie, a low-level shooter for the no-longer functioning Ganucci syndicate. He'd must've gone freelance. Kaltzas was just being insulting now. Telling Pace, You belong to me. Look, you didn't kill everybody in the organization, there's more bad boys for you to chase around with your fancy knife with the stacked micarta handle. Telling Pace, I own you.

Rollo stepped in through the smoking wood chips. He looked smooth and a bit smarmy for such second-rate muscle. He had half a bottle of mousse in his short black hair so that it looked like polished sandstone. He could fire his shotgun all day long and a strand wouldn't flutter.

Pace stood. He didn't feel rushed at all. The time aphasia struck again, but now it acted in reverse. Everything around him slowed while his thoughts sped up. He plotted the angles and positions and already knew how much force he would need to apply in order to bring Rollo to his knees.

The rage began to take on a familiar shape within him, expanding from the center of his chest and conforming to the contours of his body. Filling and strengthening him. Rollo pumped the shotgun and swung it toward him.

Pace's mind buzzed and simmered with information as he imagined a carefully choreographed waltz of murder. Icy sweat crawled across the landscape of his scars. Somebody inside him started to cry, and someone else laughed.

Funny to see Rollo again after all this time, dressed down in jeans and a leather coat. None of the Ganooch syndicate's charm to him anymore. No silk suit or imported Italian shoes. Even with the perfect hair, you could tell he was having trouble with the downturn his life had taken.

Eye contact wasn't important to most hired muscle. It didn't have to be when you were using a 12-gauge. Rollo turned in Pace's direction, holding the shotgun too high because he didn't want to take the recoil in the gut. Six inches lower and he'd kill everybody in the room. As it was, he was mostly firing toward the ceiling.

Pace covered the distance between them in two steps, grabbing the barrel with his right hand and jerking it hard, yanking Rollo forward.

Being this near to one of the Ganooch boys was like growing closer to his dead wife. A strange, wildly inappropriate warmth filled his groin. He had to squelch the abominable urge to actually hug Rollo Carpie.

Nose to nose, Pace said, "Hello, Rollo. You working on your own now?"

Rollo struggled and gasped, "You know me?"

"I know you."

"No."

"Oh yeah."

"Let go," Rollo whined, trying to shake Pace free and take the shotgun back. "Hey—" Saying it almost politely, as if it might really happen. Like you tell the guy you're trying to kill to drop your weapon so you can shoot him with it, and he actually does it.

Pace's left hand hardly seemed to touch Rollo at all. Even so, the shooter let out a shriek and fell to his knees. Pace whirled the 12-gauge around and whopped Rollo's forehead with the stock, hard but not hard enough to put him all the way under.

A loud, dull thunk resounded across the room. Rollo fell flat on his face and lay there wheezing, eyes rolling in panic.

"Is he Jack?" Hayden cried, cowering behind the couch.

"No, I don't think so," Faust said, stuck somewhere between crouching and rearing. He looked like he was about to start praying against his own better judgment. "Not yet."

"Thank Christ."

"Lower your voice."

"I'm sorry, but I'm understandably nervous, you know!"

"Who's Jack?" Pace asked.

Pia and Dr. Brandt, together behind the leather chair, neither appearing very alarmed, held their gazes on Pace like they planned on writing all this down later.

He stared at them. "What?"

"Nothing," Pia said. "Don't let us stop you. Continue."

He hauled Rollo to his feet, offended by the hair. He slapped the hair a couple of times and it still didn't shift at all. He had met the much-debated immovable object and been defeated by it. That hair, it really got on his fucking nerves.

In a daze, Rollo swooned in Pace's arms so the two of them kind of danced together for a few steps. Reeling, Rollo sagged and made tiny humming noises, sounding like Jane when she and William Pacella went dancing on their first date. It was during a Fourth of July picnic that her whole hometown had come down to the dunes. She'd worn a pleated yellow skirt, and her blonde hair had been like streaming flame in the setting sun, as they swayed by the shore and the water lapped at their feet.

When he was in Garden Falls he used to dance around with the schizoaffectives this way, remembering his earliest days with Jane. Lost inside their own heads, some of them were much better dancers than Jane ever was. Doing dips and spins, occasionally jitterbugging, hucklebucking, bumping, grinding, hustling, disco ducking, everybody in their bathrobes and slippers.

"Wait, wait," Rollo said, out of breath. Actually holding his hands out. Like all you had to do was say wait and the guy you were trying to blow away would just stand there. Rollo had a lot of weird ideas on just how much impact his pleading carried. "It's...it's you. Isn't it you?"

"It's me."

"You're the guy who came through a couple of years ago." Rollo's eyebrows began squirming all over his forehead. "The psycho."

"Don't be rude, Rollo."

"The one who did them all. The whole top-level Ganucci crew, one after the other."

"Not all of them."

"Damn near. The Ganooch, the consigliere, a lot of torpedoes. Hey, hey, I'm not hooked up with them no more!"

"Nobody is."

Jittery, Rollo started flexing his knees, like he had a nice salsa beat going and wanted to dance some more. "Hey, listen, I didn't know it was you. I don't want no trouble—if I'd known, hey—"

The darkness snickered with Pace's throat, coming from an empty alley full of fog, footsteps echoing along the cobblestones, the whores easing closer. "How much did Kaltzas pay you?"

"Who?"

"Alexander Kaltzas."

Going soft, wanting to flip over and show his belly, Rollo hung there limply in Pace's grip. "No no, never heard of him, that's the truth."

"Rollo, does it have to get ugly?"

"No! No, listen! Whoever that is, I got nothing to do with him. You got a beef with that one, go take it up with him, okay? We're square, you and me."

Pace pulled him close and searched his eyes. Rollo was very stupid but he wasn't lying. "Who fingered us?"

"A guy named Vindi. He said to pay you a visit. That's all I was doing. Shaking you up a little!"

"For how much?"

"Two grand."

That took Pace back. It was another insult, and this one kind of stung. "Two g's to do all four of us?"

"Shake you up. The five of you. You don't want the money, do you? 'Cause I don't have it on me. But it's what I got paid. My ex, she got most of it, for our kid's dental work. My boy, he eats all those sugary cereals you know, and never brushes. I get on him but—"

"Shut the fuck up, Rollo." Pace turned and studied Dr. Brandt again. She wore an expression of barely restrained excitement, passion, terror. He'd never met anybody who was so hard to read.

She said, "He knew I would be with you."

Pace checked the window. If Kaltzas's agents were anywhere around, he couldn't spot them.

Rollo's hands were still waving all over the place. "The whole apartment, he told me. Five of you. I wasn't even trying to hit you!"

"Jesus, you're really bottom of the barrel now, Rollo. None of the other families would pull you in?"

"They didn't need any more muscle." Rollo Carpie's voice dipped with desolation. "They're too busy hiring accountants and dividing up the Ganooch's business. Ten years, all those oaths I had to take, hold a burning matchbook, and I didn't even get health insurance out of it."

"You might consider another line of work."

"I'm thinking about it."

What little Pace remembered about Kaltzas came to him as if through a veil. But he figured the man could buy and sell the New York families a hundred times over. Drugs, prostitution, and construction crew kickbacks would be nickel and dime to a tycoon. He was just making another point, showing how long his reach was.

Pace still couldn't picture Kaltzas. Or the girl Cassandra. The name Vindi meant nothing to him. He glanced at the ceiling to see if there were any more faces up there.

Hayden showed his sharp teeth and said, "Even in this neighborhood the cops are gonna be coming soon. Shouldn't you be knocking the bad guy out right about now?"

"Or shooting him," Faust added.

"Or cutting him," Pia offered. "I vote we cut him up."

Rollo went even more soft and let out a whimper.

All the Ganooch boys cried in the end.

Pace had the nearly overwhelming urge to see blood. Inside him, the guy in his leather apron wanted to watch blood trickling out, alive and spreading, spurting and pooling. Pace looked over at Dr. Brandt as though he should tell her about it, but she had set her lips, already very aware.

Would killing Rollo be any less sane than dancing with him?

You could do a lot, but even a sociopath had some lines he shouldn't cross.

The Fourth of July fireworks went spiking the sky, igniting the night as the moon dipped low and red, and Jane nuzzled his neck.

Pace's hands did something and Rollo turned a pretty shade of teal and fell over unconscious.

"Who's Vindi?" Hayden asked. "That's one name I never heard before."

"Does it matter?" Pia said. Her lower lip was still cocked, the half-grin so lovely. "Someone working for Kaltzas. We'll see him soon enough, no doubt."

The dust of an ancient world weighed down Faust's words. "He's going to find us again. We can't escape him. We were foolish to think we could. Our father who art insufferable."

"We need to leave. He's had his eye on us the whole time, all the way from Greece, that prick."

"This is merely another show of his strength." Faust was resolved. The scar on his forehead glistened. He kept looking left and right, distracted, his angels chatting with him. Pace saw two glimmering streamers twining through the air. Faust leaned toward one, then the other. "He's calling us to him, now that we're all together again. This wasn't an attack. It was an invitation."

"Do we take it?" Pia asked. "As scared as I am, I'd still like to put this thing to rest eventually. I run my own life, as I see fit."

Dr. Brandt drifted closer to Pace, stood by him the way a lover would, and the two of them watched the others. Her breath warmed the side of his face. He thought, She must be even crazier than the rest of us. Why else would she throw in?

Hayden grabbed up his notepad and swung it overhead, the pages of his letter to his mother flapping. "I say we take the fight to him! Smack him in the mush!"

"How? We're still escapees from a mental institution."

"So are about a half million New Yorkers. If they locked us all back up tomorrow the streets would be empty."

"With what money?"

Faust did something he rarely did. He let out a chuckle. "Kaltzas will provide."

"Oh knock that shit off!" Hayden shouted, lunging in every direction and no direction. His notepad hit the floor. "You sound like you love the vicious bastard."

"Maybe I love all vicious bastards, Hayden. It would explain how our relationship has become almost familial."

"To hell with that. Let's just get on with it! We have to book out of here!" Hayden's hands were shaking and he closed them into fists that shuddered at his sides.

"Not just yet," Pace said.

"Why not, Will?" Dr. Brandt asked. "Do you have reservations? Are you having second thoughts?"

"I'm still confused about some things."

"You always were, Will. You'll never get any better where that's concerned, not without a lot more treatment."

"You let me go."

"I shouldn't have. I was scared."

"Why are you here?"

"We should leave."

"I want to hear your answer."

"You know it already."

"No. I want to know the real reason. Why did you devote so much time to Pacella? And to me?"

She had trouble getting it out, which proved it was true. That gorgeous face was full of honest pain. It made her even more beautiful. "My father was schizophrenic. Medication helped to a degree, but not much. My mother left. When things became very bad I was sent to live with my aunt and uncle. Finally, the day came when I came home and my father was gone."

"So that's why you try to cure us? We're stand-ins for your father?"

"An impetus, no more. I do what I can to help. This is the course my work has taken me."

"You don't like me very much, do you?"

"That's not true at all."

He reached to touch the angle of her jaw, but even his hands weren't quick enough to get there before her veneer was back in place. She looked at him without expression. "Where can we go?"

Inside Pace, the laughing darkness roiled. Its name was Jack. So that was the Jack they were talking about. Jack mentioned an address.

Pace nodded. He said, "I have a place."

seven

The scent of rain and saltwater filled the air, drifting off the East River on a harsh wind as the sun went down.

The storm had followed and seemed about to break wide again. Pace drove the Chevy hard across the Brooklyn Bridge and onto the Belt Parkway.

Kaltzas would have a real surveillance team somewhere nearby, already following. They were going to be rough to spot and even tougher to shake. The car might be bugged so Vindi could keep tabs. He was glad for it. If Kaltzas had a line on Pace, then Pace could follow it back to the man himself.

The team would stay a half-mile to a mile in back of them, running parallel when possible. That's how Jack had done it. That's how the Ganooch's people were brought down.

Crumble the pug held his head out the window. "Arf!"

The loose steering let Pace put the speed of his hands to good use, constantly shifting them on the wheel as he wove in and out of traffic, keeping himself busy. The weight of the few belongings packed into the trunk added some ballast. The squealing tires hurt his head but he enjoyed the noise nonetheless.

"What did Jack do on the ward?" Pace asked. "What did he do to you to scare you all so much?"

No one answered. Pace stared in the rearview, and nobody met his eyes. He repeated the question and specifically asked Pia to respond.

Her brow furrowed and she tugged her head back and forth. A sickly grin pried her lips apart.

"He *talked*," she said.

"About what?"

"If you don't remember then you're better off."

"Tell me anyway."

"Don't, Pia," Dr. Brandt said.

"He wants to learn about Jack." Pia ran a hand through the hair at the back of his head, a sensual move but an aggressive one too, like she wanted to push her luck with him. "You really want to know, Will? Jack would talk about what he would do to women. How he would take their kidneys and cook them. How he would carve them up. More women than the ones in Whitechapel. Many more. Not only whores, but...the elderly, little girls. History doesn't know a tenth of what he's done, but he'd go on about it for hours, chattering in the night."

"He never shut up," Faust said. "He went into detail. About the Ganucci family members. The old man in the wheelchair."

Dr. Brandt shifted in the seat beside him. Depending on the light her eyes were either blue or green. It was a little off-putting, getting used to her eyes being one way and then, as she turned aside, seeing them another. You never knew who you were getting with this crew.

"I'm sorry, doctor," he said. It was an odd thing to do, apologizing for being who you were, and who you weren't, but he felt the need. "Really, I never meant to be such an annoyance to you."

She glanced at him sadly. "Please Will, take your meds. You're just going to get worse."

"He's back," Faust said. "The in-between man. Our father who art in-between."

So that's who Pace was. In-between William Pacella and the devil. Between that drugged-up dimwit he'd been this morning and the many others milling nearby, just waiting for their chance to take over. "That disturbs you, Dr. Brandt?"

"Yes."

"No, it doesn't. You never liked the end result of all your repair work anyway."

"Not entirely," she admitted. "But you were making progress. And now you've regressed at an unbelievable rate. The medication you've already taken will remain in your system for another three or four days, but you've already thrown off their stabilizing effects. You're exhibiting your previous symptoms of DID. The amnesia, depersonalization, and identity disturbances. As well as the emergence of altered personality traits. You're growing more delusional."

"Maybe," he said, "but I feel better. Two years under intense sedation isn't progress, Dr. Brandt."

"Arf!"

"You didn't have much of a point of reference, Will."

"You pump those tranquilizers into a rhino's neck and it'll tap dance to *Swanee River* for you. Remember, you joined us for a reason."

"Yes. God help me, I'm easily frightened. I didn't know what to do. His man approached me."

"Vindi?"

"I have no idea," she said. "But he knew things about me, about my father. About the hospital, and all the patients. Things he shouldn't have been able to know."

"Why didn't you go to the police?"

"They're ineffectual."

"Why do you say that?"

"Because they couldn't stop you. You killed a lot of people as one of your alternates, Will, and they couldn't do a thing to end the bloodshed. When you were through with your mission, you stopped of your own volition and committed yourself." She lit another cigarette, took a long drag, and snorted the smoke. "If nothing else, you taught me how relentless and pure an all-consuming fixation can be. I suspect Mr. Kaltzas is also the victim of such an obsession."

Hayden leaned forward. "You're as loco as any of us, lady."

A vein in her neck snapped. "I'm not particularly proud of myself. But maybe you can do what the police can't, Will. I know what you're capable of."

"I wonder if that's true," Pace said.

Faust read the signs. "Greetings from Coney Island. Welcome to Coney Island Park. Admission to Cyclone Waterslide. W Train - Stillwell Avenue."

Pia said, "My father used to take us on road trips during the summers. My mother, sister, and me. For years we traveled all over the country. He was a Revolutionary War buff. If ten thousand guys with muskets died on a field someplace, I've probably been there. He loved roadside attractions, too. Houses made of hubcaps, corn husks, and beer cans. The chicken that never lost at tic-tac-toe. There must've been twenty of them, everybody thinking there was just this one super-intelligent chicken, and meanwhile every two hundred miles there was another one."

"Not much of that around here," Hayden told her. "Maybe they have smart chickens up at the Bronx Zoo. But in Brooklyn, the only real sightseeing you can do is maybe check out the original Nathan's."

"Visit the Aquarium," Faust read. "Deno's Wonderwheel Park. Enjoy a hotdog with spicy mustard at Nathan's Famous."

"When I was a kid," Pia said, "my old man would put me on his lap and let me steer." Her voice had taken on a placid, faraway quality. "It made my mother nervous, she always overreacted. I'd barely be touching the wheel and she'd gasp and hop in her seat like the car was skidding out of control. The bitch. The rotten bitch. My daddy would say, 'That's it, princess, you're doing beautifully.' I'd get a charge out of it, the idea that we were on these open roads, far from home, passing by men hauling potatoes or pumpkins in big pickup trucks. He'd say, 'This nation is yours as much as anybody's, never forget that. If you ever want to go anywhere, visit anyplace, then you just up and go. There's no one who can stop you.' My sister would get bored and cry. The bitch. The lousy cunt."

Faust, rubbing his scar, where they had taken things out or put more in, said, "My father always told me, 'God watches your every movement. Even your dreams, son, your basest desires. Heaven watches and judges the imperfections of your very soul. It sees the cracks you put there. The sacred storm of providence is always near, ready to descend upon you, my child.' Our father who art infuriating."

Hayden said, "My old man would just go, 'Shut up and sit down, you little shithead! Stop eating paste! Go finish your baked beans!' He was a mean prick."

As if squirming in her father's lap, feeling him under her again, Pia started to bounce. "He'd wrap his arms around me and press his face to my back as I stared out the windshield and he'd press harder on the gas pedal and we'd race through the streets. Sometimes he'd cry. My blouse would get soaked. Sometimes he'd hum songs against my back. My mother would bite her hands."

"And we're the ones they locked up," Hayden said. "The fuck is wrong with people?"

Dr. Brandt gave Pace a sidelong glance, trying to welcome him into the fellowship of judgment. He refused to meet her eyes, whichever one was blue, whichever one was green this time.

"Pia, it's important you remember the facts," she said. "Your father molested you and your sister for several years."

"What?"

"It's the truth. You know it's the truth. You must not deny it to yourself."

"What?"

Pace moved his hand to Dr. Brandt's knee but didn't touch her, just left it there hovering about an inch away. "Let her be."

"This is necessary." She stared back over her shoulder. Her words were sharp and hard as sandstone. "You cannot revert to your benevolent fantasies about him. He was arrested and committed suicide—"

"My daddy loved me. It was the other ones, the men in those foster families, who tried to force me into doing those things."

"Pia, remember our therapy sessions together—"

"That's why I had to cut them. If you don't chop off an ear or two, they just keep coming at you." Pia's face was white except for two burning bright spots on her cheeks. "I don't take that kinda shit off nobody!"

Hayden laughed, opened a window and the wind blew across his sharp forehead. "What is it with all of you and the knives? This is America. Buy a gun for Chrissake."

"They come at me and they get a nice slash across the belly. They pull out their willies and I spike that sticky *escargot* right in the slimy head."

Hayden, no longer laughing, his eyes wide. "Goddamn, girl."

Dr. Brandt tried to keep her tone rigid. "Pia, your core personality is timid, passive, and depressed."

"Until one of those fuckers lays a hand on me. Only a frigid bitch like you wouldn't understand. You could never appreciate the situation. You and your sanctimonious attitude. How often did your daddy bounce you on his lap?"

"Our father who art inflated."

"Your aggression is only going to—"

"I have parameters, Dr. Brandt!" Pia said. "You're encroaching on my safety zone!"

"I apologize, Pia."

"You just like to hear the stories because they titillate you. It's why you try to get inside my brain, because you really want to get into my pants. Tell the truth, are you going to hypnotize me again, doctor?"

"I've never hypnotized you."

"Oh yes, you did. You wanted me to recover repressed memories. You wanted to hear about the orgies. You wanted me to stop my self-mutilation."

Pace could see why so many psychiatrists wound up flipping over the big edge themselves. Always talking, and nobody ever listening.

"You aren't a self-mutilator, Pia. Hypnosis is often used to fuse the alters as part of the patient's personality integration process, but that wouldn't—"

"So why didn't you do that to me?"

"Because that wouldn't—"

"Why only to Hayden?"

"I never—"

"Yeah," Hayden said bitterly, "why only me?"

Dr. Brandt let out a soft sigh. The pulse in her throat glistened and ticked. "You're already schizophrenic, Pia. Inducing you into a trance would only further your depersonalization. I treated you with the hope of grounding you in reality. For that same reason, I never hypnotized Hayden either."

"Oh yes, you did," Hayden said.

She clenched her eyes shut in frustration and her lips flattened into a bloodless line. "You all just make each other sicker."

Faust said, "Southern State Parkway bear right."

Pace thought, Perhaps it's out of necessity. We feed off one another's illnesses because it's there we find what we need, what no one else can give us.

They drove in silence then for nearly two hours. Pace kept his eyes on the rearview, watching the storm only a few miles behind them coming on a straight run, chasing them east. Occasionally Crumble would bark or Pia would mutter about her father or mother or sister, all of them dead.

Faust read, "Twenty-seven A, Montauk Highway."

They were well out in Suffolk County now, on eastern Long Island, about thirty miles past Bayport, the town where Pacella and his wife had once owned a home. Where he tried to share his love of literature with a bunch of kids who stared at him with apathy or such outright hatred that he used to shrivel beneath their gazes. His voice would crack while he read aloud from Poe, Hawthorne, Lawrence, Joyce.

Faust leaned forward and whispered in Pace's ear. "Are you all right, Will?"

"Yes, why?"

"You're grinding your teeth."

"Sorry."

"You do that when you're upset."

"I'll try to watch it."

"Feel free to discuss anything with me that you'd like. I'm your friend."

"Okay."

They were getting to an area of the island that he didn't know very well.

Pace said, "Map?"

Faust scratched his beard and asked, "You want a map? I don't think we have any in the car. Maybe you could stop at a gas station? Do they still hand out maps?"

"Not for about thirty years. I want to talk to Map."

"You're remembering more," Pia said.

"Stop feeding his fantasy, Will," Dr. Brandt said.

"We need him to live. It's as simple as that."

She swallowed another mewling complaint and simply whispered, "For the love of God, how did it come to this?"

"Good question."

It took a couple of minutes before another of Faust's alternates rose to the surface. Map was an ex-Wall Street stockbroker who'd lost everything to cocaine and insider trading. His wife divorced him and took their infant daughter to Des Moines. Now Map lived in the bowels of the Manhattan subway system. He spent most of his day panhandling or in the New York Library, memorizing every map, address, and phone number in the world.

Headlights illuminated the interior of the Chevy. Pace checked the rearview and saw Map there. He looked like he'd spent the last couple of days binging on crack. He was thirty-eight and could pass for sixty. His hands were covered with infected rat bites, head knotted with lumps and contusions from being rolled so often in the tunnels.

"Map, we're on Old Montauk Highway on the eastern end of Long Island, about to enter Bridgehampton. Show me how to get to #11 Rudy Road."

"You've gone too far already," Map said. It was a little tough understanding him because his teeth were mostly black slivers that had slashed a fair percentage of his tongue away. He couldn't stop sniffing and the blood sluiced around inside his sinuses. "Double back at the next street. Take your first right and head north up Long View Trail. First left, then a right into a series of curves. #11 Rudy Road is off on its own, about a quarter mile from the nearest neighbor."

"Thanks."

"My wife and I used to eat out every Friday night at *Le Feu* in Southampton, and then walk along the beach afterward," Map said. The sorrow choked him as he coughed out his words. "We'd drink wine in the surf before making love in the sand bathed in blue moonlight."

"Is there a diner or a rest stop nearby?"

Map couldn't speak for a moment, hacking, keyed up with emotion. He hid his face in his scarred hands, then swallowed his anguish down. "Yes...gas and food, coming up on the left. Point eight miles."

Tears rolled down Dr. Brandt's face. Was she crying for herself or for them? In the dim interior of the car, her tears appeared like black, disfiguring scratches on her cheeks. He was surprised that he wasn't moved more, that such a lovely woman weeping beside him didn't fill him with heartache. Pia held a clutch of tissues and Dr. Brandt took one and dabbed her eyes.

"It's my fault," she said. "I knew this would happen. You've all relapsed. I should have been stronger and trusted the police."

"No, you shouldn't have," Pace said, thinking of the detectives who'd tried to crush his hand at the hospital. The cops who couldn't catch Jack. "You made the right choice."

"We have to dump the car. It's bugged."

"Are you certain?" Hayden asked.

"Yes."

"Shouldn't we have gotten rid of it sooner then? Why did we take it all the way out here?"

"I want to keep Kaltzas close but not too close."

"Ah."

"Hey," Pia cried. "I paid for this car. I love this car. This car is my best friend. Eight hundred smackers."

"How did you get the money?" Dr. Brandt asked.

"I earned it."

"How?"

"What do you care?"

"Prostituting yourself?"

Dr. Brandt put that tone right back in her voice. She really didn't have a soft hand about these things.

"Stop looking down on me, you bitch!" Pia shouted, hitting a high crazed note that hung in the car. Then, the way all the bipolars did, swinging the other way. "I'm hungry. There's a sign over there that says they've got Double Cheesy Bacony Burgers here."

"Double Cheesy Bacony Burgers made your way!" Faust read. "Our father who art indigestion."

"I want one of those."

Pace circled the diner and parking area twice, then backed into a space near the dumpsters behind the kitchen. It afforded cover and provided a good vantage point to see anyone coming in off the highway.

"We going to steal another car?" Hayden said. "Maybe one of these SUV's?"

"No," Pace told him.

"Then what?"

"One will be along soon."

Hayden frowned. "What do you mean by that?"

"Vindi. Or whoever Kaltzas has tracking us. We sit here long enough and they'll worry, thinking we boosted another car. They'll have to do a spot check in person. They'll be showing up in the next hour."

"Where are they now?"

"Either behind us a few miles or running parallel on one of the county roads."

"So what are we doing here?" Hayden asked.

"Lingering."

"And getting me a burger?" Pia said.

"And getting everybody some food. Is there a screwdriver in the glove box?"

"Why would there be a screwdriver in there?"

"Because old cars like this need a lot of fine-tuning. You use it to adjust the timing chain and carburetor, tighten the clamps on the air hoses which usually work loose after a couple thousand miles."

"No wonder this thing's been running like a piece of shit."

Pace was about to tell them that Pacella's father had a Chevy like this, but somehow, Pacella's father was his own father. Sometimes William Pacella was somebody else entirely, and sometimes they shared the same background, like brothers. "My father owned a Chevy just like this. He taught me how to drive on it."

He reached across Dr. Brandt's lap and opened the glove box, found a three-inch flathead and put it in his pocket.

"I want a damn Double Cheesy Bacony Burger!"

"Me too," Hayden said.

"We're all hungry," Dr. Brandt said. "We haven't eaten all day."

"Go inside and order enough for everybody," Pace told her. "We'll eat out here."

She did as he said, wandering into the neon glare in a kind of puzzled daze. He wondered why none of the other psychiatrists at the hospital had seen how close to cracking she actually was.

She returned with the food and Pia squealed with delight and everyone ate in silence, the car growing more and more crowded by the second until Pace had to lean his head out the window to breathe. There were kids in the backseat singing and playing with their french fries, old men having a tough time eating the hamburger because of their poorly-fitted dentures.

Pace ate little and finished quickly, the way Jack used to do on stakeout in Brooklyn keeping an eye on the Ganooch and his people. No liquids so you didn't have to take a piss break. He waited and watched while the others finished their food.

It took seventy minutes before Kaltzas's men arrived. Pace saw the white Jaguar slowly turn into the rest stop. It wasn't exactly the most inconspicuous car, but Kaltzas seemed willing to trade guile for grandeur. Perhaps impression meant everything. The Jag circled the area and spotted the Chevy almost immediately. They parked in a far-off corner, engine humming. The windows were tinted black.

"You all stay here," Pace said. "I'll be back in a minute."

"You can't, Will." Dr. Brandt touched him on the chest, smoothing her hand across him in a lover's intimate gesture. His scars began to heat. What had he done with this woman?

"Hold on," Faust said. "It might be Kaltzas himself. There might be several armed men in that car. Do you want help?"

"No," Pace said, his fear and hatred taking on a thousand forms within him. "I've got plenty."

eight

Sometimes you just stepped right up.

Pace walked across the parking lot and knocked on the driver's window of the Jag. He backed off a couple of feet and stood there with his arms crossed over his chest.

Mist rose up from the lowland grass edging the rest stop. The storm would be blowing in from the west soon. It wanted him. He could feel the desire on the wind. He could taste salt on his lips and caught a flash of Jane again. The two of them stepping across the sand, somewhere out here on the east end, down at one of the private beaches. She'd take a mouthful of wine and kiss him, passing the wine to him. He hated the taste but remembered laughing.

The engine of the Jag hummed quietly.

Maybe this cat had all day to sit around playing games, but Pace felt the need to get on with it. He cocked his head and raised his eyebrows, held his hands open in a gesture of geniality. He got in close and tapped his fingers on the hood.

Still nothing happened.

You could take a lot, but you really hated when they fucking ignored you.

"Okay," he said, smiling, and came around the front of the car.

Pace took out the small screwdriver and touched it to the center of the driver's window. He hardly had to apply any pressure at all before the glass shattered.

The door opened.

Out came one hell of an ugly bastard. Short bowed legs, thick stubby arms, wild tangle of beard, and a barrel chest. Coarse black hair twisted across his huge head that protruded like a chunk of rock breaking from the shallows. He had a large nose with permanently flared nostrils, giving him a brutish, bullish appearance. The Minotaur.

He gave off an artificial milieu of refinement. It was something he'd worked at for a long time but still didn't come naturally to him. He moved slowly, the way wealthy snobs often did, as if they refused to lower themselves to the same constraints as the rest of the world. He looked like someone who might spend the day listening to Brahms, visiting art galleries, dining on quails' eggs before kicking in the door of a retirement home and strangling an old lady in her bed.

The Minotaur, coming at you.

Wearing a three thousand-dollar suit and a huge diamond stickpin that caught a flare of headlights and sent a rainbow pinwheeling into darkness. He brushed shards of glass from his wide shoulders and shook it from his hair.

"It's a neat trick," Pace said. "Most people don't realize how easily safety glass breaks. It's designed that way in case a car ever goes off a pier and sinks underwater. There's no way to open the door or roll down the window then, because of the water pressure, so you just tap the glass with a screwdriver or nail file and it gives way."

"I shall remember," the bull said with a slight Greek accent, "if I ever drive off a pier."

"You're Vindi?"

"You do not recall?" The voice had a certain heavy resonance with the hint of a growl, a touch of implied menace.

"We've met before?"

"Yes, several times. We were quite friendly. On that ward, in the institution."

"You were there?"

"Visiting." Vindi shoved his huge nose forward and peered into Pace's eyes. His beard drifted in the breeze. "I see you have not been taking your medication. You seem as ill now as when we last met. You do not react well to treatment."

"What do you know about it?"

"I know everything about you, Mr. Pacella."

Inside him, a few different people were yelling and trying to grab his attention, but they drowned each other out. Maybe Pacella was still around despite Jack's best efforts to kill him. The schoolteacher hiding somewhere deep, grading papers, preparing exam questions. Reading Renaissance poetry, maybe drinking cocoa. The fucker actually used to drink cocoa.

Jane bringing it to him on a tray, with a dish of almond cookies. She wanted to kiss him with a mouth full of wine and he wanted to sit there and drink frickin' hot chocolate. He'd hold the cookie with just the tips of two fingers, so afraid to get stains on his books. Seated in front of a small fireplace in a leather chair that cost him half a year's salary, in a room covered with dark cherry paneling because it made him think of England, a place he'd never been. Learning how to smoke a pipe but never really enjoying it, as he paged through Browning, Keats, Burns. Sipping the cocoa, wiping those two fingers on a silk napkin.

It was no wonder the guy had to go.

Pace shifted the handle of the screwdriver in his fist, holding it the way he would grip the handle of a blade. All these wise guys packed big guns loaded with hollow-tipped and mercury-filled hotshot shells that exploded on impact and chopped a guy up to pieces inside. The bodyguards carrying oily paper bags full of zeppoles, cannolli, and Napoleons for their bosses. You never drop the zeppoles. Trying to juggle the bags and get their guns out at the same time. They liked to show off their .45's and .357 Magnums with barrels so long it took like eight seconds to draw them fully out of their holsters.

Jack could have a liver on a plate in eight seconds. By the time the goombas got their weapons free they had five inches of stainless steel in the throat or between the ribs. The Ganooch boys too stupid to know they were dead, still holding the zeppoles while a river of red froth sluiced across the floor.

"You know everything about me?" Pace repeated. "Good. Then you're the one I want to talk to. I'm a little mixed up on some things, and my psychiatrist isn't helping. She's got her own problems."

"Yes, she is ineffectual. And deeply repressed."

"Okay, so give me the details."

It tickled the Minotaur so much that he let out a snort. Vindi displayed an uneven row of thick, yellow teeth. All this effort to affect elegance and style, yet the guy wouldn't get his teeth capped or trim the beard. He was totally gratified that he could get away with being so repulsive.

"I'm serious," Pace said.

"Oh, I know you are. That has always been your most dire ailment. How uncompromising and Spartan you are. It is ultimately what led to your initial mental collapse. The first breakdown, and all those that followed."

"Stop with the compliments."

Vindi's eyes took in everything. He was aware of the screwdriver in Pace's fist, and kept himself just out of range. His arms were loose at his sides, huge hands slightly raised so he could block or attack as needed. The bull neck bulged with corded muscle. He wouldn't be easy.

"So let me hear it."

"You are William Pacella," Vindi said. "Former high school English teacher. Schizophrenic with dissociative identity disorder, better known in most circles as multiple-personality disorder. You went mad when your wife died in a restaurant fire."

Pace couldn't get his mouth wrapped around the name of the place though. He tried a couple of times and couldn't quite get it. He said, "Emily's? Emeel's?"

"*Emilio's*, yes. Named after the owner, Emilio Cavallo."

"Cavallo," Pace said, nodding. "Yeah."

"The local syndicate, run by Joseph Ganucci, also known as 'the Ganooch,'"—he had to stop and grin—"these Italians and their ludicrous nomenclature."

"Get on with it."

"Ganucci's crew had apparently been trying to drive Cavallo out of business. Your wife, Jane, the restaurant manager, was caught in the blaze along with three other employees, one of whom you saved. You had a psychotic break and hunted down several of the mobsters responsible, known collectively as the Ganucci Family. In the guise of an alternate persona called Nightjack, you killed each of them with either a knife or your bare hands. This is rather common knowledge although the police agencies never acquired enough formal evidence against you. Your alternate identities confused them greatly. After you finally dispatched Joseph Ganucci, you voluntarily admitted yourself into the Garden Falls Psychiatric Facility. You were eventually state committed after you carried out acts of violence in the hospital. Today you were released."

So there it was, laid out front to back in a few simple sentences. Pace gritted his teeth and gave a rictus grin, thinking about Jane in flames. Now he understood why it was so clear in his mind. Pacella had been there, in the restaurant, and had watched her die. Why hadn't he been able to save her?

"That sounds about right," he whispered.

"Would you like to hear more?" Vindi asked. "There is a good deal more to cover."

"No," Pace told him. You didn't go willingly to your reckoning, you let it come to you, inch by inch. "Not right now."

"As you wish."

"You're quite amenable."

The great shoulders shrugging, the mouth shifting into a brief, curious smile. "We were once friends."

"You and me? So what happened?"

"I cannot discuss that with you at this time."

"Why not?"

"It would not be in your best interest, I think. Nor that of my employer."

A family walked past them in the lot. Man and wife, five-year-old daughter holding a melting ice cream cone. The three of them tired from a long drive and moving slowly. The father perceived the situation and drew his wife and kid close, skirting away trying to get to his minivan that the Jag had almost blocked in. Pace watched them, knowing there were a half-dozen men inside him who could relate to the father, a group of children who wanted to go play with the little girl.

The guy pulled his minivan out and barely missed clipping the Jag's rear quarter panel. He kept his face down and refused to look over as he gunned it out of the lot and hit the highway, heading for one of the beach motels.

"It was stupid to send Rollo Carpie after me," Pace said.

Vindi seemed almost embarrassed. "He was no real threat to you. It was meant to gain your attention, nothing more."

"You've got it."

"Yes."

The need to do something was building up, thrashing within him, a black ocean filled with drowning people. All of them reaching up, asking to be saved. How many of them could take Vindi? How many could get him alive, and how many would need to kill him? The hinges of Pace's jaw began to throb. The kids in his head shouted for ice cream.

"But you could've just sent a fruit basket, you know."

"My employer wishes to see you. And your associates. The others from the *asylum*." Saying the word with a certain amount of veneration. Not as insane asylum, but as sanctuary.

"Say his name, damn it."

But Vindi wouldn't, as if afraid that saying the man's name would somehow invoke him, awaken the ancient gods.

Images without context filled Pace's mind. He saw a large silhouetted figure standing before a bright window, a flash of polished marble. Grim eyes ignited with undivided purpose. The kids stopped asking for ice cream and started crying, running for the corners. The dizzying stink of blood filled Pace's head, and he felt a tiny burst of pain in his throat—a love bite where teeth nipped him. The tactile presence of a hand on his chest pressed him back one step, then another.

"Where is Cassandra?" he asked.

"It is quite fascinating that you have suppressed so much," Vindi said. "How fearful you are of yourself. It saddens me greatly to see you in this state."

"I'll bear up."

"Yes, but for how long? You have trials still ahead of you."

"Everyone does."

Vindi snorted again in his bullish manner, speaking in Greek, calling to someone inside Pace. It was a challenge of some kind, Vindi urging someone to come out. Pace tossed the screwdriver over his shoulder and his hands became hard as stone. They were strangler's hands, and they had done a lot of work for him already. Vindi quit moving.

"And what's to stop me from breaking your neck?" Pace asked.

Vindi smiled without warmth. "I assure you it would not be to your advantage, nor would it be effortless. My employer does not hire incompetents."

"I wouldn't know about that."

"Oh, but you would."

Talk about a contrary prick. Pace tried to picture Cassandra Kaltzas but could only see Jane's burning face. The kids had scurried back and were whining for strawberry swirly, fudge ripple, chocolate mint chip. They tugged on his sleeve, saying, Please please please please, *oh please.*

"I was in a straitjacket when Cassandra was raped, they tell me."

"We doubt the veracity of that particular report."

"Why?"

"You and Dr. Maureen Brandt were lovers. She undoubtedly forged certain documentation. The fact that you're free now is proof that she is able to subvert the clinical system."

"But she acts like she hates me. Where do you get your information?"

"With the proper inducement, anyone is willing to talk. It is simple to bribe the proper authorities. They sought to hide the situation, rather than approach it openly. They feared repercussions. Money quells fear."

"Why didn't Kaltzas call them on it? Have a full investigation made?"

"It was decided the matter should be dealt with directly and personally."

"Is that so?" Pace handed out the ice cream cones, and each of the kids took theirs in turn, saying, Thank you, thank you, *oh thank you* before running off. He stared after them as they skipped and bounded away. "I really look forward to meeting him."

"You have met him."

"Whatever. I still have things to think through. We need your car. And money."

"Certainly." Vindi stepped aside, allowing Pace access to the Jag. Raindrops began to spatter against the windshield. "There is a billfold in the glove compartment filled with five thousand dollars."

"That's really why Kaltzas sent you, isn't it? You're here to direct our course. To make sure we get to Pythos."

"A private jet is waiting for you at Kennedy Airport."

You didn't go willingly to your reckoning, you let it come to you, inch by inch.

Maybe he was wrong. Maybe you had to meet it at least halfway, if you were ever going to get any of the answers you needed.

Pace slid behind the wheel of the Jag. The computerized tracking equipment set in the dashboard made it look like a cockpit. "Where is he now?" Pace asked. "And where is Cassandra?"

The Minotaur smiled, shards of golden bone appearing through the forest of wiry beard. "On Pythos. Waiting for you."

nine

Crumble enjoyed the Jag and stuck his head out the sunroof, tongue lolling, barking into the rain. Dr. Brandt said, "Please, Hayden, people are looking." She turned to Pace and asked, "Are you ready to discuss what happened yet?"

"No."

Finishing up her third Double Cheesy Bacony Burger, Pia let out a contented moan. All the men in the car—the hundreds of them, even the gay ones, even the dead ones—stiffened at the sound. She could do it to you even when she wasn't half-trying, reaching inside to pluck at your guts.

Faust, somehow more in tune with Pace, sensed his rising agitation and put a hand to the back of Pace's head, like he could hold everybody inside there and keep them from pouring free.

"It's alright, Will."

"Sure. We're almost there."

Pace followed Map's directions through a couple miles of wetland, along a series of curving sand-blown roads heavy with saw grass. Now that they were off the main streets traffic thinned and the towns turned into hamlets and fishing villages, the woods deepening as brackish inlets began to surround them.

The house was tucked away on a small spit of sand and weeds. The area around it peeled back into a mixture of silt, black mud, and eddying saltwater drooling across a stony shoreline at low tide. Lapping waves could be heard.

Faust threw his door open the moment the Jag came to a full stop. "It's like a church," he said. "One of those country churches where the town would huddle in the middle of a yellow fever epidemic. Where they came to die together. The town marshals would seal them inside alive to quarantine them. Our father who art inescapable."

"You're fun as a fuckin' barrel of dead spider monkeys, you are," Hayden told him.

They climbed out. The pelting cold rain hurt, but no one made a sound. Pace popped the trunk and they gathered their meager belongings and tramped up the gravel walkway in the darkness.

The storm broke in full as Pace led them to the front door. Dr. Brandt asked, "Is this your house, Will?"

"No," he said. He found a key hidden in a niche between two of the cedar shingles below the front window. He unlocked and pushed the door open. They filed in and he turned on the lights.

"How did you know where the key was?"

"Does it matter?"

"Yes, of course. You were a school teacher and your wife managed a restaurant in Manhattan. I've seen your financial records. You couldn't afford a house in this area."

"You know it all, lady."

Hayden said, "Jack must've paid cash for it after ripping off all the goombas. Those mobsters horde their payoffs, they're tighter with a buck than a Thai hooker."

"Do you know any Thai hookers?" Pia asked. "Or mobsters?"

"A few of each. After they'd get arrested they'd show up at the home to do community service taking care of me and the mongoloids. Nice folks all around, really. Taught me Texas Hold'em."

Pace tried to imagine Jack walking into a realtor's office with three-quarters of a mill in twenties and fifties. Setting up accounts to have the electricity and water paid automatically each month. The guy asking him if he was married, had children, and Jack just standing there giggling.

"When did you first come here, Will?" Dr. Brandt asked.

"Don't you ever get tired of asking questions?"

He thought, Maybe canning fish wouldn't have been so bad.

You sit there all day long in front of a conveyor belt covered in tuna, squid, halibut, cod. Pick the slimy things up, reach for one of those little cans, and just smash 'em in there. Next to you is a robot that welds the lids shut. The robot wants to learn how to be human, keeps asking you to explain things. What is love? You tell him, I don't know, Robbie. Where is the soul located? No clue, Robbie. Why do men pay Bubbles LaRue twenty dollars to lie with them in the back of her 1982 El Camino with Edlebrock valve covers and flowmaster exhaust during the designated lunch hour?

That's easy to explain, Robbie—Do you agree that it is necessary to have an underlying principle or dictum to rejoice when we succeed and to take solace when we fail? You're a little over my head there, Robbie. Is it better to live without requiring assertion of value or belief in the admittedly doubtful existence of a clinical entity thus far unconfirmed in the known structure of the visible universe? Fuck are you talkin' about, Robbie, lighten up a little, yeah? So you try teaching him how to acquire a sense of humor. Start off with knock knock jokes. Robbie tells you, That does not compute. You work your way up to the traveling salesmen making it with the farmer's daughter, her crotch smelling like corn on the cob. Robbie going, That does not compute! His metal arms flailing, claws snapping. Eradicate! Expunge! Other fish canners lying broken and dying all over the factory. The salmon staring at you while you stuff it into the fucking can.

Sniffing like he was having an allergy attack, with his head tossed way back, Faust announced, "The stink of murder is here."

"So this is it," Hayden said, holding his pad, getting ready to write to his mother. "The house that Jack built."

The one-story house was old, one of those converted cabins from back when rich New York urbanite bankers used to build this far out on the island to accommodate their mistresses in the summer. It was furnished in a quaint countrified style, lots of wicker and oak, rocking chairs and throw pillows with embroidered sayings on them.

HOME IS WHERE YOUR LOVE IS.

ALL REALITIES ONCE WERE DREAMS.

EAT AT TINY BOB'S LOBSTER PAVILION.

The weight of history bore down. Men had given way here, women had borne children, art had been conducted and completed. A broad stone fireplace against the far wall looked like an alter where human sacrifices had once been performed.

"So's the stink of love," Pia intoned, the word taking on a heavy, tragic cadence. "It's everywhere. In the walls, the very lumber."

"You say that as if it's bad," Faust said.

"It is."

"Somebody's been taking care of the place while you've been in the Falls, Will."

Pace said, "A woman. I think she comes in to clean once a month." The truth of it struck him with such force and clarity that he had to turn his chin aside like he was dodging a blow. The middle-aged woman's wide face was burnished with real character. She was the wife of a fisherman. She'd lost her firstborn to the sea decades ago and carried the guilt around with her always. The shame of a mother who could not protect her child from the dominion of the ocean.

It wasn't that odd, this far out on the island, to have repairmen and weekly or monthly cleaning services, where the owners and the help never saw one another. A lot of these homes were used only in season, a couple of weekends a year. Jack must've had several automatic withdrawals made from his account.

"This is your house, Will," Dr. Brandt repeated. When the lady got a hard thought in her head, she couldn't let it go. Talk about neurotic.

"No, it's not." He tried not to take offense at her compulsion to call him Will, always with the Will. "I've never been here before."

"You knew you had a place to go to, but you didn't know how to get here. But you knew the address and where to find the key. You've already separated from yourself again, Will. Distancing yourself from your emotions and personal history. That's why you're not healthy."

"Yeah."

"So it *is* yours."

"No, it's not," he repeated. Saying it like he was a little sad for her, that she just couldn't understand. She'd never be able to understand, which was why she was such a lousy shrink.

He knew she wished she had a tape recorder on hand. Even after two years in Garden Falls she hadn't come close to getting to the bottom of him. Any of him, any of them. He remembered her sitting there writing and making him talk into a video camera.

He'd talked for hours and days and months and he wasn't sure if he'd told a single lie, or a single truth. About himself or anybody else, even though so much of it was honest even while everything contradicted itself.

Hayden had his notepad out and was writing to his mother again.

"All this time," Faust said, sounding a little amazed and crestfallen, "and you still know so little about us, Dr. Brandt."

"True dissociative identity disorders are extremely rare, Faust. You're all quite unique."

"Perhaps even more so than you know, doctor."

That got her attention. She took on the professional air again, ready to analyze, to diagnose. "How do you mean?"

"Yeah," Hayden said. "This I gotta hear."

Pia jumped into a wicker seat. “I am all ears.”

“Perhaps we’re not suffering from DID at all.” The scar on Faust’s forehead looked pink and raw, like it was ready to give birth. “Let me submit, doctor, that we are *not* creating personalities within ourselves due to traumatic experiences which have fractured our psyches.”

“Then what?”

“That we are instead actually *channeling* these other individuals, entities, and beings. Drawing them in from other dimensions, through time and space across the cosmos. Gathering them to us. Them, and the souls of the departed. These others do not originate organically from within. They consume and subsume and the worst of them devour. We are simply the beacons. We are the vessels. We are the conduits. We are the possessed. Our father who art infinite.”

Dr. Brandt licked her lips and something inside Pace bucked. She took a moment to gather her thoughts. When they came, they were worthless. “Even you don’t believe that.”

“You might be surprised at what I believe, doctor.”

“No, Faust, I wouldn’t. I’ve heard it all before, from each of you over the years you were in therapy. But your alternate personalities are nothing more than inventions of an afflicted psyche.”

“I’m hurt,” Hayden said. “You sound like you don’t like us anymore.”

“I care greatly for each one of you, but you’re all ill. You need help.”

“You keep saying that,” Faust said. “Isn’t repetitive actions and speech the sign of an afflicted mind?”

“In certain circumstances.”

“Do you eat paste?” Hayden asked.

“No.”

“Don’t eat paste!”

Pia stood and fluttered around the room. “Maybe it’s just the fact that some badass wants to do unholy things to me, but I haven’t felt this good in years.”

“I agree,” Faust said. “This newfound independence, fueled by anxiety and tension, is quite an electrifying experience. Although I was terrified when that shotgun went off in the apartment, I was also quite thrilled. Piqued.”

Saying it but his eyes shifting left and right, back and forth, seeing two sword-wielding angels in the room.

“Are you being visited by your two friends again?” Dr. Brandt asked.

"They're not my friends," Faust said. "You know that."

"They're not real either."

"Of course they are. They're a part of me, and I'm real. The twin angels Sariel and Rimmon are no different than emotions or memories. My hopes, fears, and phobias. None of us can fully control ourselves. If we could, we wouldn't be human."

Behind him to the left, Faust always saw a fallen angel named Sariel. Wingless, looking much like a man. One of the seven honored masters in command of a heavenly host, who guides the progress of the world. Issuer of new bodies to the dead, who after the great war in heaven descended to earth to cohabit with mortal women. Sariel was the chief of the repentants, who removed his own crown on Golgotha as Christ died in the world. Possessor of the four keys to the four corners of the earth. Who will, when instructed by God, re-open the gates of Eden, which were locked after the fall of humanity and are guarded by the damned.

Directly to his right stood Rimmon, who grants success and good fortune. Governor of the first order of seraphim, angel of lightning and fire. The only seraph successful in fighting envy. Ruler of the 196 divisions of heaven, commanding 29,000 legions of burning choirs. The angel whose sword set fire to the bush that brought clarity to Moses. One of the nine who will reign over the end times.

Pace saw them too, very clearly now, the angels watching him from across the room, their swords sheathed.

"Arf!" Crumble barked happily. The pug ran forward and started humping Pace's leg. He patted the dog, scratching the deep furrowed wrinkles.

Dr. Brandt glanced over, her gorgeous face as austere as stone. "Hayden, my God, stop that!"

"Arf!"

"Good boy," Pace said.

Pia moaned and licked her lips. Twin angels, fallen and divine, moved to her, their golden locks flowing across their shoulders.

Weeping, Daedalus stared out the window and looked over the waters, searching the sea for his fallen son.

ten

"Our forefathers' forefathers have walked here in this house," Faust said. "Can't you feel it? There are graves beneath this floor. The soil is heavy with bonemeal. Stillborn children have been denied names and interred without benefit of prayer."

"Thanks for that, Captain Happy," Hayden said. "You know, living with the mongoloids was a lot more fun than dealing with you, man, even with all the dribble and headgear. Shit, they sure knew how to throw a party." He kneeled and took pieces of firewood and kindling from two neat stacks and loaded them into the fireplace. "Hey, I have a question. Do we have any idea what the hell we're doing yet? What the plan is? If we're all in agreement on our options? Our chances? If we have any?"

"No," Pace said.

"To all of the above? Jesus Christ."

Pia entered one of the bedrooms and said, "It's very homey. People were very happy here once."

"Anybody see any knives?" Pace asked.

"No," Faust said. "Not in view anyway. Why don't you search the sideboards and dressers?"

"Because it's not my house."

"Does it matter?"

"Yes."

The man Pace had been this morning was no longer the man he was now. He was already somebody else. That's the way it worked. He could become a new person by millimeters and instances and degrees, each small change allowing him to become someone else.

He turned and the others were gone. He heard them upstairs, opening doors, rummaging around. Pia tittered loudly and so did Dr. Brandt, which was a strange sound. You could get used to a lot, but there'd always be something chilling when you heard the laughter of a person who didn't laugh.

He sat in a rattan love seat and shut his eyes, wondering if any of this was real or if he was still in the hospital tied down to a bed with a huge needle jammed in his neck. He only opened his eyes when somebody moved past him, the floor creaking loudly.

It was Sam Smith, the private eye that Pacella had hired to help him find the torcher of the restaurant, right before Jack broke loose.

Sam seated himself beside Pace, smoking a three-inch cigar butt. He wore a black slicker and a fedora with a little plastic covering around it. Rain ran heavily off the brim.

"It's a bad night out," Sam said.

"I know, thanks for coming."

You could always count on Sam. The man was closing in on sixty but still went two-fifty of nearly solid muscle. Shaking his hand was like squeezing a steel pipe. He'd been one of the last ones out of Saigon in '75 and still bore the scars of an 81mm mortar shell down the left side of his face and neck, where the scars rose and twisted like knots on a log. He carried a .38 in a shoulder holster under his left armpit. You looked at him and you saw your father, any of your many fathers who'd protect you through the ugliest situation on any backstreet. You knew nothing could take P.I. Sam Smith down.

Sam was the researcher. It was perhaps his greatest skill. He could find out anything. He'd tried to teach Pacella the rudiments of shadowing somebody and casing a house, how to break into computer systems and check bank accounts, but Pacella was too busy going out of his mind.

He never picked up on it and only listened with one ear. It turned out to be Jack's ear, and that turned out to be enough.

Sam said, "There's a laptop stowed away on the top shelf of the foyer closet. Bring me that and we can get to work."

"Finding the torcher?"

"That job's already been completed," Sam said. "Now come on, I got a lot of cases I need to get to, let's hurry this along, yeah?"

"Wait, tell me who—"

Sam gave Pace the eye, a father brooking no opposition. "There's no time to go through all of that again."

All right, moving along.

Pace went to the foyer and got the laptop out of the closet, sat down again. The house was set up for wireless. Sam Smith booted it up, got on the Internet, and started typing rapidly.

"Let's start with Cassandra Kaltzas," Pace said. "Nobody will tell me much. Can you breach the security on the Garden Falls computers, get into the files?"

"There's no need to, we've already got access."

"We do?"

"Sure, with Maureen Brandt's password. It's P-S-Y-C-H-E, yeah? In the Greek myth, it's the name of a human girl and means 'soul.' She was abandoned by Eros—that means love—and left all depressed. Finally driven into the underworld. Eros is the god behind vulnerability. He's the one who cuts deepest. He exposes all of mankind—through love, betrayal, and cruelty—to the inseparable blend of pain and pleasure."

"Damn," Pace said, "you really are a good detective, Sam Smith!"

"Yeah. We private eyes like to give our clients their money's worth."

He tapped a few more keys and came to a patient video log that unfolded as if you were actually turning pages in a folder.

Cassandra Kaltzas. Daughter of shipping magnate Alexander Kaltzas, living in New York City and attending New York University. An art history major but with an eye toward abstract expressionism. Some kind of a break occurred between her and her father, and she refused to allow him to pay her way. She worked part-time as a waitress in a west Greenwich village café called the *Galleria Buffet*, a tiny place sandwiched between two small art galleries. Her second semester she began to suffer from a growing sense of derealization. Seeing walls, buildings, and other objects changing in shape, size, and color. She was given to panic attacks. Originally she was misdiagnosed by a school psychiatrist with a borderline personality disorder. They thought she was bipolar and working too hard on her abstract paintings. The meds they prescribed did nothing.

"Is there a photo of her?" Pace asked.

Smith punched a few more keys and the video pages flipped until they came to a dark-haired girl only slightly older than Pia. She had sharp aquiline features, black eyes as cold as quartz. There was strength and independence there. Her expression was reserved and remote, and she seemed to be at the point of realizing the burden might be too heavy, the consequences too severe. He could almost see how she was beginning to buckle, like Psyche driven down into the underworld by love.

Pace didn't recognize her. He read on silently while Smith read aloud, saying how she eventually failed to recognize friends, teachers, and co-workers and was as admitted into Garden Falls. She scored high on the Dissociative Experiences Scale screening test and was noted as a schizophrenic. A few months later she was found beaten on the ward. After a thorough investigation by the police and the hospital personnel, there was no forensic evidence found and still no primary suspects, although three escapees were being sought for further questioning.

"Try to find the sexual predator in a facility filled with four hundred lunatics," Smith said.

"Only thirty-five on the ward, not counting alternates," Pace told him. "But her father decided it had to be one of us three, aided by Pia and Maureen Brandt. Why? Were we really the most violent?"

"Despite your circumstances, you were in under a voluntary committal. The cops had nothing on you. You attacked a couple of guards once in treatment."

"He'd have heard about Nightjack though."

"Sure."

Upstairs, it sounded like baby rhinos were running around. "What can you find on Kaltzas himself?"

"Not much that matters. For one of the richest men in the world, he's kept a pretty low profile. Alexander Limnos Kaltzas. Fifty years old. Industrialist. Shipping tycoon. Munitions dealer. Archeologist. His father, Demes, bucked the Nazis in the big one. Drove the Italian fascists out when they attacked from Albania in 1940. German troops overcame the insurgents and invaded Athens in '41. He saw a lot of blood. The Greek government was in shambles by then. Their leaders were fleeing the country or offing themselves left and right. He could've run but he stuck it out. Famine followed along with intense guerilla resistance. The worse a war gets, the tougher and harder the resistance gets."

Sam seemed to be thinking about Nam again. "The old man was a leader in the National Liberation Front. Hardcore, living in the frozen mountains for months so they could cut supply lines. Routed the Germans in '44, and then came civil war to control what was left of the country. He started dealing with Albania, Bulgaria, Turkey, even Great Britain, making his fortune in the post-war cleanup of rebels. Made a killing in the black market when Truman came in and initiated his doctrine, offering military and relief supplies. Settled in on Pythos and never left."

Sam Smith was good at the keyboard, his fingers moving gracefully so there was hardly any sound at all. "No mention of Kaltzas's mother or any siblings. The old man died when Alexander was twenty, studying at the University of Athens. The fortune passed down to him, but he didn't return to the island until he finished interning at the Byzantine Museum and the Acropolis."

"Old school," Pace said, "ancient school. His daughter studying abstract expressionism must've pissed him off."

"Yeah. Met his wife, Catherine, also a trained archeologist, at the university. She died during an excavation on Pythos ten years ago, when Cassandra was ten. Part of a tomb wall collapsed. Cassandra was there and saw it."

"The start of her fracture," Pace said.

"Maybe. After her breakdown in New York and the troubles at Garden Falls, Kaltzas pulled her back to the island. He was already pretty much a recluse. Very little media coverage, and nobody gets on the island without his say so. He's got a private army protecting him. After she came home, he really fell out of sight. There hasn't been a word printed about him."

"And now he beckons us to his home."

"He wants to make sure he's getting the right person," Sam said. "He's deliberate and careful. Sounds dangerous and dramatic too, but I bet when he aims at a target, he's accurate. Probably comes from living with those relics, all that stone. His old man would've just used a howitzer and killed a hundred people to make sure he got the right one. This Kaltzas, he's got a flair for the flamboyant but he's incisive. You been practicing the moves I taught you, yeah?"

"Yes," Pace said, because he, or someone else, had been. Pacella had once thought a man had to be highly trained to efficiently kill someone with his bare hands. He'd been amused and revolted at how easy it actually proved to be. The simple killing strokes. Forearm to the throat. Heel of the palm to the sternum. The strangler's hands holding on. Easing the blade in under the heart. Incisive.

When Pace looked at P.I. Sam Smith again, the man had blood leaking from the corner of his mouth. Sam didn't seem to be in any pain as he coughed and brought up black fluid that dripped down his chin. He gasped twice, his lungs bubbling, and then his head sank back against the edge of the couch and the little plastic wrapper around his hat flopped off.

Pace reached over and put a hand to Sam Smith's chest but there was no movement.

Then Pace was alone on the love seat, with the laptop on his knees.

That's right, he thought, Sam Smith had been murdered three weeks after taking the job from William Pacella. He was found shot to death in his office, a couple of months after he started investigating the Ganucci family's possible connection to the death of Jane Pacella.

The screen had more information about Pythos and Pace scanned it quickly, learning a little more about the archeological digs that had gone on, what might be expected at Greek shrines. It felt as if time was running out, and he tried to absorb what he could, even though the facts kept skittering away from him.

Pace glanced up and saw Pia gliding down the stairs, pixie arms out and waving as if she might fly. Hayden slid along the rail in perfect time with her. Dr. Brandt was making her angry mama face as she followed, stomping down stair by stair.

Faust stepped from the shadows at the bottom of the stairwell, there the whole time.

"A laptop, Will? Where did you get that?" Dr. Brandt asked.

"I found it."

He looked over at the embroidered pillows.

ABIDE WITH ME: FAST FALLS THE EVENTIDE.

"You've been on the Internet?"

"Yes."

"Doing what?"

"Putting together the pieces."

"Good, I'm glad. Which pieces?"

That stopped him.

Which pieces. It was a good question. Were they big ones or small, when you got right down to it? Important or merely more subterfuge that, in the end, despite all the effort and struggle, would mean nothing to anyone? Pace didn't know.

"There's six hundred pounds on a barbell up there," Pia said. "Can you really bench that much?"

"No," Pace told her. "Not a chance."

Hayden let out a high-pitched titter. It sounded near-hysterical and he knew it did so he snapped his jaws shut. He waited a second and said, "I think you can. I think Jack can do almost anything."

"Our father who art invincible," Faust said.

You didn't invoke the names of the dark gods unless you were willing to pay a price.

Dr. Brandt stepped in close, her lips almost at Pace's ear. It wasn't a whisper, but something softer and more luxurious, throaty with a heavy hint of promise. The muscles in his belly rippled.

"Vindi said we'd been lovers," he told her.

"Ooooh," Pia said, jumping onto the couch, legs crossed, arm braced on her knee with her hand up like she was holding a glass of champagne. "Do tell."

"Is it true?" he asked.

"Yeah," Pia chimed. "Is it?"

Hayden and Faust and everybody else, all the ghosts hiding in the house, were eager for an answer.

Maureen Brandt glared at a point somewhere far behind Pace. A lot of patients used to do this sort of thing on the ward, staring so deeply into something that they went all the way into its atomic structure, watching molecular chains, electron clouds, and quarks leaping across higher quantum energy states.

Why so pale and wan, fond lover? Prithee, why so pale?

She had found photos upstairs. There were Jane and Pacella sitting out on the beach, the camera on a timer and going off two seconds before they were ready. Both of them starting to smile but not quite there yet. In the next photo they'd been grinning two seconds too long, happy expressions frozen and unnatural. The one after that, Pacella had said, Forget the camera, and him and Jane were beginning to kiss, lips about a half inch away. Pacella's eyes shut and Jane's open, adoring.

"Who is this?" Maureen asked.

"Jane."

"And the man?"

Another trick question. He could say, It's me, though it really wasn't. It didn't seem to matter that much because Jane was always the best part of Pacella anyway. Seeing the two of them together, you really wanted to be that cocoa-drinking, Chaucer-reading, wimpy son of bitch.

"It's me," he said.

"That's right. William Pacella."

All of those degrees, probably twenty of them on the walls of her office, and she'd never learned that you can't use logic to win out over a psychotic.

Really, she just had to be fucking crazy.

She drew out a photo of Pacella and Jane seated on a boardwalk sharing an ice cream cone while the waves rolled in behind them.

"And this?"

"Me and Jane."

"Yes."

But that wasn't good enough. Maureen Brandt needed to drive home her point, spearing it in there so it would skewer him. She pulled out a folded up newspaper, dated six months after Jane died. Had it been here in the house or had she carried the damn thing all the way from the hospital? His face was spread across the fifth page. It was the first time Pacella had been brought in by the cops in connection with the Ganooch hits. He looked calm and a little tired, but very amenable and incapable of even winning at arm wrestling. You had to know what to look for. Pace saw that Pacella's eyes were no more than twin blazing fissures of agony and fury.

"And this is you, Will."

"No," Pace said. "That's Jack."

Thursday's Child tells the lie that causes Friday's Child to die.

She let out an exhausted sigh. It had been a long day.

"You didn't answer my question," he said.

"Fess up," Pia said. "Come on, this I want to hear."

"No," Dr. Brandt said. "We were never lovers."

Pia laid back on the couch in a sultry pose, smiling with pride in herself, like she'd caught the cat with the headless canary. "You're a lying bitch."

Pace faced Dr. Brandt, feeling a little twitchy. He thought she was lying too. Had she hopped up on top of him while he was in that full body straitjacket, suspended in mid-air, weightless? Like one of those sex chairs with the ropes and chains, you get in and even if you can't figure the thing out it's still got to be pretty good. Was there some easy way to expose his crank in the jacket? Some kind of ripcord—she walks into the room horny as hell, yanks on a string and out falls his package.

"Will—"

"Vindi also said that Kaltzas and I had once been friends. He told me I'd met him before."

"It's not true. His daughter was in Garden Falls, but he never saw her. No one did."

"Not even Vindi?"

"Not so far as I know. A lot of reporters pretending to be friends of the family showed up, but we screened them out."

"He said he bribed people on the ward. For information. Maybe the guards let him in and out."

"Possibly. But I find it more likely that if you did know Kaltzas or this Vindi, you knew them before the hospital. Your selective amnesia allows you to remember significant amounts of your core personality's history, as well as that of your alternates."

"I am an alternate," he said. The fact didn't bother him much.

"A very highly developed provisional surrogate identity. You're William Pacella's stronger half, devoid of suffering. Without his need for revenge. You must allow those repressed memories forward."

"Fuck no!" shouted the other three as one.

It got Pace smiling. "They're right. You don't want that. The memories are what drove Pacella insane in the first place. If they come back, you get Jack."

"He's gone, Will. He had no reason to exist after Joseph Ganucci...died."

"You're wrong. He's still there, Maureen. Besides, didn't you throw in with us because you trusted Jack's skills?"

"I trust Jack's skills," Hayden said loudly at Pace's chest. "You hear me in there, Jack? I trust you, buddy. You're a-okay in my book, seriously!"

"Mine too!" Faust said, shouting.

"We love you, Jack!" Pia called.

Dr. Brandt said, "I trust you, Will."

HOME IS WHERE YOUR LOVE BURNED.

The embroidery everywhere you looked.

MY BABY, WHERE ARE YOU? WHY AM I STILL ALIVE WITHOUT YOU?

Pace went to the window. He checked his watch. It was only nine o'clock, less than twelve hours since he walked out of the hospital. He didn't have enough fingers and toes to count how many lifetimes ago. He pressed his temple against the cold glass and kept his eyes on the water, knowing there was a much longer trip ahead, a lot more lives about to come and go.

There was movement. People walking around the house. He heard doors opening and shutting but couldn't tell where.

He turned his head and looked at another pillow.

DEFINITELY DO NOT EAT AT TINY BOB'S LOBSTER PAVILION.
THAT SHIT'LL KILL YOU.

Dr. Brandt wasn't in the wicker chair, and then she was. Maybe his aphasia was kicking in again. He looked at his watch again and it was almost nine-thirty.

"What's the matter?" she asked. "You have to tell me, Will. I need to know." The urgency in her voice made him frown. She could really put a wifey tone in there when she wanted. Even if they had been lovers, even if she had unsnapped his PJ's while he was in the jacket, where did this take-charge attitude come from? Like he had to answer because it was his obligation. He searched her eyes and they went from blue to green and back again.

"Hey," Hayden said, stepping in from the hall. "You might want to see this. I found enough knives back here to stab the whole world."

eleven

They were out in the open, all these blades, proving that Jack didn't really give a damn who found them. Maybe he was showing a certain amount of camaraderie and wanted Pace to have access to the weapons. Saving Pace in order to save himself.

Nobody said it was going to be easy, trusting these people inside you.

There was a separate, small back room off the kitchen that might've once been used for storing coal or canned fruit and vegetables. There were three long shelves which contained felt-lined, glass-topped cases. The fisherman's wife had been very dutiful in cleaning the glass and leaving no streaks.

Inside were the knives, laid out in simple patterns.

Not that many, really, considering how obsessive Jack got about them. Only thirty.

A couple were from the kitchen. Butcher knives. Like Jack had been making a point—it's not the tool, it's the result. Pace still had the three inch screwdriver in his pocket, and figured he knew some of what Jack had felt. Was still feeling.

Several were antique surgeon's tools—scalpel, lancet, bone cutter, curette, and a pair of Metzenbaum scissors. Jack looked ready to start operating again.

The longest blade was a standard eight-inch Bowie with a trailing point and a brass guard. There was a 5-1/2 inch hunting knife topped with a gut hook, the handle made out of highly-polished carved antler.

There was the Trident Two, one of the most versatile field knives, used by the Navy SEALS. Powder coated, partially yet deeply serrated. He shook his head and searched on until he found the Trident, the one the cops had been looking for. A Bowie-style blade made of high carbon stainless steel married to a stacked micarta handle with a satin finish. The black, self-cleaning scabbard came with its own sharpening stone. You sat there honing your blade and your hate at the same time, until both were razor-sharp.

Hayden reached into the case, grabbed the Trident and tossed it slowly, underhand at Pace, like a father throwing a ball to his kid. He whispered, "Catch."

Pia said, "Oh God."

And then—

And then—then—

The knife was in Pace's hand.

It seemed to pulse with warmth. He was drawn to its silky feel. His throat filled with a weird giggle and Jack started thinking about kidney pie again.

The others scrambled around him, Pia letting out a sharp lament, Faust cutting loose with a plaintive cry. "Forsooth, dear Lord, forget us not!"

Hayden yelled the same thing he'd shouted back in the apartment. "Is he Jack?" This had always been a kind of game to Hayden.

Pia backed herself into the corner and tried to be alluring, sexually overpowering, like that would slow Jack down. It just made him laugh harder. Jack whirled and stared at her, knowing she did this because she wanted to die. She was begging him to kill her.

The angels Rimmon and Sariel raced about in circles. Pace shut his eyes and filled himself with the exquisite balance and profound sharpness of the knife. A total of 12.4 ounces. The grip on the handle so comfortable it was nearly impossible to ever let go.

How had he ever let go.

How could he have ever let go. How could you ever put away the thing that gave you definition and purpose.

Maureen Brandt, so effortlessly calm, her slender arm out to him, the wrist so delicate and pale you could see the map of her lifeblood.

"Will—"

Jack an extension of Pacella, the blade an extension of Jack. It was a different world now than when he'd stalked the black chilly streets looking for the wet, soft places of women. Those carefully turned-away bodies facing walls while he rutted them from behind, the arcing blood against the brick.

"Will—"

He'd spin them slowly as a final heaving breath blew in his face and those eyes—sometimes blue, sometimes green—began to dim.

"Let him go, Will."

A moment of darkness and then intense, swirling light. Pace blinked twice hearing Dr. Brandt's voice in his ear, a demanding but soothing tone. The same kind used by the whores in the East End as they called to the carriages, muddy skirts twirling, *muddy skirts hiding their dirty cunts—*

"Please listen to me. Stop it now. Let him go now!"

Flashing his sharp teeth, Hayden lay on the floor with the knife pressed lengthwise against his throat.

Sam Smith was also talking now, in an equally firm voice, telling him, Never try to cut a throat the way they do it in movies, there's too much cartilage. You gotta saw back and forth way too hard before you do any serious damage. Stick to the easy tricks. Nothing fancy needed. Go for the carotid artery. The tiniest flick of the wrist and they'll never get the blood to stop.

"Will, let him go. Now."

Pace let Hayden go.

He sheathed the Trident, and put it back under glass in the case. He reached down and grabbed Hayden by the shirtfront and hauled him to his feet. Then onto his tippy-toes. Pace dragged him forward through the air until he saw his reflection looming in Hayden's eyes.

"Why'd you do that?" Pace asked.

"You're still holding it."

"What?"

"The knife. You acted like you were putting it away, but you've got it tucked in your belt."

Pace checked and saw it was true. He hadn't put the Trident back at all, it was right there at the small of his back, where he could pull it with either his right or left hand.

The rafters groaned. The little room had a small window and the glass was covered with throbbing rain ignited by lightning. He wondered what the weather was like in Greece. He thought of Kaltzas's jet at JFK, waiting for them.

Hayden picked himself up and rubbed his throat. "I wanted to make sure Dr. Brandt wasn't right. We all needed to know if Jack was still there."

"Feel better now?"

"Christ, no."

"You play a game like that again and you might die."

"It's not a game," Maureen Brandt said.

Still in the corner, Pia looked sexy and a little sad. Faust's scar seemed to be watching Pace very intently, making up its own mind about him. Dr. Brandt appeared defeated, and she was even more beautiful for it.

"I'm going to sleep for a while in the master bedroom. Don't anyone bother me."

"Wouldn't think of doing it," Pia said, her eyes full of deadly mischief, thinking about doing it.

Pace woke with a start, heard someone crying.

He reached over and turned on the light, looked around the room.

William Pacella sat there at the foot of the bed, crying.

Pacella twisted his head side to side, his eyes clenched as the tears boiled out beneath them.

Pace laid back on the pillow and stared at the ceiling. "You did the right thing, moving aside. We all have to do it. It'll be my turn soon."

Pacella said nothing. The dead either talked your ear off or they just sat there silently.

"Just leave. There's no place for you here anymore. You did what you could. We all do. None of this was your fault."

Ineffective white-bread weakass that he was, the guy sure hung in there.

Waves lashed the rocks at the shore, sending a pleasant booming staccato through the house. A contrapuntal to his heartbeat. The rain whipped at the glass and formed vivid designs. You were always this close to figuring your life out, but you just never quite got there.

Pacella must've felt the same way.

"Why don't you go to her?" Pace asked. "She's been waiting for you for almost three years. She needs you. Go join her."

A scuffling under the bed made Pace roll over and peer over the edge of the mattress.

There was a lot going on under there. He saw a bloody hand flash out, and several thrashing legs, the stock of a rifle, a copy of *A Separate Peace*, a girl's forehead with strawberry blonde hair sliding aside.

Pacella turned his face and opened his eyes. In him remained all the fury and heartache of a man incapable of doing what must be done. It wasn't much different than the way Pacella's father had looked a couple of weeks before the old man had died. Frail, ambivalent with disappointment.

Broken by the large and small injustices done to him over his life, with the unfairness of his mediocrity.

William Pacella remained at a puzzled loss to understand what had gone wrong and when and where, with Jane's death or long before. He looked like someone chained to an anchor tossed in the shallows, an inch away from the surface but unable to get his nose above water.

Scraping sounds erupted beneath the bed. Fists were jammed up into the box spring so the mattress jumped. Pace laid there, the calming presence of the blade tight against his back. He'd slept with it on his belt.

Pacella looked away again and then, going slack, drifted forward and fell to the shadowy floor.

The noises continued. Squeaks, murmurs, and more sobbing punctuated by whispered requests and occasional guffaws. They knew how to have fun, that was for sure. Pace glanced over the edge again and saw that a woman with tightly curled gray hair was looking up at him.

She focused and said, You're not my boy. Where's William? What have you done with my son?

It was midnight. He went downstairs and Hayden and Faust were on the couch watching a repeat of the ten o'clock news, passing a bowl of potato chips back and forth. Hayden was also scrawling on his notepad, writing out tremendous looping words. They were both drinking beer and had a couple of empty six-packs stacked on the coffee table. He couldn't tell if they were drunk. He didn't know if they could ever get drunk.

"You went shopping?"

"Pia did," Faust said. "Map told her about a small shopping area a few miles up the road. She made a very passable lobster bisque while you were sleeping."

He stepped into the kitchen and saw the bisque in a huge pot on the stove. He retreated and asked, "Where's Dr. Brandt?"

"Sleeping."

"Where's Pia now?"

Hayden looked up from the endless letter. "She's gone. Left about a half-hour ago. She wanted to hit a club. Alone."

A dull frown crimped Faust's face. "She was rather rude about it. She demanded that we stay here."

"Said she'd break our asses if we followed. Not sure how we were supposed to try to follow her, but even if we could've we wouldn't have. The mongoloids knew how to dance but they never taught me."

"Quite adamant about the breaking of asses part. Even after I praised her bisque. That girl has no manners. Our father who art insulting."

Pace said, "And you let her go?"

"She's not a prisoner." Hayden's handwriting got worse and worse as he pressed harder into the paper. He was scratching deeply, stabbing his pen in. "None of us are prisoners, right? We didn't escape the nuthatch just to be locked down by you, eh? Besides, we're just going to fly to Greece soon to meet with the guy who wants us dead. So where's the harm?"

"She could hurt herself."

"You kidding me? She's nearly as good as Jack with a knife. She's sliced up a couple of her foster fathers, didn't you hear her?"

"Which club did she go to?"

Pace heard naked padding footsteps on the steps and looked to see Jane coming down the stairs.

Her red hair was an erotic chaos, disheveled from sleep. Wearing the sleek satin white lingerie he'd bought her for Christmas, the same year she'd bought him the blue bathrobe and slippers. Her freckled cleavage was prominently displayed, one shoulder strap having fallen aside. Pace's breath caught in his throat and he reached a hand out to the wall to keep from going over—all these things, no matter how small, easily pushing him over—as Jane came to him. He gritted his teeth and shut his eyes and stood there, motionless.

"Will—"

Again with the Will. Always with the Will.

"Will, what's wrong?"

He had a hundred names and he hated Will the most, even more than Nightjack. He kept his hand on the wall, his other arm pinned at his side. You could do a lot of crazy shit in front of the other loonies, but don't make a lunge for your dead wife. That would really look bad.

"Will, listen to me—"

He opened his eyes and there she was—Dr. Brandt right there before him, still dressed in her suit, but with the jacket and the shoes off, the blouse unbuttoned one button too far. The hint of her pink bra enough to drive sane men out of their trees and nutcases right out of the forest and down the mountain.

"Sorry," he said. "I didn't see you for a second." After all the thousands of pills, the therapy and treatments and group discussions, she was just another failed mother who couldn't help her fucked-up kids. "Pia's gone."

She said, "I fell asleep."

Faust chuckled again but this time it came out all wrong. Laced with hysteria and broken up with a series of effeminate burps. Maybe he really was drunk. He said, "I can't sleep, you know. I haven't slept in years." Rimmon and Sariel nodded, so tired that they sagged against their sword hilts. "God doesn't allow it. I am being punished for my many sins." He took a long pull on his beer and belched out a whine.

"We need to go after her," Dr. Brandt said, the pink drawing closer. "Somehow. The storm is much worse. It's terrible out there."

"I'll go alone," Pace said.

"I should be with you."

"No, you shouldn't." Pace placed his hand over the page where Hayden was going on and on to his mother, shredding the paper. "Where did Pia go?"

"She asked Map for directions to *Le Feu* in Southampton. That place where he said he and his wife used to go." His eyes were calm now even though his hand flashed in a frenzy. Spelling out very clearly Mama, Mama, they're going to kill me. Mama, I'm going to die soon. "Pia went out dancing. With her father."

twelve

Before he went to Nam, P.I. Sam Smith was known to boost a car or two. Him and his best friend Jimmy Lee Clark, who died in Phu Da in '72 when *Beaucoup VC* broke through the concertina wire and threw him across his own M-79 grenade launcher, an illumination round exploding in his face.

Sam and Jimmy Lee would cut school and grab a late model Chevrolet off the street in Hell's Kitchen, drive around for a day or two, and then return it pretty close to where they'd nabbed it from.

It was a skill that occasionally came in handy when Sam was trailing some middle-aged husband stepping out on his wife, heading down to Atlantic City for a night, and Smith's own '87 Datsun wouldn't start. He'd just boost a car from nearby, tail the husband, get the photographic evidence he needed outside one of the casinos, and then return the car to within a block of where he picked it up. He'd call Triple A and wait for the tow truck to come get his own piece of shit and haul it off.

Sam was drenched after a mile hike in the nor'easter. He hated the cold rain coming down and kept shaking his fist at the ocean. He didn't have many cars to choose from at the market where Pia had gotten the ingredients to make her bisque. A Civic and an old Buick Skylark that looked like it might float out of the flooded parking lot.

A row of large cabins nearby offered only a Ford Ranger with a horse trailer and a Mercedes that he knew he wouldn't be able to break into without the proper equipment. He unhitched the horse trailer, slipped into the Ranger, and found the keys already in it. Nice.

Map had given Pace directions to *Le Feu*. He found the club and was surprised at how much action there was, even in the storm. *Le Feu* was on the water, backed up to a raging channel. Fifty or more skiffs, Pro Elite bass boats, 15-footers, outboards, and water taxis were docked at the pier, vessels colliding as the turbulent waves washed over the jetty. Rich kids who didn't give a shit about safety.

He spotted the Jag parked down on the sand, marooned in three feet of water, scuttled.

The front of the place was crowded with twenty-somethings drinking under the wide overhangs. A bouncer stood framed in the door: clean-cut, muscle-bound guy with no neck. Black T-shirt with a logo emblazoned across it in white. Pace walked up unsure of the procedure. There would be some kind of arcane process to join them, he was sure of it, and was certain he'd fail the trial.

He put on his most disarming smile and approached, pushing drenched hair out of his eyes. He wasn't even close when the guy held up a beefy arm semaphore-style across the partially submerged walkway.

"You can't come in."

"Why not?"

The bouncer stood there not saying anything, just giving Pace a dead look. You had to hand it to no-neck, he had a good eye and could see trouble coming from a distance. He knew Pace was going to get into something here. Pace still had the knife but it was concealed beneath his shirt and jacket. It wasn't difficult hiding 12.4 ounces.

"Look, I don't want any trouble," Pace said, like he was reading it off a cue card.

"And there's not going to be any. That's what I get paid for."

"Right, I get that. But this is important. I need to find a friend of mine."

The bouncer let his bottom lip hang, showing a couple of empty spaces and some very cheap bridgework. "You can make new friends someplace else. Right up the road there's a couple other clubs, *The Riot* and *Oceanic*. I bet you'd like those places better."

"You're not listening."

"Sure I am."

"I have to get my friend."

"Can't help you there, chum." The arm moved a few inches but still didn't touch Pace's chest. "Now how about if you move it along, eh?" Saying it like a beat cop on the street pushing a bum aside with his billy club.

Girls wearing thin blouses and transparent raincoats shuddered in the corners of the doorway, laughing drunkenly while the music blared inside. The rain sluiced over the roof and fell in great torrents from the gutters. No one else seemed to realize that there was a hurricane in the making.

Feeling the tempest inside and outside, Pace stood there wondering how to play it. If he should fight, if he should continue to argue. Get a manager over, raise a stink. No matter how large your fate loomed, you always had to handle the moment-to-moment stupid tyrannies of life.

He would be in Greece soon with oracles providing him a hundred destinies for a hundred men, but for now he had to deal with this petty situation.

The knife was in his hand and then out of it.

Suggestion and instant rejection, without having to make any conscious choice at all. What would happen next? What would the hands do next?

Then he saw that he'd pulled out two of Vindi's hundred dollar bills.

He'd crumpled and jammed them up the bouncer's nose.

Shit, that wasn't good. That wasn't the best approach to the situation. He wanted to yell at his hands for making such a stupid move. What was this fixation with jamming stuff up other guys' noses? You had to be sick to do a thing like that.

The bouncer let out an angry warble and started to lunge. Pace brought his forearm up hard into the guy's throat. The balled bills shot out of no-neck's nostrils and he gagged and flopped back into a six inch puddle.

Here we go.

Another bouncer passing by the doorway rushed over swinging his big arms, shouting out a string of curses. Pace spun fluidly and flipped the guy over his shoulder so that the new no-neck did a complete somersault in the air. He came down in a heap and lay there moaning.

One of the girls let out a delighted cackle, a few others began to scream. Pace rushed inside, threading quickly through the crowd.

The music pounded. He passed dozens of young men at the bar using pick-up lines that were old when Jack had slipped by the fog-shrouded whores. And the girls, secure in their youth, laughed ceaselessly.

A throng of bodies pressed against him, inside and out. He flexed his shoulders and forced his way through the crowd. He scanned left and right, watching the corners. He should've known better.

Because there, in the center of the dance floor, Pia grooved with her daddy.

"Christ."

Pia's father was in his late forties, without a gray hair on his head. He had a thick, well-trimmed mustache and was a little too caught up in the whole '70's revival thing. He wore flared cuffs, a chocolate brown suit with matching vest, his shirt collar hanging over the jacket collar. Still, he didn't look as out of place as he should have.

The man liked to twirl and bump. Turned out he was a better dancer than his daughter was. Spinning on his heels, sticking his rump out. Pia laughed and tried her best to hang in there, but the guy really could pull a few amazing moves. He'd go down to one knee, do a split, whirl about skillfully, then hop back up and shake it with her. You'd never guess the guy liked to visit Revolutionary War sites.

When Pia was thirteen her father was brought up on formal charges of child abuse by her older sister, who'd been out of the house for six months. She told the cops that her father had sexually abused her for years, and only stopped coming to her bedroom once he'd started molesting Pia instead.

The day he was arrested he hanged himself in the police precinct bathroom even before they'd fingerprinted him. He'd come ready with a piano wire he'd clipped off the family piano. The wire had been wrapped around his chest, under his shirt. He must've done it the minute he saw the police pulling up at his curb.

Pia's mother protested her husband's innocence and blamed Pia and the sister for the man's death. She threatened to kill them both, went wild around the neighborhood chasing both her kids with a shovel. She was arrested about a minute after she brained the sister. Three ambulances showed up but none in time. Pia held her sister while the girl died.

The mother killed herself in the same bathroom as her husband, having sneaked in a bottle of drain cleaner. Like the man, she must've just been waiting for the chance, having packed the poison in a baggie tied to her thigh.

These people, devious as fucking ninjas.

After the sister was buried Pia was placed in foster care. The family that took her in had dealt with many troubled children before. By all accounts, it was a loving home, and Pia was treated with great patience, understanding, and consideration. She went after her foster father with a meat cleaver. They turned her over to another foster family, one made of sterner stuff. Stricter rules, more wary foster parents. She got her hands on a pair of gardening shears and lopped the guy's left ear off.

She wasn't fourteen yet. Social Services decided to give her one more try. They put her in a home run by a retired Marine colonel who had six military brats of his own and six foster kids. She stabbed him in the testicles with a trowel stolen out of the garage and was shipped off to Garden Falls.

Pia saw Pace coming at her and moved so that her father was between them. The man bumping and grinding against her, ass to ass, while Pace watched and tried to decipher why she needed her daddy so much, in this way.

When Pace was close enough she said, "It's a bad night to be out."

"For everyone. Not stopping anybody here though."

"They're having too much fun."

"So are you. I want you to come back to the house with me."

"I'm safer where I am."

He had to think about that for a second. "Maybe not."

The kids on the floor moved around Pace like one creature shifting, deaf and blind, edging forward and rearing away.

He reached out and took Pia by the wrist, realizing at once it was the wrong thing to do. He loosened his grip but didn't let go. Her father coiled past and continued grinding, bumping asses with Pace now, grooving, always grooving.

The man said, "My little girl's not going anywhere with you. She's with me tonight. It's been too long since we've seen each other. Right, buttercup?"

"Yes, Daddy," she told him, voice heavy with lust. She snapped her arm free from Pace and started dancing again.

"We've got a lot of lost time to make up for, sugarplum." The man leaning in, exposing his throat. Pia kissed him there, then began nibbling on his earlobe. "That's my good girl. My sweetie pumpkin pie."

"Yes, Daddy."

This was how she saw her father now, the dead in relation to herself. This wasn't the war buff who took his family on trips in the summer, the roadside attraction freak who traveled the country looking at chickens that never lost at tic-tac-toe. This was how she saw him now, as defined by her own self-hatred: vapid, perverse, obvious.

Pace wished the guy still had some piano wire on him. He would enjoy pulling the garrote taut, watching the bastard's head go flying.

"I love to boogie with my baby girl!" Her father thrust his groin forward at Pia, then at Pace. "You gonna try something with me, buddy? You gonna make your move now?"

"Please, Daddy—"

"Shh, honeybunch, pun'kin. Don't interrupt. Daddy is talking."

You could fight a lot of things, but you could never win out over the love a daddy's girl had for her father. Pace stared at the man, focusing himself. His hand flashed out, grabbed Pia's wrist again and held on this time. Maybe that's all she'd ever wanted, was for someone to not let go.

The music grew even louder now. The other dancers completely ignored him. Pace got up close to Pia and spoke in her ear. "We need to leave. Now. We have to get back to the others."

"You afraid of a little bad weather?"

"No."

"You like it, don't you?"

"Yes."

"You want the whole world to drown."

The squall called to him. A part of him, several parts of him, wanted to go out and battle the sea once more. He'd made the proper offerings at long last, his odyssey completed. Poseidon had forgiven him and would finally watch over Troy's favorite son. He'd been away for almost twenty years. He had a wife to win back, a kingdom to reconquer.

"Don't make me leave my father again," Pia begged.

"I won't. We'll take him with us, all right?"

The man was swinging all over the place. Pia had been trying hard to keep up and her hair was sticky with sweat. "Dr. Brandt is always telling me I have to leave him behind. She told me to *divorce* myself from him, as if I were his wife!"

"She's not a very good psychiatrist," Pace admitted. "She's got a lot of troubles of her own."

"What troubles?"

"She's in love with me."

"That bitch is so judgmental! Giving me that glower, as if I deserved what happened to me."

"You did," her father said. "Honey bunny pecan pie, you wanted my love. I had to show you that I loved you. That you were wanted. You hated being alone in your bed. You'd climb in between me and your mother. You'd roll over and sit up on me."

"I know, Daddy."

No matter how deep someone went inside, there were always more layers underneath. It was easy to find the place where fear, love, and shame bundled together into tightly-knit fibers as dense as the tissue of the human heart. But you could never cut through it. You couldn't burn it. One chamber led to another. You never got to the bottom of yourself. The discovery of who you were never really started and never fully finished. You'd be in therapy for fifty years and still say to the doctor, "*Oh yeah, and another thing...*"

Her father turned to Pace, searching his eyes. "And you, you insane murderous son of a bitch. Are you like the rest of them? Do you hate me?"

"Yes," Pace said.

"Why?"

"You abused your little girls. You took advantage of the ones you were supposed to keep from harm."

"You ever think her sister lied?"

"No. If she had, you wouldn't have been ready with the wire."

"That's just careful planning. You'll be ready with your wire too, when the time comes."

Pace thought that was probably true.

"It wasn't my fault, you know," Pia's father went on. "She wanted it. She used to crawl into my bed and cry and cry if she didn't get it."

"I heard you before."

"I did my best to resist but nobody's that strong. You'd lose the struggle too. When she's whispering, pleading, nibbling on your ear. Her sister was the same. You know why she turned me in? Jealousy. Plain and simple. It was between them. They both wanted me. They both—"

"How about if you clam up now, man?"

Another thing you couldn't do was you couldn't shut the dead up once they got going. They went on and on about every shittin' little thing. You'd wait for them to give up the secrets of the grave, offer clarity about God, the process of demise, the grandeur of deliverance, and instead you just got someone cutting a rug and spouting off about their sickest guilts.

"So you want to kill me? You want to stick that knife into my gut and twist it?"

"Daddy, please—"

"And keep turning the blade, with my blood spurting into your face?"

"No," Pace said.

"Why not?"

"Because she still needs you."

"This little slut doesn't need anyone! She's got it all figured out! She knows just how to get by in the world. She's cheap on the street, let me tell you. Three bucks for three minutes, on her knees. How they fall in love with her. They line up around the block. And if somebody doesn't fall for her, she'll just chop off their ears. Maybe you'll be next. You're gonna look damn silly with no ears, let me tell you."

The night was screaming now, but nobody on the dance floor seemed to notice or care, about that or anything. Pace wondered what it might take to capture their attention, if a guy talking to a ghost couldn't do it, if a hurricane couldn't do it.

He said, "She needs her daddy. Maybe only for a little while longer, maybe forever. I don't know. I hope she gets rid of you soon. But for now, you're still a part of who she is, what makes her so special."

"You're just another lunatic," the man told him and swung away through the crowd until he vanished.

Pia stood there with an unsettled expression, as if she wasn't completely certain what had transpired, or what the consequences were likely to be. Pace drew her to the front of the club, where just inside the door a couple of waitresses were attending to the two bouncers Pace had fought with. Pia followed him into the deluge. He led her to the stolen truck and she said, "I'm sorry about the Jag."

"It doesn't matter."

"We'll never be able to fly to Greece tomorrow."

"Probably not."

"It's like the heavens are trying to protect us."

"Or protect Kaltzas."

"You still don't remember him, do you?"

"No," Pace said. "But tell me, why does he think you had something to do with his daughter's rape?"

"Because," she whispered in his ear, nibbling on his earlobe. "I'm a sick bitch. Didn't you hear anything my father said?"

thirteen

When they got back the house was already going full-throttle with an end of the world party. In droves they approached and said hello, kissed Pace's cheek, patted his shoulder. He hadn't seen some of them for a couple of years. Features softened and blurred and redefined themselves. Some personalities were so faded and ephemeral he couldn't touch them, could barely hear them.

Smoker, the half-breed outlaw from 1880s Arizona, held up his Colts and grunted in Mescalaro Apache. He'd jumped the rez and wanted Pace to join his men as they raided towns along the Mexican border. A part of Pace wanted to go, to be with his tribe again. Across the room, obscured by a wall of bodies, he saw Dr. Brandt trying to make her way toward him. Every time she got close, the crowd would heave and she'd be shoved aside.

Thaddeus, friend and companion to St. Paul, was still spreading the word of Christ across a troubled new world. He whispered in Pace's ear and told him of the death of Paul, beheaded on the Ostian Way at Tre Fontane, just outside of Rome.

Faust appeared for a moment with tears in his eyes. Behind him to the left, Sariel guided the progress of humanity. The four keys to the four corners of the earth jangled on his belt. Rimmon continued to fight envy in his never-ending battle. The 29,000 legions of burning choirs blazed around the room, lighting the rafters.

Hayden had brought along Cravenborn the warlock and his demonic familiar Bloomboy, who performed occult rituals in the kitchen. Black motes of energy rose around them as hexes glowed on the walls.

Pace recognized some of the faces from *Le Feu*. Jesus Christ, had they followed him here? Had Pia invited them? Or were more identities emerging every minute now, from himself and the others? He couldn't tell anymore. Dr. Brandt was right about one thing, they were making each other much sicker. He looked down and he was holding the head of St. Paul in his right hand.

Crumble waddled past chewing on a sock.

Pace said, "We have to go to Pythos." It came out sounding odd, and he realized he'd said it in Apache. He touched his mouth and tried to straighten his tongue, get his lips working the right way.

He knew he was weakening, beginning to slide out of form. He felt himself starting to diminish. His resolve—it was the only reason Pace was even here—wasn't enough anymore, and he hoped the next guy would do better.

He drew the knife and pressed it into his palm. Blood welled and a surge of satisfaction filled him, just from feeling the blade entering flesh, even his own. Jack's mouth began to water. There wasn't as much pain as there was sudden clarity. The din subsided, the pressure of crushing bodies eased.

The room emptied quickly, the crowd draining away even as the windows shook from the nor'easter. He slid the knife back into its sheathe and tightened his wounded hand into a fist, holding his own blood in. Symbols had their own power.

When you couldn't find any allegories, you made your own. You moved aside when it was your time to go, but you never let anybody push you out of the way.

Dr. Brandt stood beside him, whispering words a little too faint for him to understand.

"What?"

"You did well, bringing her back, Will. Was it terrible?"

"It was confusing. I think she'll always be attached to her father despite what he did."

"You're protective of them. That's a good sign."

"A sign of what?"

"That your primary personality is beginning to re-emerge."

He turned to her and said, "You have got to be the dumbest person with twenty degrees that I've ever met."

"Don't be insulting, Will."

"Get away from me, lady."

Pace looked over at Hayden and Faust on the couch, watching him sleepily. Pia joined them, the excitement having dissipated from her. He gestured at the stairs with his chin and said, “Go to bed, we leave for Pythos in the morning.”

Pia said, “We can’t, the storm.”

“I have a feeling it’s going to clear.”

Faust’s scar was hardly even there anymore. There was barely a mark. “We’ll die on that island, you know. In the ruins of some temple to a forgotten god, we’ll be buried alive under a mountain of stone. We’ll be entombed together, breathing each other’s stale air for our remaining hours. He’ll leave us with one dwindling candle to hold back the endless, eternal darkness.”

Hayden said, “Oh, why don’t you just suck the pipe already, Mr. Happy Pants?”

The lights flickered and thunder groaned. The roof creaked as if a dozen children outside pounded on it with their fists. Pia moved to the stairway, her lips full and bruised from kissing her father’s throat. “Don’t we still have to go through customs? We don’t just get on a plane and it flies to his doorstep, do we?”

“No, I wouldn’t think so,” Pace said, but he didn’t know.

“Then there’s more to come. More things have to happen.”

Pace knew exactly what she meant. He nodded. “Yes. Probably in the morning. Vindi or somebody will come knocking on the door.”

“I’m too tired to care right now.”

“We all are. But don’t worry. Nothing will happen to you.”

“I’m not worried.”

“I’m a little worried,” Hayden said. On the pad he had written to his mother, Momma, oh Momma, I’m fucking seriously worried right here.

“I won’t let anything happen to any of you.”

Faust said, “I wonder if that would be more soothing if someone other than a murderous lunatic had said it.”

“Probably not much,” Hayden told him, and the two of them followed Pia, single file up the steps.

Watching them go, Pace had a very strong sense that he was seeing three children going up to bed, maybe on Christmas Eve. Three kids wearing jammies and trailing teddy bears that had only one button eye.

Dr. Brandt slid onto the couch and he sat beside her.

“I’m sorry I yelled,” he said.

“It’s all right. You’ve suffered a great deal today.”

"Not really," he admitted. "Actually, it's been sort of fun. You're the one who's suffering worse than any of us. You haven't accepted yourself the way we have."

She turned to face him, and he was reminded of the first time he'd seen her in the hyper-white room, in his straitjacket tied to the steel rails of the bed. What had she felt at that initial moment: Revulsion? Empowerment?

"The fire's dying," he said.

"There's more wood out back but it's too wet to burn."

She gazed into his eyes. Analyzing and making assessments. Inquiring and discounting. Distrusting and overwhelmed by anxiety. That stunning, sorrowful face turned on him in full. His heart strained toward or away from something.

He said it again. "We go to Pythos. Tomorrow."

"I refuse," Dr. Brandt said.

"You threw in with us for a reason."

"Yes, to get away from that man, not to go to him."

"There is no way to get away from him. Or anybody, really, if they come at you hard enough."

"You would know." Saying it with an acidic tone.

"Yes, I would know. The only chance you have is to meet them head on. That's why we have to face him."

"Ridiculous. He owns the entire island and resides in a fortress, surrounded by a private army."

"How do you know that?"

"It's not a secret. He's very famous."

"You tried to save his daughter, didn't you? Why would he hold that against you?"

"He doesn't. It's what came after. I should've kept her safe. But I couldn't."

"You mean you couldn't keep her safe from me."

"From you. Or one of your alternates. Or someone else on the ward."

Pace kept wanting to touch her. Not out of lust, but hoping for reaffirmation. A homecoming of sorts. It would be a lot nicer to make love on the couch than it had been tied to the railings, if that had happened.

"Vindi said we were lovers. Is it true?"

"Stop asking that."

"Answer it then."

"I already have, but you push and persist. No, we were never lovers."

"You don't sound very persuasive."

"I'm not trying to persuade you, I'm simply telling you the truth."

Even while she sat there, staring bleakly, with many lifetimes between them, he knew she was lying. "Kaltzas thinks you were covering for me."

"Yes, I believe he does."

"Were you?"

"I didn't cover for you. I don't know what happened to Cassandra."

He opened his hand and there was a piece of blood-stained paper in it that read:

She's lying. Don't trust anything she says.

It was enough to make you laugh, if you weren't a little worried about laughing at this sort of thing. He quietly wadded the note up and tossed it into the cooling fireplace.

A low, humming current ran through Pace's skull. It made him grit his teeth and shut his eyes for a second. When he opened them his other fist was closed. He unclenched his hand and there was another note there that read:

Don't trust these notes. You've written them to yourself, and you're completely insane.

He crumpled that one up too and tossed it after the other. Maureen Brandt didn't notice. She just sat there, facing front, like a scared girl on a first date in a movie theater, waiting for the boy to make a grab for her tit.

"You had a laptop and access to the Net," she said.

"Yes."

"Your strength is research."

"Well, Sam's is."

She either knew who Sam was or decided to ignore the comment. "What did you do while you were online, Will?"

"Tried to learn about Kaltzas."

"Did you find out anything important?"

"Not really."

"Or the island? In case you need to escape? If it comes down to that? If it's what Jack needs?"

"No, I didn't think to look."

"Why not?"

"I don't know. I'm not Jack."

"Maybe it's because you've been there."

"Maybe."

Dr. Brandt shifted on the couch and stared at Pace, the condescension mixed with *bereavement*, the way you feel for the memory of someone who's been dead for years. This lady, she could never look at you with just one emotion. Everything she felt was in conflict. He wondered how someone could live with that for any length of time. Maybe she'd been in love with Pacella, the cocoa-drinker. Maybe she liked men who took better care of their books than they did their wives.

She said, "I think Faust is right. I think if you go there, you'll die."

"It doesn't matter. The course is set."

"You're so self-destructive, Will," she told him, standing and moving quickly away.

"Sure. Even I know that."

Only somebody who had nothing to live for would sound so cavalier. Pacella had never sounded like that, and neither had Jack, back when he used to write mischievous letters to Scotland Yard. Pace wasn't sure that he'd ever been afraid of anything. Maybe that was the signature to this aspect of himself.

He wanted Dr. Brandt's professional opinion on that sort of thing, but only a diminishing shadow at the top of the stairs remained of her, and then not even that.

The night spoke in a voice of darkness and regret.

Whispered reminders of lives already gone or waiting to be born. Crying children and quiet lullabies. The words of your mother, the laughter of your wife. The decisive snarl of your eighth-grade gym teacher, barking down at you on the wrestling mats. Hating your father because you thought he hated you. The lost chance to forgive.

You hung back in alleys and watched the Ganooch boys swagger down the street to their Coupe de Villes. Using grease in their hair like the old days, a couple of them with ducks' asses. These guys still thinking they were part of the Rat Pack, as if Dean Martin and Frankie were about to bust into song, call them up on stage, share a tall one with them. You never drop the zeppoles. You didn't even have to be half-good to run through these guys, not even when they were supposedly on their toes. It just meant more muscle packing more heat, carrying more sopping oily bags. Your whole life you thought the mob was full of all-powerful men, and when the time came they went easy as snuffing out votive candles.

Are you cured?

Chin in hand, with his face damp, Pace awoke sitting at the foot of the bed.

He glanced over and saw Pacella lying under the covers, looking comfortable and well-rested. He wore a kind of post-coital leer that actually disturbed Pace a little.

Pacella said, “It’s all right. You did what you were supposed to do.”

“No, I haven’t.”

“Just leave. There’s no place for you here anymore. You did what you could. We all have. Now take a powder.”

“It’s not supposed to work this way,” Pace said. “We’re going backward.”

“Move aside, crybaby.”

“So when did you become so tough, huh?”

Waves lashed the rocks of the shore, sending an unpleasant booming staccato vibrating through the house.

A contrapuntal to his heartbeat. The rain poured down the panes in vivid designs, some of them recognizable. He saw Dr. Brandt and Jane there, moving across the glass separately, then together. He watched himself performing strange functions of death.

Pace dried his face with the sheets and glared at Pacella, who was supposed to be long gone by now. The hell was happening when you couldn’t count on the dead wimps staying out of your way?

He drew the knife and slipped up the mattress, eased himself forward and pressed the blade to Pacella’s throat.

The guy just kept smiling

“You’re not William Pacella, are you?” Pace said.

“Who do you think I am?”

“You’re Jack.”

“No, you still don’t get it.” Showing teeth the way Pacella never would, unless Jane was with him. “It’s you. You’re Jack.”

Are you cured?

And Pace thinking, I’m not stepping aside for you or anybody else. I’ve got too much left to do.

fourteen

Jack had saved the Ganooch for last.

He'd taken out all the major capos, a few of the made guys, a couple of dirty cops, and about a dozen of the Ganucci family soldiers.

Big Joe Ganucci, like all the old-time mobsters, pretended to be a regular businessman in waste management and disposal, too cheap to have a first-rate burglar alarm put in. Even now, with the syndicate in shambles, he still believed in a show of muscle, surrounding himself with stupid bodyguards.

The first thing a pro learns is to never compromise your hands. Don't read the paper on duty, don't have donuts and coffee, don't run off to the john. Don't hold the fucking bag of zeppoles. Drop the fucking zeppoles, idiot. These guys, they spent most of their time trying to find the TV remote behind the couch cushions.

When Big Joe and Jack were finally alone, the Ganooch just sitting in his wheelchair in the center of the room, with the sacred heart of Jesus picture overlooking the gutted bodies, the old man looked around a little sadly like he expected to leave more behind in this world.

"You've done a good job of taking me out of the game," the Ganooch said calmly. "Who the fuck are you?"

Pacella told him.

"The schoolteacher. The fucking schoolteacher. Jesus. Never count out the common man."

Jack liked that. The old guy showing no fear at all. Jack was a grinner not a talker, so he slid aside and let Pacella answer.

"Yes."

"I always *thought* maybe it was you doing all this, something in the back of my head telling me it might be you, but nobody believed me. You're a pantywaist. No one could pin anything on you."

"You're not very good."

"No, I guess not. You hire the private eye that was watching us?"

"Yes."

"Things are falling into place. He used to steal cars around here, that one, first when he was a kid in the Sixties, and then lately to follow my men. Drive around in their cars, the prick." Nodding, glad that he could finally scratch some of the itches that had been bothering him. "How have I wronged you?"

"*Emilio's* restaurant," Pacella said.

Ganooch thought about it. "Place on 67th and Madison. Where your wife died."

"You burned it to the ground."

"Me? No. Not personally."

Like that might matter, after everything that had gone down.

"You ordered it done."

"That's what this is all about?"

"Three people died."

"Yeah, yeah, that I knew, but I didn't think you'd blame me. The whole job was sloppy. Bad for business. But it was a favor. You understand? Cavallo asked me to do it. You skip him and come at me and all my crew? What are you, a child? You should've just taken him out. He's the one who had it done."

Pacella's jaw hung open at that. He'd known Emilio Cavallo for almost five years, since Jane had first become manager of the restaurant.

"Why?" he asked.

"You really got to ask that? You gotta ask why? In this economic climate? Why else? He was losing his shirt and wanted out of the business. He did it for the insurance. Everybody does every goddamn thing for the fucking insurance, I have to explain this to you?"

Blinking, Pacella realized just how naive he was. He wanted to go back to sleep and let Jack return, but Jack was having fun watching Pacella twisting like this. "Cavallo did it himself? He torched his own place?"

The old man started to get excited in his chair, sorta hopping in it now, his fists jumping in the air. "I took a small interest in the restaurant at the beginning, back in '67. We grew up on the same block in Ozone Park, me and Emilio. You always help somebody from the neighborhood, that's old school, it's the rule. I lent him money a year or two ago when things started to slide for him, but nothing helped him dig his way free. So he took the only way out he had left."

"Three of his own employees burned to death."

"You wanted to kill somebody, you *pazzo* son of a bitch, you should've killed Cavallo! My men had nothing to do with it. But you want the truth, it wasn't Emilio's fault either, or mine. My consigliere set that up with some pyro on the outside. My right hand man, you killed him two months ago. Strangled him, from behind. Broke his neck. I got guys...had guys...who told me how hard that was to do. Breaking somebody's neck from behind."

Jack, the mad surgeon inside, was starting to cackle, because it had been so easy.

"Who was the torcher?" Pacella asked. "I want a name."

"I don't know, and that's the truth. I never had anything to do with that side of the business anymore. Even when I did, I never knew the details. I gave the order and others got it done. You *pazzo* prick, you murdered all my guys for this? You got it all wrong. You weren't even close."

"You should've hired a smarter consigliere, it would've saved us both a lot of grief," Pacella said, rolling over and sinking down to where it felt like death, even though he couldn't die. The old man only managed a small whimper before Jack finished the job.

So the Ganooch wasn't last after all.

Emilio Cavallo.

Pacella had always liked the guy. He'd eaten many meals at the restaurant and shared a lot of wine and Italian beer with Emilio, who was seventy and had been in the country nearly all his life but still talked with an Italian accent. Emilio was always admiring Jane from afar, telling Pacella how beautiful she was, what a lucky man he was, how he should never let her go. Pacella always agreeing, knowing it was all true.

If you weren't already insane, a betrayal like this would push you over the big edge. Thinking about every time you laughed with the man, broke bread with him, listened to him the way you had never listened to your own father or grandfather. Believing he loved you and was forever looking out for you. That man, who made you promise aloud to protect your wife—that one, he was the one who took her away.

Pacella boarded the train into the city, took a cab out of Penn Station up to the east-side brownstone where Cavallo had lived alone since his wife died from a stroke a decade earlier. Pacella and Jane had visited the place a couple of times, attending Christmas parties and stopping over when Emilio celebrated his 70th birthday. Jane had bought him cuff links made of Italian gold, and Pacella had brought a rare biography of Dante Alighieri, written in Italian.

Pacella paid the cabbie and, as he turned and hit the first step of the brownstone stairs, Jack started urging him to move it faster, faster. Pacella sprinted up the steps and leaned on the buzzer, Jack's hideous giggle at the back of his throat.

Cavallo was surprised to hear Pacella's voice over the intercom, but buzzed him right in.

Pacella walked in and there was Emilio Cavallo, standing with his arms wide open. By then, Cavallo was going almost three hundred pounds but still carried it pretty good. He had a deeply bronzed tan, the kind that takes two months in Miami Beach to get.

Pacella walked into Cavallo's huge arms and hugged the guy, pressed his cheek to Emilio's chest, shut his eyes. He'd missed his friend.

"*Beltrando*," Emilio said, supposedly an Italianized version of Bill. "*Mio amico. Che se dice*? What brings you to the city?"

"An important matter."

"Che cosa?"

Cavallo had wept until he'd nearly collapsed at Jane's funeral, this close to being one of those old world types that scream and throw themselves into the grave, pounding on the casket. He'd hugged Pacella this same way at the funeral, like a father, and Pacella could hear Emilio's heart beating out rough, painful rhythms of grief.

"What matter, ah? You tell me."

When they broke away from one another, Cavallo moved to a bottle of wine already open on the dining room table. He poured two glasses and he and Pacella sat across from one another, sipping the wine in silence. The surgeon inside hated the smell of any type of alcohol because it reminded him of the hospital where he was forced to take care of orphan children to keep up appearances.

Cavallo just sat there with a big smile, his false teeth way too white in the brown face.

Pacella put the glass down and said, "Why didn't you clear them out first, Emilio?"

A shudder went through the fat man. It started at his ears and worked right down through him inch by inch. It was beautiful to see—to know they weren't going to have to race around the bush for an hour before

Cavallo admitted to it. The old man knew exactly what Pacella was talking about. His eyes lit with fear and shame.

"What's that? *Che cosa*? What's that you say to me, *Beltrando*?"

On the wall, another sacred heart of Jesus picture. These killer Italians, all of them under the watchful eyes of Christ, like they'd never be called to judgment. "You should have made sure the restaurant was empty."

"I don't know what you're saying." Cavallo poured himself another glass, drinking it down fast. "What are you saying? Explain this."

"You were right, I should've looked after her better. I got there too late. I almost got the torcher but he slipped away. I nearly got trapped in the fire myself, Emilio." He wrenched open his shirt and showed off his scars. Repulsive as they were, he hardly ever thought of them anymore. It was good to get a chance to show them with some pride. "I watched her die, Emilio. Everything that's happened, it's your doing."

"Will—"

The name lingering there without enough substance.

Will, always with the Will.

Pacella's rage took on its form—a process of growth and movement—as he stood quickly, the seams of his soul stretching to their breaking point, everybody inside wanting out.

It wasn't time yet. He still had questions. He struggled to continue talking, as demands and promises began to fill his head. "You knew what night it was set for. Why didn't you protect your own employees? They were your family. You always said the people who worked with you were family."

Cavallo's false front totally collapsed and he went on the defensive, angry and self-righteous. He waved his arms, the thick fingers covered in rings fluttering in the air. "I couldn't be there, it wouldn't look right! I was in Atlantic City for the weekend, I had to be seen, don't you understand? I did not do this thing, I was not even there!"

"Maybe you weren't there, but you did it."

"You don't know, Will! I did everything! Everything to keep *Emilio's* alive in this economy. My dream, and they took it all away! Taxes, they increase my rent, the licenses, all the kickbacks—the people I have to pay. Everybody getting a piece of me and my dream—"

Pacella, grinning a little like Jack now, the killer seeping through. "Sing me a sad song, Emilio, tell me your troubles."

"*Vaffanculo*, talking to me like that!" The fat man had to make a last try of it, lumbering to his feet, driving his fists down into the table. It should've been a powerful blow, but Cavallo still thought he might get out of this and he didn't want to scratch the table top. The wine in Pacella's glass hardly rippled. "Damn you, it was not my fault, Will! It was supposed to happen after midnight, after everybody finished up and had gone home. Nobody was supposed to get hurt! I loved Jane! I loved her! I loved them all!"

"Who was the torcher, Emilio?"

"I don't know that! I asked Joe Ganucci for a favor, he set everything up. He owned a couple'a points on the place. It went through his consigliere. But that one, he's dead."

"So's the Ganooch."

Finally, Cavallo started catching on. His eyes brimmed with understanding, realizing who he had to be talking to, what was happening now. What was about to happen.

"No. No, Will."

"Yeah, Emilio."

"It—it—"

"Yeah."

"It's been you, Will?"

"Yes." Pacella felt a wonderful warmth flood through his belly.

"You...*Beltrando*, you've been doing those things to the syndicate guys? The capos? Carving them up like that? Taking their hearts? Their kidneys?"

Pacella wanted to say, No, not me, Emilio, what we have here is a fractured psyche that allows for the release of tension and frustration via disassociation and yet keeps the primary personality intact, at least for the time being. A psychological mechanism that allows the mind to split off traumatic memories or disturbing ideas from conscious awareness.

He said, "Yes, it's been me."

"How could you do this? How could you do any of this, Will? With the knives? Snapping necks? Cutting open the...*dio mio*! You're a schoolteacher!"

"Sometimes."

Pacella, one of the many Pacellas, moved fast now, lithely leaping onto the dining room table and easing himself over it. Pressing Cavallo back down into his chair, the chair against the wall, the picture of Jesus and his bleeding, broken, thorn-entwined heart bearing down.

It wasn't quite Pacella's voice anymore. The timbre was off, the tone pulled taut like it was ready to snap. "Please think, Emilio—think extremely hard now. Put some effort into it. I want a name."

"I don't know, I swear, on the eyes of my children! I don't—"

"Shh, think about it a second. Who is the torcher? They must've told you something, given you a clue."

"No, nothing like that!"

"A favor, just do me a favor, Emilio, all right? Just a hint."

Jack was thinking about the eyes of children, staring back at him from a little jar.

The fat old man struggled to get out of the chair but was unable to move because there was a hand like iron pressed against his chest. His jowls flapped as he started to mewl. He saw the edge of the knife reflecting the chandelier light, so bright that he couldn't even look at the blade in Pacella's fist. He had to turn his face away. "*Madonna mia*! Will, it wasn't my fault. You have to believe me. I loved Jane! Like my own child, like my daughter. You know this! *Dio mio*, I'd do anything for her!"

Showing all his teeth, Pacella's voice was almost gone, little more than a high-pitched shrill cry. "*You shouldn't say things like that, Emilio.*"

"Jesus Christ! *Dio*! *Jesu*!"

The blade Jack used at the time was the six inch hunting knife topped with a gut hook. Jack liked the way it moved through flesh—not too easily, you actually felt the ripping and shredding as you cut sideways, yanking at the muscle and tendon. He had fun aiming the arterial spray up into the compassionate face of Christ above, until the forlorn nailed god was dripping with red ribbons.

fifteen

Are you ready?

Pace woke at dawn and walked downstairs, expecting Vindi or other men to be standing in the living room. There weren't any.

Instead, a black leather briefcase sat in the foyer, just inside the front door. It contained their passports, other identification and paperwork, tourist maps of Athens, five thousand Euros, and fifty thousand drachmas. Altogether that was more than fifteen grand Vindi had handed over.

Kaltzas wanted them to be tourists for the afternoon, have a good time, before heading on to Pythos. There were instructions on where to find his private jet, and what to do when arriving in Athens. The best places to eat, the most hospitable *tavernas*. Where to catch the ferry to Voros and its scheduled departures. Where to rent a boat.

While he was studying the contents of the case he must've had another attack of aphasia because when he turned the others were at the kitchen table having breakfast. He didn't know where Pia had learned to cook so well, but she'd made a full meal of pancakes, eggs, hash browns, orange juice, everything you think about when you imagine having breakfast with your family when you're a kid. Your brother stealing your bacon, your Dad reading the paper but keeping a watchful eye. Sissy with a doll in her lap, trying to feed it toast.

It had never happened this way, but it was truer than anything that had ever happened to you.

Now you imagined having breakfast with your wife, who swept past you moving from the stove to the sink, the floors shining, the kitchen windowsill filled with sunflowers. Your tow-headed son chattering on about his model cars, his video games, baseball cards. Lovely baby girl with a new doll in her lap, trying to feed it toast. Your dreams were pedestrian but honest. Your anguish common, your insanity only average. Jane asking you how much work you'd done on the book last night.

Six pages, it was going good. They're already pretty clean, just need another pass to tighten up some dialogue, clear out a couple of fragments.

Pia spun from the oven and told Pace to sit. He ate quickly, listening to Faust and Hayden discussing torture. The Greeks liked to do dramatic things like putting a guy inside a large metal bull and then making a roaring fire under it and roasting him alive. Funky stuff like chaining somebody to a cliff side and letting the birds chew him to death. But besides that, it seemed like the Greeks preferred straightforward murder. Ramming a sword diagonally through a man's collarbone to chop him almost entirely in half. Plunging a spear through somebody's guts. No prisoners, no waiting around, clean your blade and get on with your day.

Sitting about a foot too far from the table, Dr. Brandt stared at them, a mixture of loss and shame inscribed across her radiant features. This lady, never one thing on her face, always fifty different emotions working her over.

"If you don't practice your smile," Pace said, "you'll forget how it's done."

Dr. Brandt only frowned further.

Pia said, "Should I leave the dishes for the lady who cleans the house? That might be rude, but maybe she'll be glad to do them. To see there were people in the house again. It's the kind of thing my mother would have liked."

The mother who had chased her around the neighborhood with a shovel, who had brained her sister, and drank the Drano.

"This is the kind of thing we should be worried about right now?" Hayden asked. "You didn't hear us talking about the Brazen Bull? They cook you alive in it!"

Faust sounded resigned, like he just wanted to get it over with. "More likely we'll be disemboweled and our entrails will be burned in a pyre as a sacrifice to the oracles."

"All of our organs?" Pia asked.

"The preference seems to be for livers and lungs."

"I'd rather not part with them." Saying it almost happily while she cleared the table, sticking plates in the sink. "If the choice were mine to be made."

Nightjack thinking he had never had lung before, wondering about the consistency, whether to cook it with oil or butter.

"Nothing like that's going to happen," Pace said.

"Then what?"

"I don't know, but nobody's going to burn up your entrails."

"You hope."

"I won't let anyone hurt you."

No one appeared to believe him much. They headed for the door, this leg of the journey becoming something both too large to deal with and also too small.

With her bottom lip protruding into a little girl pout, Dr. Maureen Brandt's demeanor at once appalled and excited Pace. He gazed deeply into her face and saw all the varieties and versions of Maureen Brandt, the amendments and modifications and revisions she had gone through long ago and minute by minute.

The inflated ego casting judgment, always reflecting disappointment. The hunger for authority and domination over others, the willingness to call someone else insane. The drive to actually help, to cure, to alleviate distress and misery. Her failure in the world to find a man she could not consume or eclipse. The kinkiness that led her to hump the bound.

"Don't go," she said. "None of you should go."

All four of them turned to look at her, waiting for more, but there was nothing else.

"Kaltzas never threatened you," Pace said. "He bought you off, didn't he? That's why you signed all the reports saying I was stable and deserved to be released. He needed you to get me out. Isn't that right?"

"You're in cahoots!" Hayden shouted.

"No," she answered.

"Smack her in the mush! Make her eat paste!"

Her face of devastating glory. It was easy to forgive such painfully open beauty. Something inside Pace's chest seemed to expand. A sob nearly broke free. Moments occur that are larger than they should be, with a meaningfulness that isn't apparent until much later.

"It's okay, Maureen. We don't blame you."

"I do!" Hayden shouted.

"Me too," Pia said. "You arrogant, condescending bitch. I'm getting one of Jack's knives and I'm going to cut her tits off."

Pace stepped closer to Maureen Brandt until the others faded behind him, blocked from view. "I'm sorry you got caught up in it. You're a lousy psychiatrist, but you did try to help us. Don't be so hard on yourself."

"Will, listen to me. There are things you need to know."

He waited, and again, there was nothing else. She was a woman heavy with pregnant pauses and faltering purpose. He'd met a lot of sad people and she was more depressed than any of them.

"I'm sorry," she said.

He couldn't help himself. He could never help himself. He swept her into his arms, pressed his lips cruelly to hers, thinking of her on top of him in the white. Even as she began to respond and leaned into him with a selfish groan, she broke the kiss and stepped away. He shook his head sadly and walked out the door.

The others followed him to the stolen truck. While they arranged themselves inside, Pace muddied the plates.

He got in and felt a bulge in his back pocket.

He found several torn pieces of notebook paper, taken from Hayden's million-page letter to his mother:

Rudy Road. Rue the Day. Get it? Another of your bad jokes. That's why the book will never be published. Nobody ever liked your jokes. It's one of the reasons why you're all alone, tied to a bed.

The truck was full of noise and querulous voices, arguing in a dozen tongues. Something like a tentacle reached over and pinched at the back of his hand.

On another sheet, in the same ornate handwriting:

Ignore the previous. You've got too many ghosts already, don't take on any more. Your friends are inept but you need them. Cassandra is on Pythos along with your fate. Go to her.

And then, a last shred of paper:

If you listen to that shit you deserve what you get, you stupid fuck.

PART II

The Portents of Gravitas

sixteen

The nor'easter had dissipated so thoroughly that except for a few flooded streets and downed tree limbs there were no other reminders in sight. You'd think that the morning after a hurricane you might see a few people outside crying, cars flipped over on lawns, mothers looking for their lost children, a cradle in a treetop. You'd think not everybody else got off as lucky as you did.

The sun was intense, the day actually pleasant. Pace kept off the streets near the shore, hit the parkway, and drove to JFK without any trouble. They all passed through security without a hitch. Kaltzas's people did good work. Nobody cared about the knife in his bag. Or the broken ashtray.

They were led out over the tarmac by a gate agent, an appealing but priggish young woman affecting a bad British accent. She walked stiffly and kept murmuring things that she thought were funny, then raising her hand and daintily tittering beneath it.

Pace didn't understand what the hell she was saying or what was going on until Pia dropped back, took his elbow, and shunted him aside. The gate agent peered over her shoulder twice, smiling warmly at Pace.

"She's trying to impress you," Pia said.

"She is?"

"That's why she's talking like a constipated Queen Elizabeth."

"How is that supposed to win me over?"

"You have dark curly hair. She probably thinks you're a rich Greek, maybe a member of Kaltzas's inner circle, another magnate. She figures the British are more refined and upscale. She's trying hard not to appear like a stupid American girl going out of her way to dazzle you."

"How ironic," Pace said.

The gate agent paraded them to Kaltzas's private jet and made a little *ta-da* hand gesture like she was showing off the prizes of a game show.

Pace told her, "There's a stolen Ranger parked in lot 31C. The keys are in it. Could you make sure somebody finds it soon?"

"Pardon?"

Hayden said to her, "Hey, you want to come along? We're going to visit an island owned by a tycoon who wants us all dead. It's gonna be lots of fun. At least it will be once we drop Faust out over the ocean."

"Our father who art insignificant," Faust said. It was as good a retort as he could muster.

"They're gonna eat our lungs and livers!"

The woman giggled under her hand again and started back to the terminal.

The name on the jet was written in Greek. It had a cockpit crew of five men who spoke only Greek and apparently didn't understand English. Pace wondered if Vindi would show himself. Once the pilot said something sharply in Pace's direction, and Smoker the breed gunslinger grunted back in Apache.

Pia said, "Kaltzas makes his fortune in shipping. Couldn't he book us on a cruise instead?"

"Are any of these the men that threatened you on the ward?" Pace asked.

"No. And they didn't exactly threaten us."

Pace tried to remember her exact words. He directed his thoughts and felt a subtle pressure, and then the pressure gave way and he was through and the words were there. *They asked questions like they were our friends, but they had us marked from the beginning. They knew all about us, everything in our files, all about our lives.*

"Are you sure they weren't just investigating everyone?"

"Are you calling me paranoid now? I'm telling you, he wants to hurt us."

"Maybe *Zorba* will be the in-flight movie," Hayden said.

Faust looked at the Greek lettering on the side of the plane, his mouth moving as if he was this close to figuring out what the word meant. He clutched a hand over his chest, plucking himself lightly, trying to draw something free from his heart. "Kaltzas might sacrifice his whole crew to kill us all in one fell swoop."

"Yes," Pia said. "But not the jet. He's a man of belongings. He'd give up people but not his possessions."

"That's an astute observation."

They boarded and took their seats. Pia sat beside Pace. Faust and Hayden sat behind them, window seats opposite one another. The crew completely ignored them. Pace wondered if any of them would make a move at any point. Throw a smug smile, pull a gun, play a video made by Kaltzas. He stared into the cockpit until they closed the cabin door and started the engines. The small jet gave off the impression of lean, immense power.

Takeoff was smoother and faster than he'd been expecting. He could hardly feel the ascent at all. Pacella had never liked flying, and now he kept trying to rise to the surface so he could grip the armrests and clench his teeth.

"I don't suppose any flight attendants will be coming around to offer us drinks and a meal," Pia said. "Good thing we packed the leftover food. So, when do we land on Pythos?"

"We arrive at the airport in Athens," Pace said, "in about ten hours."

"Holy shit, ten hours in this sardine can?" Hayden glanced around like he wanted to skip out the door. "Nobody told me that!"

"Then we take a ferry to another island. Voros."

"And then?"

"We charter a boat to Pythos."

"You know," Hayden said, "is it just me, or is anybody else starting to feel really frickin' dumb going to such extremes just to visit a guy who wants to kill us?"

Faust held up his hand. "I do."

Pia held up her hand. "Me too."

"If he really wanted to kill us, we'd be dead," Pace told them. "He's a billionaire. He could afford to hire somebody better than Rollo Carpie."

"So he only wants one of us dead."

"I'm not so sure about that either."

"Then what's it all about?"

"I don't know. That's why we're going, so we can find out."

Hayden said, "We're going there to find out what we're going there for? That's just crazy talk now."

The ocean appeared bluer than Pace had ever seen it before. Pia shifted beside him and brushed her hand over his knee. Now that the powerful allure of Maureen Brandt was no longer present, he started to feel a tug at his heart, the cascading emotion he'd originally felt around Pia. Not so much sexual as it was the idea of comfort. Somehow she gave off the vibe that she would care for you when no one else would.

She asked, "Why would he extend us the courtesy of his private jet, and then make us take ferries and boats afterward?"

"Part of the game," Faust said, "is the challenge. The trial. The labors. All ancient heroes had to be tested. He wants to know if we're worthy. He's showing us he's polite but unwilling to overindulge us. That he's got dominion over us but will only use it in his own time, as he so chooses. He brings us a part of the way to his world, and we must journey the rest on our own." Sariel nodded, Rimmon shrugged, trying to get comfortable in his seat. "It's proof of our desire and our will to continue on. He requires more than just our compliance. He wants *collusion*. Participation. Our father who art independent."

"Why?" Pia asked.

"The mad king hasn't merely summoned us, he's *invoked* us. This is going to be *his* pilgrimage as much as ours."

Pace thought about it for a while and decided maybe it was true. Kaltzas didn't only want revenge or justice for his daughter. He wanted something else from them. Needed them for an unknown purpose. How much easier it would've been just to meet with the man at the Plaza over a nice dinner, where they could get everything off their chests.

"This guy," Hayden said, "is proof that money can't buy you peace of mind." He unlocked his seatbelt and searched the cabin. "Are they really not going to feed us? Breakfast was good, but ten hours on here without even a glass of water might take its toll, you know? I'm hypoglycemic, man. I could have a mood swing, and trust me, nobody wants to see that."

Pia drew out her backpack, stuffed with food. "I told you, I packed the rest of what we had. I've got sandwiches and bottled water, you won't starve."

"A true goddess," Faust said drowsily. "Any more bisque?"

"No."

"Ahh."

Hayden sat again, tilted his seat back, and promptly fell asleep.

Pia whispered, "Why did Jack kill those whores in Whitechapel, Will?"

Sometimes she was sexy insane and sometimes just insane. Pace turned and looked at her as Jack pulled his leather apron off a hook.

"I mean, did you ever ask him? Does he want to murder me too? I bet it was really rough holding him back from slicing apart Dr. Brandt. That bitch would piss off anybody, and my core personality is timid, passive, and depressed."

"Shut up, Pia."

"I'm a slut, you know, just like she always said. I've been paid for it. Sometimes I rip the bills up right in their faces." Eyes gleaming, she bent toward Pace's chest talking directly to Jack inside. "I bet you didn't have half your usual fun cutting those wise guys to pieces. Where's the fun in chopping up fat old guineas?"

"Stop."

He could press his hand over her mouth, but the very thought of it made Jack start licking his lips, his breathing becoming more rapid. There was no way to quiet her without making his heart beat faster. Pace gripped his thighs.

"Do you want to put your blade in me, Jackie boy?"

"Nobody's going to hurt you," Pace said. "I promised you that. Now shut up."

"My mother should have killed me," Pia said and burst into tears.

Jack started going through his doctor's bag, drawing out bone saws, laying them side by side preparing himself for Pia. Three quid. You could have a woman like this for three quid, but you had to do her standing up against the bricks while the horses clopped by in the streets. You had three minutes. After that, they always started talking, wanting you to move along, *'Ave at it, Guvnah, get the ole leg over, eh? I've business to attend to tonight.*

The cockpit door opened and the pilot stepped out. He spoke rapidly in Greek, pointing out the window to the east. In the distance, the sky bloomed with oppressive, churning black clouds.

"We're running back into the storm," Pace said.

"It's been waiting for us," Faust said.

Rimmon, governor of the first order of seraphim, angel of lightning and fire. One of the nine who will reign over the end times. Pace saw what was about to happen and tried to get out of his seat. Rimmon stood and aimed his burning sword ahead. Lightning arced down from heaven and struck the wing.

"We die," Faust gasped as the jet bucked wildly. A ghastly all-consuming din erupted from the sky, the engine, and every throat of every creature and ghost on board except Nightjack. Jack was laughing.

seventeen

Pacella spent most of that last afternoon and evening working on his novel. If anybody asked him what it was about he told them he didn't know. It wasn't a lie. He'd been working on it for two years and still didn't understand what he was trying to express, why his characters were doing the things they were doing, saying the things they were saying.

Every time he opened the manuscript and reread a section of it, it was like reading a stranger's work that he found not to his liking. It was vapid, a touch pretentious, and rather pointless. He'd let Jane read his finished chapters and she'd tell him how much she enjoyed the book even though she was clearly as confused by it as he was. So were the publishers. They returned his submissions with either short bracing rebuffs or long effusive commentaries that were kindly worded but amounted to the same thing.

The latest rejection letter had come that morning. A thoughtful analysis and honest appraisal of his convoluted themes and cluttered narration. This one, like all his rejections, arrived in the plural.

We suggest you untangle the many subplots, delete the extensive flashbacks, and streamline the protagonist's often unnecessary forays into understanding his own failures. We feel his "life" is rather histrionic but uninvolving. We feel the reader will become too confused and shall prove unwilling to extend themselves the great lengths the work requires. The humor is sometimes amusing but too often lacks true wit. The prose is taxing. We feel you too frequently evoke unpleasant emotions. Too many questions go unanswered in the end. There is not enough assertion. There is not enough resolution. We are left wavering and wanting.

As usual, Pacella agreed with the comments but had no idea how to go back and rewrite the damn thing. It had long since grown too unwieldy, abstract, and unnecessarily complex. He'd started off writing a semi-autobiography, but since nothing interesting ever happened to him, his alter-ego had grown sort of crazed. The situations he found himself in became more and more intricate and unbelievable.

Jane called to tell him she'd be late getting home from the city. "Somebody's got their hand in the till," she said. "I think it's the new girl. She's clever about it, but I can't approach her until I finish double-checking the books for the entire week."

"I'll come in on the train and we can have a late dinner," he told her, only half-listening. He kept rereading the rejection. He liked the word histrionic.

"I'd say don't bother, it'll probably be close to midnight before I finish up, but we haven't seen much of each other the last few days. Won't you be too tired tomorrow?"

Their conflicting schedules didn't often bother them since they usually spent afternoons together, after he got back from school and before she left for the restaurant. But lately Emilio had been asking her to come in earlier, and the novel had been taking up too much of Pacella's time. Without Jane as a stabilizing influence, he felt himself growing more irritable, his temper getting shorter.

"It's no trouble. I'd just like the chance to sit with you for a bit."

"The cook and one of the bussers will still be here. There's some kind of problem with one of the ovens and they're trying to fix it. I think they're just making it worse though. They're taking turns hitting it with a big hammer."

"Sounds like they're about as mechanically inclined as I am."

"Don't worry though, before he ruins it completely I'll have him make you a plate of Chicken Parmesan. And I'll have a bottle of Chablis waiting. There will also be candlelight."

He said, "Thank you, baby."

"What's the matter?" she asked, and then answered herself. "Another rejection? The book is good, Will, it'll sell soon." He was about to read it to her when she said, "Need to run, see you soon."

He took the Long Island Railroad and spent the time grading essays on Eliot's "The Love Song of J. Alfred Prufrock." It was always illuminating to see how teenagers viewed a poem about the fear of aging. Despite his discussions, few of them understood the root of the work, which—while it was to be expected—still showed a depressing lack of sensitivity and acumen. Three kids thought Prufrock was upset because his cats died. Others thought it was because the oceans were so polluted he couldn't get good crab legs anymore. Pacella wondered why the hell he kept assigning the piece.

He bundled the paperwork up in his briefcase as the train pulled into Penn Station. It was 10:40 and the line at the cab kiosk on Seventh Avenue was short enough that it only took a minute for him to hop in a taxi. The driver crossed over to the east side at 33rd, passed the Empire State Building, turned up Second Avenue and headed uptown to *Emilio's*.

Pacella enjoyed Manhattan at night and again regretted that he and Jane lived so far out on Long Island. Jane spent over two hours a day on trains, subways, or in traffic, but she'd been raised in the city and never seemed to mind the travel time. He was a suburban boy through and through and Jane was often amused by his capacity to still be dazzled by Manhattan action.

The cab let him off at the northeast corner of York and 67th and Pacella walked the half-block to the restaurant.

He was immediately aware of the smell of smoke.

He thought, They really were using a hammer. The dumbasses threw a spark into the gas line and now they're burning the place down.

He dropped his briefcase and sprinted to the front door, burst through and saw flames rising across the faux olive trellises surrounding the coat check. He called out for Jane. The heat blasted against him before he saw the full extent of the fire. The skin of his face tightened and ash circled him, rising and falling, sweeping along as he moved through the smoke. Flames rose in a funnel-shape through the center of the room, extending outwards as it crawled across the ceiling. Several tables had been consumed already.

Jesus Christ. He rushed through the dining room and screamed for Jane. Already his voice was a dried-out husk and he went into a coughing fit. He found one of the busser tubs and came up with a linen napkin that he tied around his face. It didn't help much and he kept lifting it free of his mouth so he could shout for Jane as he stumbled through the fire.

The overwhelming noise surprised him—the crackling and snapping of all the wood, the constant popping of superheated embers and clanging of expanding metal. He finally thought of the sprinklers and looked up. There wasn't even a dribble from any of them. What the hell had gone wrong?

He spun and shouted again and saw someone else was there in the fire.

A figure near the open door to the kitchen. He moved to it thinking it was Jane. Relief rushed through him. He said, "*Thank God*."

Pacella's eyes were tearing so badly he could hardly see, but after he took three steps toward the figure he realized it wasn't Jane or the cook with the big hammer. He could barely make out a guy over there in a tight-fitting overcoat cinched at his waist. Just a silhouette really, but with these strange details about it. Looked like maybe he was wearing small racing gloves and actually smoking a cigarette, leaning back as if he enjoyed the show.

The fuck?

Pacella had a split-second view of the kitchen and saw the cook and the busser back there on the floor beneath a thick layer of black cloud. Tied and gagged, already dead from smoke inhalation, having choked on their own vomit. Their bodies were quickly being covered with flames shooting across their chests in zigzag patterns, like the way somebody spritzes lighter fluid across a charcoal grill.

Pacella knew then that the guy had started the fire. Maybe even using the candle that Jane had set for Pacella's meal, making it look like an accident. Pacella's mind raced as he put pieces together. Jane might be in the office, hiding there. The guy would've come in through the back door, tied up the cook and the busser. Maybe a fight breaking out, shouts. She might've heard him. She might've hidden beneath the futon, in the corner between the filing cabinet and the wall. She might've made it that far, except the fire had already moved across the office door. There was no other way out of the office, no windows. The smoke would be killing her.

Even as he thought it the door flew open and she emerged. She'd taken off her blouse and used it to cover her head. He saw the edges of it dripping and knew she would've only had a glass of wine back there. She must've pissed on the cloth to try and protect herself.

You went mad by fractions.

You went mad by the stress cracks in your fingernails digging into your palms.

You went mad when your love took five faltering steps from the manager's office through the inferno and emerged on the sixth step a beautifully ignited pyre that stared at you with boiling eyes.

Pacella moved through the smoke and reached for Jane as she floundered blindly forward, but it was too late. She held her melting hands out to him, sensing him there somehow, and understanding the futility of another breath.

He screamed. The scream started in his chest and worked up his throat and kept going up, slashing through the soft tissue of his brain, and still rising. Jane shrugged away almost as if she were terrified of the scream and had flinched from it. She fell backward into the fire and joined it, became one with it, remaining in his vision as a brightly lit smear of dancing orange that soon receded beneath the rest of the blazing waves.

Even after the scream ended, it was still there rebounding inside his skull. It had been joined by many other voices also shrieking. A few were crying, begging, lecturing. He heard his father yelling at him, telling him to take out the trash.

Some of them suggested he untangle the many subplots, delete the extensive flashbacks, and streamline his often unnecessary forays into understanding his own failures. They felt his life was rather histrionic but uninvolving.

Pacella stumbled toward the torcher but he'd become very weak and could barely breathe and went down against one of the busboys' tubs. The guy was still over there, smoking his cigarette, his face hidden in smoke and flame. He had to be crazy to have stuck around. He had to be suicidal not to move after all of this. The guy watching his work. He flicked the butt away and started for the kitchen.

You went mad by trying to decide your next step.

You went mad with the wonder of Why.

You opened your mouth and a hundred tongues fell out beneath the linen napkin. The force of them tore the cloth from your face.

The garbled shouting voices were loud enough to be heard even over the raging fire. The torcher froze and turned back.

Pacella's hand shot forward and brushed against silverware in the busser tub. His hand was open and a steak knife leapt into it. He felt a rush of gratitude, not merely for the blade but *to* the blade.

The hand wasn't entirely his hand anymore. His legs lifted him and carried him forward, the scream still going, some of the voices giving advice now on the best way to get free of the room.

The torcher turned and moved more quickly but he still wasn't running. Pacella went after the guy, easing through the scorching colors and coiling ribbons of smoke. There was a great sense of speed and capability as he was ferried by the crowd, people appearing all around him and pressing him onward.

He was going so fast that he nearly overshot the figure. He lunged and the guy sidestepped but not fast enough. Pacella felt the blade scrape bone.

His attack heaved him forward into the kitchen. He tripped over the dead cook's burning body and blundered into a wall. He turned and the scream told him to go back into the dining room and finish the job, but by then he was starting to burn.

More tongues fought their way free of his throat and he spit them on the floor. His father was still yelling about the garbage. *Wash out the tuna cans. Separate the papers and bottles.* Why was the old man always going on about the trash?

The ceiling groaned and a flaming rafter dropped down straight in front of him. The dead busser was on fire as well, but beside the corpse, beneath the back counter, Pacella saw someone else. A girl whose hands were tied to those of the dead busser, lying semi-conscious, trying hard to breathe through her gag and crawl away pulling the corpse along with her.

It was the waitress who'd started working at *Emilio's* a couple of weeks ago, the one Jane thought might be skimming. Pacella had only met her once before, a week ago while he drank Italian beer with Emilio Cavallo and she served him a dinner of Seafood Alfredo that he didn't want but Emilio insisted he eat. A Greek teenager with dark hair and sharp aquiline features, black eyes as cold as quartz that seemed to be ninety percent of her face. You looked at her and that was almost all that you saw, her eyes.

He could imagine Jane figuring the books, calling the girl back in, wanting to get it all out in the open.

He lifted her still bound and carried her out the back door, dragging the busser's corpse a few steps before the broiling skin of the dead guy's wrists slid off like a glove and the body fell away.

The instant Pace hit fresh air he threw her down because he was on fire. It almost felt good. It was nearly enough to draw him away from the screaming. He hit the ground and rolled across the cement in the Manhattan night, vomiting tongues in the gutter.

You went mad by multitudes.

You saved Cassandra Kaltzas's life.

Pace finished his leap to stop Rimmon from igniting the world but the plane tossed again and he lost his footing.

He was wearing a different shirt and he could taste the faded taste of vomit. Pia turned in her sleep beside him. He checked his watch. More than four hours had passed. The aphasia had hit again and he'd been frozen through the storm.

Faust was the only one awake and he was staring at Pace. He looked like he'd been awake the entire time, his gaze focused.

"We survived," he said.

"Obviously. What happened?"

"We survived."

"Yeah. Tell me what happened while I was out, Faust."

"It wasn't an agreeable experience. In fact, it was rather horrific. The storm battered and attacked and cudgeled. We were swept down toward the sea. The pilots were screaming. Hayden cried. Only Pia enjoyed herself. She still wants to die, you know."

"I know."

"One of the engines blew out. The jet wanted to shake apart. We were doomed, as we've always realized. You threw up on yourself. We all threw up on ourselves. I spoke the great prayer."

Pace cocked his chin. "The great prayer? Which one's that?"

"The one you taught me."

"The one I taught you?"

You could spend your whole life repeating what other people said and just adding a question mark to it.

"The prayer of power. Our father who art invoked. And the Lord our God answered. He showed mercy and stayed the hand and sword of his champion archangel." Faust gently rocked in his seat, his fingers trembling. "The engine restarted. We passed through the storm. The weight of our debts continues to grow. Soon we'll each have an entire mountain on our backs to carry."

"Don't we already?"

"Of course not, that's why we went crazy in the first place. To relieve ourselves of such burdens." The starlit sky gleamed behind him through the window. "We go to our deaths now. Our deaths come to us."

"No one's going to hurt you. I won't let anyone do that."

"Every time you make that false promise you condemn yourself to a deeper corner of hell."

"Fine by me."

Pia murmured in her sleep and eased the side of her face against Pace's shoulder. He couldn't help himself and pressed his nose into her hair and took a deep breath. It sent Pacella's ghost into spasms, thinking of cold nights on the shore when Jane fell asleep in his arms and he did this same thing. Breathing her in.

Pace thought, They own me, these three. Faust, Hayden, Pia. I own them. That's what this is really about. They're as much a part of me as Pacella or Jack or any of the others. They're only here because they couldn't cut free from me. Kaltzas hasn't brought them here, I have. I'm going to get them all killed.

Pace opened his fist. There was another torn, curled slip of paper:

Forget what I said about Tiny Bob's Lobster Pavilion. They're under new management and the current menu is superb.

eighteen

They reached Elliniko Airport at five a.m. local time. The sun had come around the earth to meet them and the finely-hewn dawn erupted across the bow of the jet. They passed over a congested port surrounded by whitewashed houses that led off to a wildly choked stone metropolis already in full flurry and bustle.

As they circled, Pace noticed that the Aegean Sea was at least three different colors: turquoise, a compelling deep-ice blue, and a burnished black. Faust put his hand against the window and Daedalus's eyes welled.

They landed fast and simply, taxiing for less than a minute before the jet came to an abrupt halt. The cockpit door opened. One of the flight crew opened the main cabin door and slid a small stairway out.

As she exited, Pia smiled blandly and said, "The American consulate shall hear of the simply atrocious fashion you treat your passengers, boys. Expect U.S. sanctions. My father's an ambassador and the President of our free United States won't put up with this."

"Not even a goddamn ham on rye!" Hayden said. "Tell your master that next time, we meet in Newark where even the thugs have better manners. Clearly money can't buy grace."

Faust said, "Thank you."

As Pace reached the steps, the pilot lashed out, gripped Pace's shoulder, and snarled something in Greek. The rest of the crew laughed. The pilot patted Pace's back, trying to get him in on the joke, tell him how they were all brothers, how good it was to be alive.

But Pace didn't think so. He asked, *Jimmy?*

Aye, laddie.

Jimmy Boyd shrugged the hand off, spun and let loose with two left jabs that knocked the pilot on his ass. "Next time, boyo, ye'll be wantin' to speak in a proper tone when ye address me. Else I'll slap the snottiness out the other side a ye head."

The co-pilot leaped to his feet and started jabbering. He looked greatly offended and threw a wild punch. Jimmy sidestepped easily and unleashed a swift uppercut that snapped the man's head back so hard that blood from his mouth spurted onto the cockpit ceiling.

"That'll be enough of that nonsense, ye fuckers."

Pace moved down the stairs and the heat reached out and gripped him by the heart.

Pia cried as if she'd been struck in the face with a hot towel. "Ugh! My god!"

"People vacation here?" Hayden said. "They come here willingly?"

"We'll get used to it."

"Just lead me to the nude beaches and leave my ass in the sand."

They walked through the airport, had their paperwork checked again, and were welcomed to Athens.

Pace had never seen a city like it. The garbage towered in the streets. People were crammed everywhere, with so much traffic pressing along that you wouldn't be surprised to find old men or children crushed into the asphalt. A living sea of motion swept you along with it whether you wanted to go or not. It made Manhattan look rustic.

"I never thought I'd be homesick for Alphabet City," Hayden said. His eyes were panic-stricken. "By the way, what time is it?"

"Not quite six a.m."

"Jesus, what are all these people doing awake?"

"Heading to work. This is a port city. Fishermen and their families get up with the tide."

Hayden pulled a face. "I just stepped in something that if I called it shit would be an insult to shit. This has no name. God turned his back on this when he was handing out names."

"Adam handed out names," Faust said.

"Shut the fuck up. I need new shoes."

Pia's father liked the action and started dancing among everybody, grinding against the women passing by, his shirt open to the last button and his furry chest covered in salt streaks. Pia watched him, swallowing deeply every time he turned her way.

"Do we know where we're going?" she asked.

"We need to get to the ferry," Pace said. "But according to the schedule, the next won't be leaving until noon."

"Maybe we should get a hotel room and rest up. We still stink of vomit."

"So does everybody else."

For a moment, Pace lost sight of Faust, as they slid further into the city and the city sealed itself up after them.

"Faust? Faust!"

Daedalus, the Athenian architect, had now returned home. He dropped to his knees, threw back his head, and let out an overwhelming wail for all the lost centuries he'd been away. His great mechanical wings attempted to unfurl but were battered back again by the crowd. Chunks of wax and feather fell to the street.

Hayden said, "Is it just me or is this guy really a downer even on this side of the planet?"Pace positioned himself to keep the foot traffic from crushing the winged architect. They showed no respect for their own living history. He stiff-armed them away, the anger beginning to gain purchase within him. People hissed in Greek and other languages. Would they be so bitchy if they could recognize one of their own solar deities?

Daedalus had designed the labyrinth for King Minos, built to imprison the man-bull Minotaur. The dungeon was so skillfully built that no one who entered could escape the great beast. But Daedalus revealed the secret of the maze to Ariadne, daughter of Minos, so she could aid her lover, Theseus. She unrolled a length of string that she and Theseus could follow back to safety. In a fury, the mad king imprisoned Daedalus and his son, Icarus, in the labyrinth.

As if that could stop the man who'd created it. Daedalus made two pairs of mighty wings so that they could both fly out.

But sons never listen to their fathers. It's a rule, a dictum. A formula meant to be pursued even to death and beyond. You don't wash out the tuna cans. The brash boy flew too near the sun even as his father called for him to return, the way he was calling now, thrashing in the garbage. Icarus had merely laughed, spurning his father's orders, drifting toward Sicily where he'd always wanted to join the army. With his eyes full of sunshine and adolescent lust for peasant farmer women, his wings melted, and he plummeted to the sea shrieking for his old man.

Daedalus heard it still.

So did Pace.

The kid crying across the sky.

Pace's father telling him that the flat rock he used on top of the garbage can wasn't heavy enough to keep out the raccoons. They got in and ripped through the plastic bags, and there was trash strewn all over. Always with the trash.

With his artist's hands thrust down to the street, gripping Athenian stone, Daedalus was home again. He stood and looked in the direction of the sea, his view blocked by ugly buildings and angry-eyed strangers. Seeing nothing of his drowned son, he took three running steps preparing to fly. He stumbled, fell on his face, and lay there panting.

Hayden tried to get Faust back onto his feet, but he'd gone completely slack. "We're going to set tourism back a few years if he doesn't get up soon. Maybe cause an international incident, you know? Somebody's gonna call the cops. Will that be a good thing for us? I mean, maybe it would be."

Stooping, Pace said in Daedalus's ear, "Fathers must let go of their children. Even if they drop into the sea. It's been the way of life throughout the ages. The father feasts on guilt but cannot take blame. You're no different than the rest."

Still hearing his old man asking him, Did you separate the paper, bottles, and cans?

Daedalus turned his face aside and wept. The throng continued to swarm around them. Pace let his lips curl into a humorless grin, thinking how it would look to die five minutes off the plane, flattened by old Greek ladies heading off to their bakeries to make the morning bread.

"Faust," Pia said. "Faust, you need to get up!"

The scar on Faust's forehead was covered with dirt. Pace brushed it off and felt the ridge of tissue hot beneath his hand. An almost electrical buzz worked through his fingertips. Faust opened his eyes and said, "I'm thirsty. I would very much like a drink."

"We could all use one," Hayden said. "There's a *taverna* right across the street. Some local color, but it kind of looks real touristy too. Christ they start early in this town."

"*Tavernas* are open twenty-four hours," Pace told them. "Let's go."

"We're a long way from Zorba's little hut with all the dancing and singing, let me tell you. How much money do we have?"

"About fifteen grand," Pace said.

"What!" Hayden gripped Pace by the shoulders, grinning but angry, his sharp teeth coming out to catch the bottom lip. It looked painful. "You've been holding onto that much? What're you going to do, retire with the cash? At the very least we could've had something better than Double Cheesy Bacony Burgers in the last forty-eight hours of our lives.

Jesus Christ, man! Let's go have some fun! I could use it. So could Mister Misery over there."

The crowd kept coming, lumbering like the dead, and Pace had to work faster to keep them off him. There was no laughter, hardly any talking. He thought, It's a good thing Pacella never got to take Jane to Greece on the honeymoon, she wouldn't have liked it. Not here anyway.

"I just want a glass of water," Faust said. "This land...I feel very uncomfortable here. Distracted."

"Let's have a hell of a morning." Hayden peered into the mob. "I'd have to guess that an Athens prostitute is of equal net worth per engagement as a New York pro."

"By what standards do you make the assumption?" Pia asked.

"The generally accepted standards."

"But where do they fit in where Thai hookers are concerned?"

"Probably not even in the same league. But I'm willing to put it to the test."

"Our father who art *in dilecto flagrante*."

"Let's go have a good time! We're on vacation until we get killed!"

"No," Pace said.

Pia started to laugh. "How'd I know you'd say that? We can't have fun because that's what Kaltzas wants us to do, right?"

"Right."

"In the future," Hayden said, "I have really got to get some less insane acquaintances to travel with to evil homicidal tycoons' island paradises."

No one argued.

nineteen

Tourists sat with Greeks watching the repeat of a soccer game on the TV set over the bar. They appeared to have been up all night long. They were drunk but nobody seemed tired.

The waitress had already sized Pace's group up as Americans and asked them their order in perfect English. Hayden wanted something strong and she brought them each a glass of metaxa, an amber-colored alcohol. Six in the morning and they were already into the hard stuff.

Deep in the guts, Pacella withdrew another layer, revolted.

Pace took a sip and it was hot and smooth. A lot of the ones inside him liked it, a lot of them hated it. Sam Smith was indifferent, he'd had better in Saigon. Some of the children spit it out and began to cry. Pace kind of enjoyed it.

"When's the ferry to Voros again?" Hayden asked, taking out his pad and getting back to work on his letter to his mother.

"Noon."

"I have pages missing. Who's been taking my paper?"

Faust threw the metaxa back, frowning as if he might hate the taste, but then nodding. He waved for another. "What do we do in the meantime? Shall we take advantage of Kaltzas's guidebooks and visit the hot tourist spots in the area? Do we trek to the temples and commune with the ancient ones?"

"Fall in love," Pia's father said. He was looking around at all the Greek girls going by. Pia got up and stood beside him, fuming, her back teeth grinding. The jealousy written so plainly in her face that women at nearby tables started doing double-takes.

Pace wondered why they were all coming so unglued here, the edges to each one of them peeled back to expose more of the mess beneath. Maybe it was lack of sleep, or the true onset of fear. The desire to go home, hide on the ward, get back with the program. If Dr. Brandt hadn't set him up, he could have happily stayed at Garden Falls with the other lunatics, maybe forever. Wearing his blue bathrobe and shuffling along past the grimy locked windows.

He became lost in the soccer game, unsure of who was playing whom or when the game was taped. Last night, a week ago? The footage looked a little grainy, it could've been from the Seventies for all he knew.

He heard three men at another table speaking animatedly in French, mentioning Apollonaire, Sendak, Rimbaud, Guy de Maupassant. Inside, Pacella began to twist in pain, the names of the poets reminding him of papers he had graded. Pacella's mouth was dry and he was thinking of cocoa, hungry for the little marshmallows.

It didn't take long for everything to go straight to hell.

Amazing how quickly you could bring out the worst in somebody. You just show your face and somebody wants to murder you. Sometimes you didn't even have to show your face.

Pace got a sense of it about a minute before the action started, when he noticed Pia wasn't at the table anymore. He scanned the bar and there were twice as many people clustered in the place now than when they'd first walked in. The pressure of history smashed these people to pieces and drove them into the shadows reaching for their bottles. The land where art and myth was born. It even crushed the tourists.

He saw a kind of ripple going around one section of the *taverna*. Men trying to keep hushed but unable to keep it down. Pace immediately knew it had something to do with Pia. Maybe she was fighting with her father, maybe she was trying to tackle five guys at once.

Faust saw it too. "She's in anguish but hasn't learned any wisdom from her hardships yet. Perhaps she'll accomplish her suicide before she ever does. What do we do, Will?"

"You two stay here."

Hayden wrote: Momma, I'm dead, I've been dead forever.

A glass shattered and Pace slipped through the patrons, got himself wedged right into the middle of things. Pia was on her knees, writhing, her arm bent too far behind her back. A handsome Greek youth with turbulent eyes sat drinking beside her, gripping her wrist and pulling harder. The agony made her coil across the floor but she didn't let out a squeak.

"Take your hands off her," Pace said.

Sometimes you couldn't help but sound like a puffy, second-rate action star in a straight-to-DVD release.

The kid sipped his drink, taking it slow. "Do you know what she said to me?" His voice was charged but almost amiable, as if asking the question of a new friend.

"I can guess. She's a sick girl. She's cursed. You're better off not touching her."

"You take me for a stupid, superstitious Greek, hah?"

"No, I'm just telling the truth."

The kid, showing his perfect white teeth that must've driven all the middle-aged lady travelers out of their girdles. "You Americans, you are all the same."

"Believe me, buddy," Pace said. "We are definitely not all the same."

"You know what this one did? This lovely tiny one? You know the promises she made in whispers?"

"She's ill. Please forgive her."

"You think it is funny to do these things to the ignorant locals?"

"No," Pace told him. "It's just been a mistake."

"There was no mistake."

The crowd wafted, waiting for blood.

Crumble ran over, the small, curled pug tail wagging just a bit. "Arf!"

Jack was snickering, thankful that Pia was helping him out here. He wanted all the fishermen to draw their long, thin fishing blades, watch them twirl in the morning sun. A glorious dance waiting to be consummated, fulfilled.

The kid had a blade tucked into his belt. Mediterranean fishermen are noted knife fighters, and Greek fishermen some of the best in the world. Pace didn't even know if he had the Trident tucked into the small of his back anymore. He reached and drew it and held it up before his eyes, realizing, Yeah, there it is, I still have it, and then sticking it back in its sheath hidden away, all in about a second. The youth's eyes widened and he started to go for his own blade, then realized Pace had sheathed his so very quickly and now had no weapon. The kid didn't quite know what to do, and he still had Pia on her knees.

Pace drew the knife again in a blur, reached down and gently tapped the point of it on the back of the kid's hand. The act itself so delicate that not even a bead of blood welled up. The sting of the knife perhaps feeling no different from a spider bite, but still enough to make the kid let Pia go.

She got to her feet, rubbing her shoulder. She glared at Pace and said, "You didn't have to do that."

"I know."

"I mean, you shouldn't have."

"I know what you meant."

The kid rubbed the back of his hand, plucking at the skin so he could see what bit him, what touched him, what happened.

Pace asked, "What's your name?"

"Stavros."

"Listen, Stavros, I—"

Stavros shot to his feet. He was tall, six-three, with a long reach. "I do not wish to dialogue!"

"Arf!"

Stavros worked his tongue over his teeth, bobbing on his toes, ready to lunge. He looked from Pia to Crumble to Pace and back again. He didn't want to ask the question but couldn't help himself. "Why is that man barking like a dog?"

"He's insane," Pace said. "We all are. You should go away now."

"This man thinks he is a dog?"

"Yes, sometimes."

Crumble rushed over, licked the back of Stavros's hand, and immediately started humping his leg. The crowd thought it was hilarious.

"This man seeks sexual congress with my knee!" Stavros shrieked.

He was too shocked to even think about drawing his blade. Pace didn't have much choice but to grab Crumble by the collar and rap him lightly across the nose. The pug let out a sneeze and sat there panting.

That got to the kid and the rest of the patrons. Stavros tried to hold on to his anger but it was already lifting from him as the others began to laugh. He tried to clench his jaws shut but the laughter started in his chest and eventually broke free. He held his sides and really whooped it up, the spittle flying. The laugh caught on and the rest of the place began to join in. Soon they were all howling. Crumble howled too. Another round of drinks was ordered. Someone began singing. Pia looked at Pace like she wanted to fuck him to death. Jack wanted to kill everybody.

twenty

Maybe you just needed to get back to New York and rent a cheap apartment on the Upper West Side, try to play catch-up on all the time you've already lost. Check in at the fish cannery. Find a friend you could go out with, take in a ball game, hit the margarita bars. You sit there on a stool eyeing the girls across the way. Robbie starts going through all the best pickup lines he's downloaded into his memory banks. Hey baby, what's your sign? You remind me of someone, haven't we met before? You tell him, I don't know, Robbie, I get the feeling those might not work anymore. A little bullhorn pops out of Robbie's chest and starts doing wolf whistles at the pretty chicks. You think somebody's going to come over and start some shit, but the girls are all tittering. You give Robbie a look and all his lights are lit up, he's beeping like a son of a bitch. His chest opens again and a little catapult fires stuff at the girls. Candy hearts, plastic flowers, tabs of X, packs of purple condoms. The girls come over and circle Robbie, start rubbing his shiny metal parts going oooh and aaah. You ask him what the hell's going on. He tells you, I shut down the Cognitive-Analytic Progression Matrix in my positronic phalanx module, I'm just letting the ride happen now, sport. A slot opens up between his eyes and a girl pops a quarter in. Robbie blasts out techno-pop dance tunes. The girls are grinding and bucking, Robbie gets up and starts clanking and gyrating along with them, his metal claws groping nubile breasts, the girls tee-heeing. His chest opens again and out comes a leash, a bridle, fur-lined handcuffs, a loofa sponge, an eggbeater, a Roto-Rooter. They all leave together in a hushed, eager air of sharpened expectation.

Pace tried to get everybody together in time to meet the noon ferry to Voros. But Pia was dancing with men other than her father, Faust was actually laughing with the soccer enthusiasts, and Hayden had managed to put down his pen after writing only five pages to his mother. The world turned by these small miracles.

You could almost believe in the possibility of joy. Pace thought, Okay, one night, we'll try to relax for a night. We need that much.

They drank and ate and talked with people for hours. The conversations ranged from the informative to the delightful. Faust was almost enchanting, and Hayden told stories about how he and seven mongoloids from the group home would steal the school bus and sneak into Madison Square Garden to watch the Playoffs. Two of the mongoloids had even gotten basketballs signed by most of the players on the Knicks. Hayden had once been shoved by a ref for straying onto the court. The Knicks got so pissed at the ref that the guy had to be escorted out under armed guard. *What the matter wit you? This boy retarded!*

At some point a *bouzouki* band came in and began playing their *bouzoukis*, *baglamas*, guitars, and violins. The Greeks started teaching the tourists folk songs and traditional dances.

Stavros had grown enamored of Pia and mooned over her from across the table, smiling dreamily while she pranced around the room. Pace kept taking the money Vindi had given him and paying for round after round. He wanted to find out information about Kaltzas and Pythos, but didn't know what kind of a reaction it might get from the locals, if any. He subtly tried to weave the name into the various conversations. No one had anything to say. Maybe if you threw a stick around here you could hit fifty shipping magnates with their own private islands.

The French men had left, but the names of the writers continued on and on, rocking Pacella where he lay hidden. Baudelaire, Mauriac, Proust. His eyes twitched, opened for an instant, rolled up into his head, and then he continued dreaming in the dark.

The dead will follow.

The afternoon waned. A third of the money had been spent. Pia had received five marriage proposals, two from Stavros.

Pace had been drinking steadily but wasn't drunk. Sam Smith, though, was having a ball. Jimmy Boyd was singing "Kathleen."

It took a while, but finally Pace managed to gather everybody and get them out of the *taverna*. He had to carry Pia along while she swooned and laughed against his neck. Hayden and Faust were dancing and singing *To Vouno*—"The Mountain"—a slow song that several of the Greeks had performed.

Hayden sang, "I'll climb the highest mountain—"

Moving heavily, Faust turned and turned again. "—and I'll sing, in the wilderness—"

"—with the playing of my *bouzouki*—"

"—my sorrow will be heard..."

"They sure are a fun people."

"But it's quite understandable why their economy's so deflated. How many of them drank all day and never went to work? Never left at all?"

"There are drunks everywhere. At least they don't get mean. Well, most of them, anyway."

"It got a little uncomfortable when you were aspiring to have carnal knowledge with Stavros's leg."

"I trust in the power of forgiveness."

"It's so different now," Pia said, looking about the streets. "This morning I hated it."

Pace knew what she meant. The city was still too congested and choked with people and traffic. But the beauty beneath had made itself known.

"I want to visit the Acropolis! Syntagma square and the Plaka. The Archeological Museum, the Cathedral, the town hall. The Temple of Zeus!"

Hayden finished up the dance and joined in. "The Parthenon. The Theater of Dionysus."

"On the return trip," Pace said, "we'll stay a week and see the sights, all right?"

"We won't be able to then. We'll be dead."

"No one's going to die."

Breathing lustily, her voice growing more and more smoky, Pia said, "You're an idiot, Will."

"Don't be mean."

"I'm not, I'm a very loving young woman."

Ten minutes later they passed a hotel. "How about we stay at this place for the night?"

"It's not accommodating enough," Faust told him. "I would very much like to stay in a five-star hotel. Four at the very least. We should keep our standards high."

"Why?"

"Because we are cultured and civilized."

"You pick it then."

They continued on through Piraeus, the open air market, heading toward the Plaka District near the Acropolis. The area was made up of pedestrian streets that coiled and diverged wildly.

"Here," Faust said in front of a luxury hotel, the *Athenian Palace*, close to the port where the ferry would take them out to Voros in the morning. Bellboys circled them, unsure of what to do. They'd never seen tourists checking in with so little baggage. "This appeals to me greatly. I haven't had room service in years."

"When did you ever order room service?" Hayden asked.

The smile on Faust's lips froze. He stared off into his memory and whatever he saw there filled him with a keen, well-acquainted dread.

"I don't know," he said. "It was there for a moment, but it's gone now. I don't think I'd like to remember."

"You don't have to," Pia said. "None of us do. Maybe someday, but not tonight."

"It was back when I was in the lettuce."

"Don't think about it, Faust. Push it aside. You can tell it to go away."

"The long green spinach!"

Hayden let out a surprised snort. "The hell? You were a short-order cook?"

Faust wavered and refocused in a way Pace had never seen him do before.

"The job was all that mattered," Faust said. "They put the call in and I came rushing to them, heeling, you see? It's all that mattered, getting it done, seeing it happen. Accomplishing the task given to me by my grotesque taskmasters. It was beautiful to do and wonderful to see because it meant something at the heart of all things. It wasn't art, it wasn't actually a discipline, no matter what anybody said. This was just the gorgeous deed that led to all the other exquisite achievements out there, waiting for me."

"I knew it," Hayden said. "I knew it couldn't last. I was actually starting to like him for a minute there. Now he's fucking up my *bouzouki* songs."

"The lettuce, it got me whatever I wanted," Faust went on. He grinned through his beard. Pace thought, he's staring like he wants to try himself against me. Like he wants to take me out of the game. Faust glared as if from a different place, looking younger, as if he was moving back in time. "I rolled it in and rolled it for all the most beautiful ladies. In the restaurants, the clubs, all the joints up and down the strip. Park Avenue. The Gold Mile. Philly's Main Line. Malibu. Beverly Hills, oh yes, L.A., I did a great deal of work there too. If the wine wasn't perfect I would spit it back in their faces. The women, there were always so many glorious women, they'd kneel under the table and I'd pet the cheeks of their magnificent faces with the loose lettuce. I'd throw it on the floor. It would stick to their sweaty knees. If the waiters or managers or patrons said anything, I'd smash the thick end of a broken broomstick into their faces."

"Smack them in the mush!"

"That's what I did with the long green spinach!"

It was the most Pace had ever heard Faust say, on or off the ward. Pia could only stare, and after a minute Faust—the Faust they knew at least *a little* better than the other—returned. The scar burned a bright pink.

He said, "Our father who art insane."

"You got that right, Major Downer," Hayden told him. "Can we go inside now? I'm drunk and tired as hell and little hungry, and I'd like to get some sleep before our hideous agonizing deaths tomorrow, right?"

twenty-one

The night porter spoke perfect English and wore a stylish uniform with epaulets and an odd looking cap that he kept on the counter. He wouldn't take the drachmas, insisting on Euros. He hid his discomfort well, fearing that a group of foolish tourists had wandered in without having converted any money. Pace took out a wad of Euros and paid for a suite. Three bellboys eddied about them and took their tiny bags.

The suite had four lavish bedrooms connected by a extravagant common living area with a huge bar in it. It took Hayden ten minutes to figure out the phone system, but when he did he ordered up several Greek dishes. He didn't know what any of them were and didn't care. There were bottles of metaxa and ouzo at the bar and he poured a round for everyone. When the meal came, they shared the dishes and discussed which foods appealed to them and which didn't. They watched television with English subtitles, napped for a while, and then ate some more.

Pace left them laughing and went to his room. It was ten o'clock. If nothing else, Kaltzas had given them this night.

He got undressed, eased into bed, and lay there thinking about how it all might've gone differently if Pacella had only known how to write.

How much could the book have sold for? Enough to keep Jane at home? At least afford her a job closer to home? William Pacella, the dull high school teacher made good, turning a nifty check from a major publisher. Movie rights selling at auction. He'd make a cameo in the film. Jane on the red carpet at the premier, as beautiful as any movie star.

He wandered into the bathroom. There was a large hot tub with an intricate mosaic tile floor showing a myriad of swimming women. Water nymphs, sirens, mermaids. He turned on the jets and sat in it for a minute and then got out again. What was he feeling?

Something was wrong with his knuckles.

He looked down and noticed they were bleeding. A thin trail of blood led into the tub, where the red curled and bubbled through the water. He glanced over the edge and saw several tiles were missing, shattered at the bottom of the tub. He'd must've punched the mosaic several times without knowing it.

These hands, always trying to tell him something.

A strange chuckle slid from between his lips.

His own chuckle. His own lips.

He felt angry. It was a true emotion. And his alone. It was a bizarre, intimate experience, feeling what had always been reserved for others. Pacella was so furious it drove him out of his head. Jack felt it over the smallest transgressions, the kill switch always flicked on in his skull. Smoker had it for the white man, and Jimmy Boyd used it in the ring.

But why was Pace feeling it now? His job was to walk the line, even if the body didn't always respond.

So, what was this for? Probably for the girl, the thief. Cassandra Kaltzas, the siren who had called him to the islands. If the billionairess hadn't pilfered a few bucks out of the restaurant till, Jane wouldn't have stayed late to work the books. It was Pace who had remembered the scene, and now it was within him, inside his head. Somehow his own memory. He kept feeling the weight of the girl on his shoulder, like he was still carrying her bound body. He'd been around long enough now to begin forming his own hate.

His bedroom door opened and Pia entered. She was naked. He was still surprised at how lithe and petite and young she was. Her small breasts bounced lightly as she walked to him. His blood began to surge. He thought about what two lunatics would be like in bed and was sort of intrigued by what he imagined. He hoped to hell her father didn't pop up.

She stood before him and whispered, "Did you like the way I danced today in the *taverna*?"

"Yes," he said.

"I enjoyed showing off for the men."

"I could tell."

"Do I disgust you?"

"No."

"Why not?"

"Why should you?"

"Because I've done bad things."

"We've all done bad things."

"I'm the worst."

"You're nowhere near the worst."

He could put her mind at rest about who was the worst, but now wasn't the time to tell her about the six inch hunting knife topped with a gut hook that had ripped through Emilio Cavallo's guts and sent arterial spray across the sacred heart of Jesus. The men's necks broken from behind. Catherine Eddowes, Mary Jane Kelly, Frances Coles and the kidney pie, the vaginal incisions, the glory of mutilation.

The moon washed over them, cold and distant but with a divine, immense grandeur.

"You're ill," he said. "There's nothing to be ashamed of."

"Yes, there is. Just because you're sick doesn't give you a right to hurt someone else. We're still accountable."

"Maybe you're right."

"Your hand...is that your blood?"

"Yes."

"What happened?"

"It's nothing."

"Were you trying to kill yourself?"

"No."

"Are you sure?"

Having this conversation while they were naked in a suite in a five-star hotel in Greece with a billion years of silver beauty shining in. If you put your mind to it, you could screw up any paradise.

Her pale blue eyes burned in the dimness. She sat on the edge of the bed and pulled him down to her. She took his earlobe in her teeth and held it for an instant.

"Do you want to know what I did to her?" she asked.

"To who?"

"Cassandra Kaltzas."

Pace felt very remote. It was part of being disassociated, depersonalized and derealized. Back on the ward in his straitjacket hammock, lost in the dark, waiting for the needle in the neck, Dr. Brandt would utter such words with an intensity akin to poetry. He would sometimes hum along with her voice, turning all her evaluations into love songs.

Pia moved against him, pulled him down to the mattress, her breasts pressing against his chest. "Will?"

That lower lip cocked in a half-grin, like she knew something you didn't, and she was never going to tell you.

"Yes," he said. "I want to know what you did to her, Pia. I want you to tell me about that night."

"First you have to give me something."

Of course, everything had its price. You couldn't eat a piece of fruit in a garden without having it cost the love of your god.

"What?"

"I want you to make love to me."

He said nothing, did nothing. He lay on the pillows staring at her silhouette, her white teeth ablaze.

He thought how she should be at college mixers meeting boys her own age, going to football games. Falling for the handsome quarterback who'd treat her like crap and break her heart just before she realized the sensitive best friend bookworm she'd previously air quote loved like a brother end air quote was actually the better choice.

Same thing that had happened with Pacella and Jane.

She took his hand and placed it on her thigh, easing further up over the bedspread so his knuckles brushed against the soft, trimmed hair between her legs. "Why aren't you touching me? Don't you like me? Don't you think I'm beautiful?"

"Yes, I do."

"You're not William Pacella. You don't owe anything to his dead wife."

But maybe Pace did. Jane was inside him even more deeply than all the others. The reason he was alive, had been given this life, was because of her. He had Pacella's face but wondered how he'd stack up against the guy, side by side, in Jane's eyes. If Jane might love Pace for who he was, even if he didn't drink cocoa or smoke a pipe. Even if he had never read Chaucer or Proust and had never tried to write a book and fucked it up.

"Tell me what you did to Cassandra, Pia."

"They have enormous hot tubs here."

"I know."

"Let's get in. I want to get in with you. I want you to hold me. With those strong hands of yours. I know what you can do with them."

Saying it with a kind of love but her knowing smile told him she wanted him to tighten his fists around her throat.

Despite all he'd done—that all the many *hims* had done—he still felt slightly offended.

"Is the knife under your pillow?"

"No," he said, although he wasn't sure. It might be there. Only his hands knew for certain.

She straddled him and licked the burn scars on his chest, nibbling at the gnarled tissue. He couldn't help himself. He became aroused and wasn't sure why he *should* help himself, why that should be such a necessity.

How about just letting go for once where nobody died? It was a heavy burden carrying the guilt of a hundred, maybe a thousand, other men. He thought, I have my own hate, maybe it's time for my own love too.

"If I cause you enough trouble," she said, "if I push you too far, will you stab me?"

"No."

"Yes, you will."

"No, I won't, Pia."

"Jack will." Biting hard at the scars, talking into them. "Won't you, Jack?"

"Why do you want me to kill you?"

"Why?" She stared at him as her icy blue eyes ignited with the moon. She laughed and stopped herself, started to say something and stopped herself. She began to kiss him and stopped an inch before their mouths touched. Her breath swept across his chin. A throaty snarl broke from her. "Because it would be so *romantic*."

What had happened to the Ganooch and his boys, what had occurred on the streets of Whitechapel, was anything but romantic. She just wanted to go out of this life with some kind of a dramatic display, like her father with the piano wire wrapped around his chest, the mother downing drain opener. Nobody took themselves out of the game anymore just sitting in the car with the engine running, the garage door closed. Where was the grand gesture in that?

"What was your sister's name?" Pace asked.

"I don't have a sister."

"You did. What was her name?"

"I never had a sister. She didn't have a name."

He shut his eyes and tried to remember. He must've heard it at some point on the ward. Perhaps Dr. Brandt had mentioned it in group therapy. He pressed himself and asked the others for help. The kids shouted. Vera. Angie. Nipple Jones. Freddie "Double Tap" Freeman. Lucy. Caramel

Skankie. Siobhan. Katie. Yokahama Yolanda. Duchess Crotch Stink. Pookie.

Katie. Katie, that was it.

"It wouldn't be wrong, you know," she said, reaching down to stroke him. "The two of us making love. We're both alone. No matter who else hangs onto us, or wants to take over, or tries to shove us aside, we're still alone. There's no need to go through the world like that. I don't want to go through life like that, it's nothing but torture."

"Pia—"

"Don't be afraid, Will."

"I'm not afraid and my name isn't Will."

"What is it?" she asked.

"I don't know."

"That's okay. Do you want me to give you one?"

"No, I don't think so. What did you do to Cassandra Kaltzas, Pia?"

"First tell me who you are."

That one stopped him. "I'm...the In-between man."

"In-between what?"

He watched the moon in her eyes. Nothing came to him. Finally a voice, not his, said, "The sins on the left hand and the sins on the right."

"You just mean you're not Pacella and you're not Jack. You're the edge of the coin."

"Yes, I think so."

"You aren't going to let Jack loose to cut me up, are you? No matter what I do?"

"No." He drew her closer and kissed her, hard and wanting.

She pulled away viciously, hissing. She got out of bed and headed for the door. The moonlight receded, following her in a heavy white tide that left him in deeper darkness. Over her shoulder she snarled, "What the fuck good are you to me?"

Then she was gone.

He looked down and the knife was in his hand.

twenty-two

The ferry to Voros reminded him of the ferry crossing from Port Jefferson, Long Island to Bridgeport, Connecticut. Pacella and Jane would cross the Sound and spend the day driving around the antique shops looking at colossal, centuries old furniture with high five-figure price tags.

If he had the money he might pick up a music box for her or something else small. A salt & pepper shake set from 1920, a dollhouse piano he could set on his fingertip that cost eighty bucks. Pacella might buy a carved meerschaum pipe stained by ten thousand pouches of tobacco. Even these small mementos of history made him feel vaguely connected to a greater world he didn't really belong in.

The tourists heading to Voros exhibited a contained enthusiasm, as if afraid to show too much excitement in front of the locals. Pace let the sea wind blow in his face and tried not to imagine what would've happened if Pia had actually wanted to love him last night instead of only wanting to die.

Hayden said, "We could still probably skip out, you know. Make a run for it."

Pace started to answer and Faust cut him off. "There's no going back, at this point. Don't you feel that now? The draw forward?"

"We don't have to go back to New York. We can hide in Athens. Who the hell could find anybody there? You could stick the whole Red Chinese Army behind the stacks of garbage. We could form our own *bouzouki* band. Pia could dance. Or we could become fishermen. Sponge divers. These people never sleep and never work. I say we fit right in."

Stroking his beard into a finely-crafted point, Faust said, "I think I'm beginning to look forward to meeting our unseen host."

"Me too," Pia said. "It's time to finish this."

"But what is this?" Hayden asked. "I'm still unsure what it *is*."

"This."

"Yeah, but what is it?"

"This thing we're in."

"Which is?"

"Stop bothering me, Hayden, or I'll stab you in the nuts and kick you overboard."

Hayden looked mildly hurt. Faust said, "Pia, your disposition is getting markedly more miserable."

"Imagine that."

No one asked Pace's opinion on anything, so he didn't offer it.

Faust leaned into the breeze and said, "I enjoy the water. I find it calming. There's almost a sweetness to the air, isn't there?"

Swaying her hips as if she might begin dancing again, Pia touched him lightly between the shoulder blades. "What's the long green spinach, Faust?"

"Excuse me?"

"The lettuce that got you whatever you wanted. In the clubs, the restaurants, all the joints up and down the strip. Park Avenue. The Gold Mile. Philly's Main Line. The lettuce that would stick to their sweaty knees. The long green spinach."

There was apparently no domino effect going on in Faust's head, one memory toppling forward into another. Her words didn't mean anything to him, even though they were his own. "I don't know, Pia."

They passed fishermen in the harbor, children in brightly painted green and yellow dinghies calling to the tourists and wanting to dive for coins. Pia threw some and the young boys disappeared like dolphins.

The ferry docked at the Voros port and they walked down the beach to an inlet where the charters and sailboats were busily going out.

The guy they chartered the boat from was also a handsome Greek youth. He also had a fishing blade stuck in his belt, and he was also named Stavros. Pia ignored him. This Stavros asked to be paid in drachmas because he had a friend who could still get a very high exchange rate. No wonder Vindi had given Pace the outdated money instead of only euros. He'd known the sailing men would prefer the obsolete notes.

"How long will it take to get to Pythos?" Pace asked.

This Stavros spoke with the same proper diction as the other Stavros. "In my boat, which was also the boat of my father, it is no more than an hour east of us. Not many go there, but I believe I can find it again. I have not visited for almost five years, a time when I went diving beneath the island."

"Beneath it?"

"Yes. There is a pit at the south end of the village, a large hole that goes directly through Pythos. During the war, the Germans invaded and tried to drive their vehicles down the road around the pit. They'd fall in and vanish. When I was sixteen, friends and I would go diving to salvage in the reefs. Many Nazi weapons and armor are still in the depths. There is good money in such items, even rusted and damaged. Many tourists buy them for their collections."

"Nazi memorabilia."

"Yes. We could have been rich but we dealt with a deceptive antiquities dealer."

Porpoises swam alongside the boat as Stavros confidently handled the large outboard motor. Pia and Faust sat back and laughed like children as the waters frothed. Hayden asked, "Are those marlin?"

"Dolphin," Pace said.

"Naw, maybe tuna."

"They are dolphin," Stavros said. "Do you not know dolphin when you see them? Don't you visit them in your ocean parks and watch them do flips and pretend to laugh and walk on the water? Did your parents not take you there?"

"My father would lock me in the crawl space when he got drunk," Hayden said. "And slide me cans under the door like I was a cat. I'd have to smash them open on the concrete and pull back the lids with my teeth. I hate tuna."

"Me too," Pace said, surprised that it was true. "Somebody wanted me to go work in a cannery where I would've spent the rest of my life jamming tuna into cans while the fucking fish stared back at me."

Hayden appeared perplexed. "Is that how they do it?"

"Forget it."

"No, seriously, I'd like to know. You just grab it with its head and eyes and everything and just smash it into the can?"

"Forget it."

The sun burned brightly. Their skin began to redden but no one had thought to bring sunscreen. Faust's scar was hard and red as a ruby.

Stavros looked over at the porpoises and grinned in the sunlight. The ocean was a cobalt azure with a blazing sheen. There was no land in sight.

If the little boat capsized or the motor failed, they'd all go straight to the bottom. Except Stavros who could probably swim for days without tiring.

The kid turned with a seductive smile and leaned toward Pia. "They say that dolphins are the ghosts of drowned sailors. They swim beside the boats because they remember what it was to be fishermen."

"You sound like you believe it," she said.

"Because I do. I must. My father and grandfather and two uncles died at sea during storms. They are here to protect me from the same fate. It may only be a delightful legend to outsiders, but to us, this is truth. They know I am of their blood, they show their love and guardianship by swimming beside me."

"I would've thought you'd feel guilty."

Stavros peered into Pia's lovely face, still giving her the sexy smile. His curly hair drifted across his exotic features. "Guilt? How do you mean?"

"You know, that they all drowned out there in the ocean trying to make enough money to feed and clothe you and put a roof over your head. If I went down like that, you better believe I'd be pissed at the little shit I had at home who didn't appreciate a damn thing I'd ever done. Working until my hands were blistered every day, burning from the salt. You know? I mean, can you imagine the last thing your father must've thought while he was going under the waves, sinking deeper and deeper while the pressure built in his head and he clawed for the surface, the ocean filling up his throat and his belly, I mean, he was probably wishing he could've been a sheepherder instead. All alone on a mountain somewhere, safe with his sheep. But no, he had to fish, just so his whiny, snotty kids could have shoes and crayons. Your whole life knowing your father is dead because of you."

Stavros held onto the shaft of the motor and blinked rapidly at Pia. His breath came in bites and his chest worked harder and harder.

"Well, it's true," she said and turned away.

Pace said, "Stavros, listen to me—"

"I do not wish to talk to you people anymore," the kid said. "I do not consider this a pleasant conversation. I have met many friendly tourists but you are strange and very unlikeable. I am filled with sorrow that I allowed you to charter this boat, which was also my father's boat. I will not return for you, you must make other arrangements."

"All right."

The next thirty minutes went by in silence. Pace took out the knife and fondled it, running the edge of the blade at an angle over the meaty part of his palm. His hands were so strong that the blade, as sharp as it was, couldn't easily cut him.

He could feel Jack and many others circling just beneath the surface, like sharks, waiting to chew him to pieces and take him down to the bottom. He realized, the more this knife meant to him, the more purchase it gave Jack.

The dazzling Grecian morning like a flaming cathedral.

Are you cured?

Pace thinking, I'm not stepping aside for anybody else. I've got too much left to do. But I need to do it on my own terms. Not Pacella's, not Jack's, no one else's. Just mine, whoever the hell I am.

He took the knife and held it over the starboard rim of the boat and let it go.

Princess Eirrin, ten thousand-year-old sorceress and heir to the Atlantean throne, eased her head back and her gills opened as she breathed above the waves. She slid to Pace and pressed herself against him. He sucked air through his teeth because her chain mail was so cold on his heated skin.

The ten-mile-deep trenches in the ocean depths rumbled with the force of her mystic spells. A dolphin leaped twenty feet out in front of the bow of the boat.

Stavros said, "I have not seen that occur for a long time. They do not venture that close because of the motor."

"Maybe Dad wanted to say hello," Hayden said. "Wanted to see how you were making out."

"Do not mock me, sir."

"Not me, man. You go to a Knicks game with a bunch of mongoloids and you learn never to mock *anybody.* You like the Knicks?"

Princess Eirrin's lidless eyes turned on Pace and tears dripped across her blue cheeks. She placed her webbed hand against the side of his face and said, "If you ever need your fetish returned, then my knights of the deep shall retrieve it for you."

"That won't be necessary," he told her.

"If your trials ever become too great and you need your weapon, call on me and it shall be yours once more."

"Thank you, but I still have it." He lifted his hand and showed her.

He'd tried to drop the blade and it looked like it had gone into the water, but here he was still holding it.

Faust said, "In the sky, toward the west. There's something coming this way. Is that a plane?"

It took a minute to make out the sound of the propeller over the boat motor. A black shape dropped lower and lower, as if it might buzz close enough to knock them into the water. It was a helicopter. It swept by maybe a hundred feet directly overhead and continued on in the direction they were heading.

Ten minutes later a wedge of darkness spread out across the water broke from the horizon, quickly growing larger, wreathed in gulls and mist.

Pythos.

twenty-three

Grottoes opened at either end of the horseshoe-shaped harbor. A swathe of funeral cypress angled along the banks. Limestone caves in the cliffs sparkled above the glittering beaches. Moaning exhalations issued from the great fissures.

At the summit of the island sat Kaltzas's fortified villa, with gates to the south, east, and west. Guest cottages, stables, and huge garages were plainly in view. Sheep grazed in the grassy hills nearby.

The main house was a rambling four-story white stucco building covered with steep ceramic roofs. Pace could make out towers, patios, balconies, and ornate wrought-iron railings.

"Like Olympus, rising on high," Faust said. "Can you see it? There's actually ice up there in the crags of the mountain."

It was true. The shadowed cliffs had a slight sheen of snow even in this heat. "There must be a completely different air stream that far up."

A flashing red aircraft warning beacon filled the sky with splashes of crimson. The helicopter had flown toward the flare of color and vanished from view behind the mountain.

Stavros told them that the bay of Pythos was seven miles long and three miles wide. The blue-black waters shifted to a burnished green along the coast. Stavros maneuvered the boat past several fishing vessels, through the cove to a huge stone mooring.

He said, "As I've stated, I will not be coming back for you. You will have to find other arrangements if you wish to return to Voros or continue on to one of the other islands."

Pace paid and thanked him and the kid left without another word. Pace turned to see a steep set of stone stairs leading up from the harbor to the village.

"Holy crap!" Hayden said. "There's hundreds of them. We've got to climb up all those? That's probably as many steps as they've got in Madison Square Garden!"

"But you walked those, didn't you?" Pace said.

"Yeah, but at least we had big pretzels."

"Come on."

"That ref knocked mine onto the court. The prick."

The steps were so narrow they had to walk single file, huddled close to the ancient cliff wall. Pace led the way wondering how much blood had been shed on these sharp corners. Old men carrying their day's catch getting almost to the top before a slippery step sent them all the way back down. Pacella was a little frightened of heights the way he was a little frightened of most things.

Pace kept looking back over his shoulder to make sure the others were following. It would be very easy for all of them to go over the side and die on the rocks below. Pace kept waiting to feel Pia's hand tugging at him, drawing him down. Or maybe Faust's. Or maybe Hayden's.

At the top, herds of goats and sheep drifted through the wild golden grasses of the area.

You could feel the antiquity of the land, all the chronicles of mankind witnessed by stone. Rutted dirt roads twined across the countryside. Deep ravines revealed mastic trees and yellow crown daisies. Groves of olive trees receded along the hills.

"It's so beautiful," Pia said. "That way is to the village, you can see it from here. The other way...Olympus."

The village was a primeval myth taken form. You looked at it and you looked at the places where Homer wrote his poems, where Achilles was born. Clusters of buildings were arranged tightly along the hilly streets blasted from rock. Carts raised clouds of chalky dust.

"I need a drink," Faust said. "I just want a glass of water."

"The last time you said that we were stuck in a *taverna* for twelve hours and you started your own *bouzouki* band."

"Now what?" Hayden asked. "We walk?"

"Looks like it," Pace said.

"Maybe that guy Vindi will be along in another Jag soon."

"We're in a land hewn from tradition and legend," Faust said. "He's making us walk as part of our trial."

Pace said, “Like Christ along the Via Dolorosa.” He had to suppress the sudden desire to bolt toward the mountain. The driving need to face Kaltzas at last was upon him all at once. His had to fight to keep his teeth from clenching.

“So the whole town can see us for our sins?” Pia said. “Is that what he wants? All he had to do was ask. He wants a parade, I’ll give him a parade. He thinks we’re afraid of that? He wants me to wave a black flag, I’ll wave a black flag. He wants to see me naked?”

“The village appears empty, or nearly so,” Faust said.

“This isn’t like Athens. The fishermen probably go out at dawn and stay out until dusk.”

“While a billionaire lives in his high castle above them.”

“They must hate his guts,” Pia said. “They must plot his death every waking moment.”

“I doubt it. They live the lives they’ve got. The man shares the same dirt roads, drinks from the same wells.”

The sun had tanned Pia to glistening gold, and when she flashed her grin Pace felt a pang of remorse that they hadn’t made love last night. Maybe it was just another one of his crimes that should be promenaded before the world.

“Let’s go see the bastard and find out what he wants,” Pace said, and the others once again fell in line behind him as he led the way to a minor god on the vast throne of Olympus.

You had to at least chuckle. No matter how guilty or mad you were, when you were walking along a dirt track toward a high castle in the distance, your broken ashtray and pajamas in the bag on your shoulder, your little troupe stomping along behind you humming Greek songs, plumes of dust rising from their heels, the knife you’d thrown away a couple times still tight against the small of your back, another man’s dead wife bright in your mind, wondering if you would have to kill or die before the end of the day, you had to at least let out a chuckle.

They walked along the rutted road and Pace was surprised at how much greenery there was to the landscape. Judas trees and shrubbery dappled the hilly terrain, sparse along the seaside but growing richer toward the center of the island.

Down a separate path, Pace thought he saw a young woman peering at him through branches. Perhaps it was Cassandra. He thought, She wants to get a close look at us. He turned down the path and followed, and the others followed him.

The way grew steadily more steep and rocky until they reached an embankment with a suddenly down-sloped grade. The road they were on had dipped away from Kaltzas's plateau, and they were now wandering into a craggy bowl canyon.

At the bottom was an excavation site centering on a set of ruins dappling the mouth of a cave. It had clearly been a very long, ongoing dig. Tons of rubble had been moved aside, the dirt filtered for artifacts. It looked like it hadn't been worked for a while though.

They approached cautiously, except for Pia, who skipped forward as if across the lawn to grandma's house, letting out girlish laughter along the way. If she hadn't been one of the most depressed people Pace knew, she would've been one of the happiest.

Shafts of sunlight illuminated the cave entrance, which opened into the first chamber of a temple or a tomb which continued on into a deep passageway, flanked by mortar and lumber.

"It was a trap," Faust said. Pace looked in his eyes and saw a growing awareness there, a blossoming sense of purpose. "We shouldn't have come this way. There must be another road around the far side of the slope, leading up to the villa."

"Who gives a shit?" Pia said. "So let's just go in."

"Into those black tunnels?" Hayden asked. He rubbed at his widow's peak, smoothing it back until it was sharp as a box cutter. "You're kidding, right? This is what we want to do? I don't want to go in there. We don't have enough problems? Seriously, let's backtrack."

"I'm not sure we could make it back up the incline," Pace said. "The grade didn't mean much coming down here but the rocky terrain is precarious. It'll be a lot harder getting out of the canyon."

"You can do it."

"Maybe."

"So? Go kick his ass and come back for us in a helicopter. You know how to fly a helicopter, don't you?"

Sam Smith had flown Hueys in Cambodia toward the end of the war. Pace's hands could probably work the copter that had flown overhead earlier today.

Faust stepped in closer to inspect the excavation site. Pace followed and saw that several battered bronze, oil-burning lamps sat aflame in niches in the rock just inside the cave mouth. "An underground temple?"

"Built inside a cavern that collapsed. Probably covered over by rockslides centuries ago."

"Whose temple is this?" Pia asked. "Or is it a tomb? Didn't they used to sacrifice virgins to Poseidon so their ships would have good fortune?"

"Think virgin blood might still help?" Hayden asked, bullets of sweat streaming down his face. Pace saw a nun with a yardstick waiting in his eyes. "My Sunday School teacher, Sister Lurteen, could prick her finger for us. Of course, she is a lesbian. She's done some weird things with plastic. You think that counts?"

Faust appeared more and more sure of himself now, growing stronger. He stared into the depths of the chamber. He let out an uncomfortable laugh. "I think you have to walk through the site to gain entrance to his home. The tunnels seem to twist back toward the mountain. Another labor. Moving underground. We're already part of a fable thousands of years old. Everything in Greece is symbolic."

Including us, Pace thought. "This is the underworld," he said. "Our psyches have been driven down by love. Eros is the god behind vulnerability...who exposes all of mankind, through love, betrayal, and cruelty...to the inseparable blend of pain and pleasure."

"That sounds kind of sexy," Pia said. "How do you know all that stuff?"

"Sam Smith told me."

"Who?"

Alongside the sun, the flashing red beacon bore down on them. The ice on the distant cliffs sparkled. Faust studied the layout of the land, the mountain towering overhead with the retreat waiting for them.

"These lamps are filled with oil. They had to be filled within the last day or two. Kaltzas set this up, but did he do it for us or himself?"

"Well, we know he's got problems," Hayden said. "And he likes drama."

Pia peered into the darkness. "Jesus Christ, these Greeks and their trials. We studied this in middle school. Hercules and his twelve labors. Sisyphus and his boulder. Atlas and the pillars of the sky. What the hell is it with these people?"

"They've had an unpleasant history," Faust said.

"Who the fuck hasn't?" She showed her teeth in a hateful smile that Pace found alluring. He stepped to her and put a hand on her elbow. She wheeled away from him. "The big crazy Kahuna wants us to go through the cave, we'll go through the cave. Come on."

Faust actually held his arm out, stopping her. He'd never done anything like that before. Pace wondered where this new change would be leading the man, leading them all.

"Wait."

Pace said, "It's the trigger. This is where Kaltzas's wife died while they were excavating the site. This is where Cassandra watched her mother get crushed to death."

The start of the fracture.

He thought about what it must have been like, to watch your mother die beneath tons of rubble, trying to free some speck of the past from the rock. At least as bad as watching your wife burn to death holding her melted hands out to you.

"There should be electric lights."

"There are," Faust said. "I can see them in the glow of the burners. They're strung along the roof of the tunnel, but I can't see a switch."

Pace entered the cave and felt his way along the wall. Jack had strange eyes and could see very well in the darkness. He found the switch and hit it, but the lights didn't go on. "No power. Another scare tactic."

"Can you see daylight out the other side?"

"No. The cave must be catacombed."

"We might grow lost and die in some wretched dark corner."

"We've already died in wretched dark corners."

Pace watched Faust, waiting for Daedalus to reappear. But the masculine solar deity stayed hidden in the shadows. He thought maybe they should use Ariadne's trick of unfurling string through the maze so they could return safely.

"Fuck it," he said.

"Fuck what?" Pia asked.

"Nothing. Let's just get it over with. Everybody grab a lamp. He left them for us, might as well use them."

"Seriously," Hayden said. "Wouldn't you rather just go back up the ridge, walk up to his house, take the big knife out and stab the hell out of everybody, and then bring the copter back for us? I think that's a much better plan. Isn't it? Isn't it the better plan? You're not listening to me."

Faust took one of the bronze burners from its nook and stepped ahead of Pace. “Shall we enter?” he asked, already inside, the light from the ancient lamp receding step by step as he proceeded deeper into the underworld. The rest followed.

PART III

The Lost Art of Odyssey

twenty-four

The children were scared of the dark and started crying. Pace offered them ice cream but they refused. He thought back to when he was a kid sitting in the bleachers of the circus and how his father bought him a little blue flashlight on a strap. You held the strap and swung the light around and waited for the ringmaster or the dog act or the tiny car with a million clowns hiding in it. Pace gave little blue lights to the kids who swung them around and ran up and down the cavern alcoves and started playing Marco Polo. Their laughter eased his heart but irritated Jack and made Pacella wrench to one side because he and Jane had always wanted kids, and the sound of them made him ache even now.

Pace was struck by the beauty of the arched walls and colonnades of the temple, the scale of the stone structure. The cave roof was thirty feet high and the columns nearly touched the top of it. Friezes on the walls showed scenes of tree worship from the prehistoric goddess cults. The temple appeared to have been built on a holy site from a much earlier period. Pace ran his hands over the pocked stone and felt some kind of energy alive in there.

"Old gods die, and new ones are built on the bones of them," Faust said, his voice taking on the quality of a history professor lecturing. "Their temples vandalized, their flesh and rituals cannibalized by new belief systems."

Hayden said, "Sister Lurteen would've busted your ass with a yardstick for saying such things."

"You had Sunday School at the home?" Pia asked.

"Oh yeah. Mostly we just sat around and made pictures of Jesus out of construction paper, but sometimes the nuns would give a sermon while we did it. If they caught you eating your paste they'd really wail on you."

The cave branched. Triangular stone chambers opened. Sometimes the ceiling was only inches above their heads, and sometimes it slanted upward three or four stories high.

"There's a kind of courtyard here," Faust said ahead of them. "In the center of these rooms. There's a round section that contains a tomb of some kind, I believe."

"Any markings?" Pace asked.

"No symbols or Greek letters. Some of the stone doesn't seem to be as old. They've been cut with modern equipment. And food's been set out. Some kind of cake and dried fruit."

Kaltzas must have rebuilt the tomb for Cassandra's mother. But why place it here where the woman died? What did that say about Kaltzas's personality? Maybe he was trying to merge the present with ancient history, reality with myth.

A conical structure rose up near the tomb. A twining design had been carved around it as it rose, serpentine and polished to a lustrous white that shimmered with reflected lamplight. "It's an omphalos stone," Pace said. "It means 'center of the world.' They're found in most shrines. In Greek mythology Python is a guardian serpent. It was the original name of Delphi, which means dolphin, before it was renamed after Apollo. He took the form of a porpoise in order to lead sailors to safety and become his priests."

Pia said, "How do you know all that?"

"I'm not sure."

"Think about it, Will."

"I'd rather not."

But he did. He recalled that he'd read about it on the laptop in the house on Long Island, the night he and Sam Smith had done research online. He hadn't even realized he'd remembered it all until it started coming out of his mouth. His hands far ahead of him, and now his mouth too. Pretty soon there'd be nothing left behind, and Pace would be gone.

"There's a fire," Faust said, moving into another chamber. The rest of them walked forward and met him at a small pyre.

A gas pipe led along the edge of the tunnel. More of Kaltzas's updating of the ancient. An eternal torch burning for his wife.

"This is a *heroon*," Pace said, wondering what his mouth would tell them now. "A kind of monumental tomb built for heroes and VIP's and their families."

"You sure got smart fast," Hayden said.

"Not fast enough," Pace told him.

"Tell us more, Will," Pia said. She held her lamp high, near his face, so she could see him clearly. "You know more. Tell us."

He wanted to say, I don't know anything. Sam Smith was the researcher.

His lips parted and he listened to himself as if from an adjacent but unseen place. "On a typical visit, it was adorned with colorful ribbons or anointed floral wreaths. Vases filled with oil were the most popular gifts brought on a visit to a crypt or cemetery. A feast was laid out at the tomb in honor of the deceased. However, it is unknown whether the living ate any of the food or not. Among the foods left were honey cakes, celery, pomegranates, and eggs."

"Honey cakes and pomegranates," Faust said. "That's what's on the tomb lid."

Pace imagined Cassandra coming here, with or without her father, to visit the place where her mother died, and relive the moment over and over again. Each visit driving a deeper wedge into the fracture, splitting her psyche farther apart.

Staring at the pyre as if he wanted to immolate himself, Faust's eyes wavered, shifting in color from gold to orange to red as the flame flickered. He brought the lamp up higher until it looked like he might set his beard on fire. Pace's hand lashed out and gripped Faust's wrist and forced him to extend the lamp away.

"Something's happening to me," Faust said.

"I noticed. Can you describe it?"

Faust's mouth moved absently and he gagged trying to form words. His tongue jutted a few times and withdrew. He swallowed and shook his head. "No."

"Does it have to do with the long green spinach?"

"I don't know what that means."

"What's going on now?" Hayden asked.

Pia said, "Sh."

"Sh? Did you just shush me?"

"Shh."

"Do not ever fucking shush me!"

"Shhh already!"

"Sister Lurteen used to shush the shit out of us all the time!"

"Shut up!"

"You afraid I'm gonna wake somebody?"

Whatever hex Faust had been under, he snapped free of it. His shoulders relaxed and slumped, the strange force having seeped from him. "We're all going to die here," he said. "We'll be entombed together, breathing each other's stale air for our remaining hours. These lamps are all we'll have to hold back the endless, eternal darkness."

"Nobody's going to die," Pace told him.

"You can't be certain of that."

"But I am. Let's go on."

Some of the small stone rooms and alcoves held more burning lamps. The dark rock of the cave walls was streaked with light-colored powdered minerals. They stepped through pools of water on occasion. The tunnel narrowed farther on and they had to walk single file again.

Hayden began singing *To Vouno*. His voice carried into the far corners of the cavern, echoing across all the black crevices.

"There's another incline, feel it?" Faust sounded almost joyous.

"We're moving up the mountainside. Toward Kaltzas's villa."

"There's a draft. The flame is brighter."

"We're reaching the end of it."

"That means we're nearly to Kaltzas," Pia said.

"And to Cassandra." Pace's stomach tightened. He just wanted to see her face.

"We're almost dead," Hayden said. "So much for my band."

The far end of the tunnel broadened and brightened with daylight.

Pace opened his fist and there was another note in his hand. An entire sheet of paper folded up several times. He held the lamp closer.

The symbolism is obvious. You're in the bowels of your own brain, with these various aspects of yourself, weaving through the dark labyrinth of your diseased mind. Here are more tangled subplots, another foray to understand your many failures. This too is uninvolving. This is not resolution. The story is convoluted, blurred, confusing, and jumpy. You are not as funny as you think you are. We are left wavering and wanting. We do not find you a likeable or sympathetic protagonist. We hope you die soon.

Sincerely, The Editors.

twenty-five

They stepped out into the world and Vindi stood there before them with a group of three men holding machine guns.

The Minotaur, coming at you.

Even in the heat he wore a suit, and that huge diamond stickpin caught the sun and flashed it back into Pace's eyes. The man-bull snorted through his flared nostrils and blew little dust devils at his feet. The tangled beard wafted in the breeze and he held his strong stubby arms out to his sides like he wanted to charge forward and wrestle somebody in the dirt.

Jack had good eyes in the sunlight too. He put on his leather apron and got ready to make his move. Pace placed the burner down on a shelf of rock, took three quick steps forward and got within arm's reach of the men. Machine guns at such close range were stupid, they'd chop each other up in the crossfire. All Jack had to do was take a step left or right and he could kill them all with four quick swipes of the blade.

"Welcome, friends," Vindi said. "You're just in time for lunch."

Hayden said, "Hah?"

"You must be hungry. And thirsty. Here, we've brought canteens of water."

"No hideous death?" Hayden looked unconvinced. He crouched with his feet half-turned so he could sprint back into the tunnel if need be.

"Pardon me?" Vindi asked.

"You're not going to put us inside a large metal bull and cook us? None of that chaining us to a cliff side and letting the birds chew us to death for days, picking away at our livers?"

Pia whispered out the side of her mouth. "Don't be giving him ideas, idiot."

Vindi let out a grunt of puzzled laughter. The security men either didn't know English or didn't find any of this amusing. Pace looked up at the villa and wondered if Cassandra or her father were staring down at them right now.

"Oh, do not fear," Vindi said. "The Kaltzas family has many enemies, industrial and otherwise. A defense force is necessary. These men are certainly not here to threaten you." He spoke softly in Greek and the guards made a show of angling away their weapons and putting on accommodating smiles. "You are our esteemed guests. I apologize for not meeting you at the harbor. We expected you yesterday."

"We were held up," Pace said. "In a *taverna*."

"I hope you enjoyed yourself."

"We did, and you really weren't expecting that, were you?"

"No. Although you were left with maps and guides of the tourist spots, I did not think you would participate. Forgive me for my breach of etiquette, as well as for misjudging you."

"It doesn't matter."

"But let me ask," Vindi said. "Why do you have these lamps?"

"The lights wouldn't work in the caves."

"No? How can that be?" He turned to a guard and barked an order. The man rushed off into the tunnel. "But tell me, why did you go through the caves?"

"It was the only way."

"That is not even on the main road. How did you find your way there?"

The others looked at Pace. Pace wasn't sure if he should mention that he thought he'd seen the face of Cassandra through the Judas trees and had followed her to the excavation.

Hayden, bolstered by the fact that he wouldn't be roasted in a bronze bull this afternoon, said, "Stop messing with us, it was the only way, man. You think we wanted to go through dark tunnels? We don't have enough problems?"

Pace asked Vindi, "How did you know to meet us right here?"

"There are monitors at the site. They are necessary due to archeological pillagers. Museums and unethical private owners would pay handsomely for even fragments of these ancient finds. Those lamps you were holding are over thirty centuries old. Each one is worth tens of thousands of dollars."

"Then why were they just left around in there, burning?"

A shadow of confusion crossed Vindi's broad face before his expression changed to anger. His jaw tightened and he began to snort. "I do not know."

The wind rose and blew a heavy musk in from the sea. The sky had shifted to a vivid glaring violet, lined with crimson, the color of cracked flesh. You looked at it and thought of contusions, punctures, lacerations. Dark clouds swept in like the tide and moved steadily in front of the sun.

Vindi said, “It’s about to rain. Please, let us retire to the villa.”

Pia looked up. “It’s the storm. It’s found us again.”

They were led up a lengthy mosaic, balustraded walkway that widened into a marble courtyard at the villa. They stepped into a large entrance hall. Marble pillars supported the roof. On pedestals sat statues of warriors and goddesses missing limbs, heads, faces. Relics and artifacts brought up from digs, shattered pieces of history that ought to be in museums.

There were several servants who moved about with great efficiency or else stood aside primly awaiting orders. Maids filled a long banquet table with fruits, wine, meat and fish dishes. There were actual gold goblets and silver chalices.

An expansive staircase rose to an upper galleried floor. The walls of the tremendous rooms were covered with a profusion of paintings and bas-relief carvings of mythical beast-men and -women. Satyrs, centaurs, mermaids. Ariadne the daughter of Minos, shown as a beautiful woman with the beginnings of spider-like features. Faust walked over and stared at Daedalus with his mechanical wings sweeping open. Daedalus looked at Daedalus and almost smiled. Small spotlights highlighted the details of the statuary and artwork.

You looked at the marble long enough and it started to appear alive, like the victims of Medusa’s gaze.

Pia said it first, what they were all imagining. “Makes me think this is where we’re going to wind up. Frozen in stone and stuck inside this gallery. The maids dusting us each day so Kaltzas can see his own grin in our polished skin.”

“Is he even here?” Hayden asked.

“No,” Pace said. “He’s missed his chance for a big entrance.”

“All of this and the guy’s away? What do we do?”

“We wait for him.”

“Even the mongoloids didn’t act this stupid.”

“I’m quite hungry,” Faust said. “I’m going to get something to eat, and suggest you all do the same. Our father who art insatiable.”

Pace moved up the stairs. He wanted to see what Kaltzas’s view from on high would be like.

A butler eased along behind him at a polite distance. Whenever Pace looked over at him, the servant would drop his gaze. He wondered if the guy ever got the chance to look somebody in the eye.

Pace stood on the terrace, taking in the view from the top of the steep mountain, spotting the remnants of three other archeological digs in the distance. To the south, security men prowled the area and, heading toward the village, Land Rovers raised dust all over the summit. Directly below, a plaza swelled with fountains and mosaics, opening into panoramic gardens filled with fruit and nut trees, palms, and exotic birds.

The storm rushed in like an angry animal. The waves tore into the harbor from the open sea and smashed against the cliff walls. Trees groaned and wavered. Somewhere, somebody shut off the fountains, and as he stared down the first drops of rain splashed heavily across the marble. The statuary lining the courtyard darkened as it grew wet. He looked at the columns, pillars, and colonnades that had withstood ten thousand such gales.

He sensed that the house had risen up around the landslides and ruins, a merging of earth and man, past and present. He didn't get the feeling that Kaltzas was trying to bring these remnants into the modern age, but rather the man was trying to retreat through the millennia, to become one with a plane of life lost long ago.

Pace turned and stepped back into the house, the butler following close behind as they moved down the stairway. Pia angled her chin at him and sipped from a chalice. Faust and Hayden were eating heartily. The three of them were seated at the far end of the long banquet table while Vindi enjoyed his drink all the way at the other.

Vindi gestured for Pace to join him.

Sure, what the hell.

Pace walked past the others and Pia whispered, "You sure he's not Kaltzas? He could be lying."

"Kaltzas wouldn't lie about who he is," Pace said and proceeded down the length of the table, twenty, thirty, forty feet until he took the chair beside Vindi. A peal of thunder broke like a colossal bell over the ocean.

Vindi poured him a goblet of wine and a nearby maid let out a gasp and jumped forward. He spoke a gentle word and she retreated to her station.

He said, "I believe you will enjoy this wine. Try it."

Pace took a sip and found that liked it. Will Pacella made a face and his lips bubbled like a baby's.

"Where is Alexander Kaltzas?" Pace asked.

"My employer...is away at the moment."

"I thought this entire visit was orchestrated so he could meet with us."

"He will only meet with you. He does not wish to speak to the others."

"So why did he invite them along?"

"They are here because you need them. You are united to them in a way I do not fully comprehend. Through violence. Through love and torment. It was the reason that Rollo Carpie was hired. Not because it was what we wished, but because it was what you needed."

So, we've been wrong from the beginning, Pace realized. Kaltzas didn't really suspect the others of hurting Cassandra. He had no real interest in them, except so far as Pace had been using them as emotional crutches from the minute he left the psych ward.

"Who was in the helicopter?" he asked.

"That is not your concern right now."

"Then by implication it will eventually become my concern."

"Yes, I believe so."

"I could make you tell me."

A small smile appearing on that bullish face. "Perhaps. But let me ask you a question, Mr. Pacella. Why are you in Greece?"

"You invited me. And I'm not Pacella."

"Yes, of course, apologies. But why did you accept the invitation?"

"I'm here to see Cassandra."

"Why?"

"I want to know what happened that night on the ward." He searched Vindi's face. "Can you tell me?"

"I cannot."

"Are you saying you won't tell or that you don't know the answer?"

"I am saying that I live in a superstitious land, and I am a superstitious man. Despite education, opportunity, and even affluence, many of us are still burdened by our rituals and religion. I am saying that you make me afraid. The fate that has encompassed the Kaltzas family often makes me very fearful."

"You said we'd met before and had been quite friendly."

"That's correct."

"You spoke to me at the hospital, the regular hospital, where I was laid up with my burns."

"Yes, many times."

Pace nodded. "You stopped in to see me while you were visiting Cassandra. You wanted to thank me for saving her life."

"You remember this now?"

"I remember the fire. The rest just makes sense. But why the intrigue? Why make me think you wanted to hurt us?"

"It was a mistake on our part. But again, it was what you yourself needed. You and your friends are all paranoiac schizophrenics. You all harbor great amounts of guilt feelings where your pasts are concerned. And where Cassandra is concerned. They chose to believe that they were threatened with harm, giving them a reason to escape the facility."

"Dr. Brandt said she was frightened by your men as well."

Vindi looked to the floor and appeared to have trouble finding the correct words to explain himself without revealing too much. What was he still hiding? He started to speak and stopped, started again and once more curbed himself.

When Vindi glanced up again, Pace watched his eyes. Vindi had come to some decision much more important than he intended it to appear. "Yes, I know. Dr. Maureen Brandt...that woman...her life...it is a troubled one. Made worse by her feelings for you. She hated and feared you, and yet was attracted to you. As I mentioned to you several days ago, it was common knowledge that you were behind the Ganucci family murders. And yet the police could prove nothing. She was terribly frightened, and yet intrigued. She studied you, and sought to build her career based on your unique case. But I believe she was greatly influenced by the distrust, anxiety, and illness of the others. And yourself. Your many selves." He took a sip of wine and stared over the rim of the goblet. "If you have not realized it yet, she is quite insane."

"I realize it."

"Ah."

"You still believe we were lovers?"

"Almost certainly."

Pace thought about how lonely she must be. How difficult it must've been to let him go, and not follow. Maybe she didn't do it out of fear at all. Maybe she'd let him come this way on his own out of love for him.

"Call me paranoid if you like, but I still don't fully understand the hiring of Rollo Carpie to take me down."

Vindi sighed. "He was meant as a gift."

"A gift?"

"For you. He was one of the few members of the Ganucci syndicate who avoided Nightjack's wrath."

"He was a low-level shooter who never got in the way."

Vindi's snorting breaths blew wide ripples in his wine, making it slosh over the rim. "This Rollo Carpie, he killed your mentor, Sam Smith."

Before he could stop himself, Pace let out a fierce, cruel laugh. "No way could a second-rater like Rollo take out Sam."

"But it's true."

Inside, Sam was shaking his head in disbelief. He didn't actually remember getting iced, just sitting in his office pouring back a tumbler of whiskey, a little high and very tired and feeling very old, and then turning in his seat to an instant of blinding pain coming in from the window. He supposed it could've been Carpie. It could've been anyone.

Still, Kaltzas had no right to offer up blood gifts. They weren't his to give.

The rain throbbed across the windows and the growing wind beat at the glass. The storm raged down, a giant infuriated child. Perhaps, in some fashion, it was just another alternate, out there alone in the endless sky, pursued by the burgeoning night, trying to get back inside a safe, warm cage of bones.

"Why should I believe anything you tell me?" Pace asked.

"That I cannot answer. You must find your own way to the truth, whether you choose to believe me or not."

"When can I talk to Kaltzas?"

"Perhaps tomorrow, or the day after. Until then, please, enjoy yourself. The servants shall show you to your quarters."

twenty-six

The third story of the villa opened up into several suites very similar to those found at the *Athenian Palace*, but even more extravagant.

Faust sat in a chair staring out at the black ocean, his hands folded under his chin. Every few minutes he'd flinch, as if his thoughts were at war. Hayden lay on a bed large enough for five people, drinking metaxa and flipping through the satellite stations, watching American sitcoms from the Sixties in Greek. Funny what didn't make it into translation. The Skipper shouting down Gilligan, smacking him in the head with his sailor's cap, the heavily masculine Greek voice ending a string of hard consonants with "*little buddy.*"

Pia was taking a bath in a step-down pool-like tub so large that Princess Eirrin was able to swim several strokes underwater. The double-doors to the bathroom were opened wide and Pace watched her nude blue body arching and curving. Every so often the Atlantean heir would lean over the edge with her green hair dripping across her eyes and she'd beckon to Pace with her webbed hands.

He leaned against the far wall of the suite, near the main door. Servants moved past in the corridors and he tried to split his focus, keep an ear out for anyone who might sound important, Cassandra or her father. He had a bottle of ouzo in his hand and drank from it without feeling. The anti-climax of the visit had left him even less grounded than before. He felt as if his mission, already vague and tenuous, had become even more ethereal.

Night had fallen early, quick and tremendously hard. The storm continued its siege. Pace felt a little sorry for all the fishermen that wouldn't be able to go out in the morning to make a living, and for all the others who might try and yet have their boats wrecked, their lines torn, perhaps lives lost. All because Pace had a tempest on his tail.

"Did you notice," Princess Eirrin said, "that the shipping tycoon has no paintings of ships? No seascapes? No statues of Poseidon or the naiads? For a Greek who's made his fortune on the ocean, he has no love for it in his soul."

Pacella had lived on Long Island his entire life and he never had a picture of a ship in his house either. He and Jane had loved the beach and going out to Fire Island and spending time in the Hamptons, but the walls of their home were covered with prints of Manet, Van Gogh, and Pollock, an oversized photo of the Manhattan skyline. In the dining room there was even a sacred heart of Jesus. Just like the Ganooch. Just like Cavallo.

A blur of motion made Pace turn his head. Sister Lurteen sat there on the bed dressed in her habit, smacking her palm with a yardstick. She looked at Pace and said, "Are you eating paste?"

"No."

"You'd better not be!"

"I'm not."

"Let me see your drawings of Jesus."

"I don't have any."

She raised the yardstick and brought it down against the back of Pace's hand. The wood broke in two and the old nun stared at him furiously.

"Hayden," Pace whispered, pulling the bottle of Metaxa away from him. "You've been drinking too much the last few hours, you should eat something."

"Not paste!"

"No, not that."

"Shh!"

"Have some fruit. Drink some coffee."

"Shhh!"

Pace opened the door to the suite and only had to wait half a minute before one of the servants rushed down the hall to him. Pace was trying to figure out how to gesture for coffee when the man said that he spoke English. Pace asked for some coffee and something to eat. Five minutes later three maids wheeled in three carts of food and a cappuccino maker.

Faust never turned his head from the window.

Wearing a large cotton robe, her hair wrapped in a towel, Pia came out of the bathroom and sat on the bed while Pace struggled to get a few cups of cappuccino down Hayden's throat. Eventually Sister Lurteen faded and Hayden settled down and started eating.

Pia asked Pace to dry her hair. He took the towel from her and his hands knew the gentle motions because Pacella used to dry Jane's hair this way. Pia sighed and began to fall asleep in his arms. He wondered if there was any chance of happiness for him, or if it would have to wait until he became the next alternate down the list.

"Kaltzas is planning to take us out, one by one," Hayden said with cream on his lips.

"No," Pace said while he drew Pia's hair back and forth with delicate precision. "I don't think so."

"Look. His daughter flees from him and goes where? To America. New York. So he's already got a hard-on for Americans. Then what happens? She loses her shit completely, has a nervous breakdown, winds up eating fucking rats in alleys."

"That's not what hap—"

"America drove her insane. Now he's got even more reason to hate us. Now she winds up in the booby hatch, where bad things happen. Now her father thinks that all these nuts chased after her, beat her up. All of us sticking our crazy cocks in her."

"Did you?" Pace asked.

"Did I what? Fuck her? No. None of us did. Except maybe you."

"What was she like?"

Pia relaxed against Pace's chest. "A total bitch."

"What was she like, Hayden?"

"She was a sweet girl. Very quiet. Black circles under her eyes. You can see she wanted to die. Like Pia. That's why Pia hates her."

Pia looked at Hayden and went, "Shh."

"Do not fucking shush me!"

"Shh."

"Did you hear me, I said do not—"

Pace looked over at the window. "Faust?"

Faust said, "I don't remember."

"Are you sure?"

Faust tilted his head aside, chin aimed toward Pace but his gaze going through him. "Why would you ask that? You don't remember, so why would you expect me to?"

"Because I do remember," Pace said. "Some things."

He told about the night of the fire, and how Pacella had saved Cassandra Kaltzas from the flames. How Jane's death could be tracked back to Cassandra, if you wanted to think about it that way. Pace didn't but Pacella did.

His hands tightened on Pia's hair and she let out a gasp but didn't pull away. She whimpered once, a beautifully sweet sound of highly charged sexuality. His voice was that of a schoolteacher trying to excite passion in his students about some great tome of literature. He spoke about the hospital. Pace listened as if from very far behind himself, running to catch up.

"You two have blood ties," Faust said. "It has nothing to do with us at all."

"That depends on what happened on the ward," Pace told him.

"No," Hayden said. "All that matters is what she thinks happened there. She's a nut. She could've told her father anything. The man still wants vengeance. I can smell it, the hate is all around us."

"That's the hate in us."

"Same thing!"

They watched television the rest of the night, hardly moving at all. Eventually Faust left his seat and stretched out on the enormous bed. Even with the four of them on it there was still plenty of room. They settled in deeper while more sitcoms moved in front of their eyes speaking in a strange language. On occasion one or the other of them would laugh. Sometimes it was Pace. His hands were still twined in Pia's hair. She couldn't slip away if she wanted to, but she didn't seem to mind. Someone would get up and grab some food and share it. One by one they fell asleep, all except for Pace and the storm, which continued to pound at the walls, hoping to slip in and escape back into his flawed human heart.

The next day went by quickly because of the party.

Pia and Hayden asked the servants to teach them Greek songs and dances. They wanted to recapture some of the fun they'd had in the *taverna*. The maids and butlers looked away shyly until Vindi said something in Greek that gave them permission. It was all part of keeping the guests happy. Someone drove down to the village and brought back one of the *bouzouki* bands. The members entered the house dripping wet, wide-eyed and alarmed at being invited into the temple of Olympus.

Over the course of the day Pace learned that the English words chorus, chorale, choir, and choreography all come from this same Greek word HOROS. Dance, song, and music were such integral parts of the theater that the single word covered all of it. Pacella liked learning new things. Pace stood aside while the others enjoyed themselves. After the first two times the maids asked him to join in on the dances, they kept away.

At first Faust was a little distracted, but he eventually got over it and he joined in on the *Yeranos*—the Crane. They learned how to do the happy, exuberant *Syrtos,* the national dance, written about by Homer in the *Iliad.* It was done with a smooth, flowing style by the women, while the men bounced and leaped wildly.

Pia and Hayden did amazingly well right from the beginning. Faust got better and better as the afternoon progressed. The celebration became an expression of the moment. The Greeks went on to mix step variants. Improvisation that became open challenges, the men trying to outdo one another, the women becoming more and more sensual.

More people showed up, more food and drink were brought in. More seating and tables. The wide marble floors seemed made for this reason, for gala and rejoicing. Pace sensed that deep-rooted emotions were being purged or expressed, that these people were showing love and hatred and pain in a way that was denied to him.

He watched the men and women openly weeping during the sad, heavy *Zeibekikos*, and a lot of bared male chests during the heroic, masculine *Tsamikos* and *Beratis.*

It started as a kind of show—with Vindi telling him, Look upon us, the gods are kind to the peasants—and it became a hell of a party. Vindi joined in on some of the songs. He had a lovely singing voice. His laughter boomed around the villa. The festivities becoming richer and more vibrant by the hour. Young men swooned over Pia—young men would always swoon over Pia, forever. Pace spotted two fistfights about to start but Vindi got there before anything could happen. Old men and women sat clapping their hands, enjoying the food, a little puzzled and astonished by it all.

Pace watched and drank more ouzo. Eventually he wandered the villa and spent time studying the statues and paintings in the gallery. There were no photos of Cassandra, Kaltzas or his deceased wife anywhere on display.

He stood on the terrace in the driving rain. In seconds he was as wet as if he'd been dropped into the sea. The fountains below were overflowing across the mosaic tiles, the fruit and nut trees bending savagely in the wind. The storm flung itself against him and he held on to the stone balcony with both hands. The waves crawled into the harbor, wanting to get at him. The statuary below watched him with pitiless eyes.

When Pace finally released his grip and stepped back inside he wiped his hair from his eyes and immediately felt the hot breath of Vindi upon him.

The Minotaur, snorting, said, “My employer will see you now.”

twenty-seven

He was led to an immense library down the corridor from the suite where they'd slept last night. Twenty-foot-high shelving with rolling ladders set in tracks surrounded the room. There were tens of thousands of volumes. The smell of acidifying paper was overpowering. Busts, carvings, sculptures, and parchments under glass sat on lit pedestals. It was the kind of room that Pacella had dreamed about all of his life.

Vindi ushered him inside, then retreated and closed the door.

Alexander Kaltzas sat in a broad leather chair facing Pace, his back to a large window that trembled, the darkness beyond flowing and pulsing as bucketfuls of black water were hurled against the glass.

Pace had been expecting a broad, powerfully built man, someone imposing, as awe-inspiring as Zeus or one of the Titans. But Alexander Kaltzas was diminutive, fragile in appearance, almost petite. He was completely bald, his angular chin covered with a well-trimmed beard. Extremely red lips gave his mouth an obscene quality. His nose was as sharp as a hatchet.

He wore a black suit with tails, a high-fastening collar with a perfectly double-knotted thin tie, and a brocaded vest. The man appeared ready for a funeral. His hands were clasped, index fingers steepled under his chin gently stroking the tip of his beard. His gaze rested near Pace but not on him.

Kaltzas was in complete *repose*. A word that William Pacella liked to use repetitively in his book. Everybody in the novel was always in repose—after they got laid, after an argument, after the final revelations of a situation were finally made clear, those fuckers were in *repose*.

Alexander Kaltzas, father of Cassandra—unmoving, and at peace.

"Hello, Mr. Pacella," he said without any accent.

The voice had a little grit to it, deeper than you'd expect from such a small man, as if thickened by constant use, shouting orders.

Pace decided not to correct him. Dripping, he stepped forward and his wet shoes squeaked on the tile floor. He stood and waited to see what kind of opening gambit would be made. "Mr. Kaltzas."

"Thank you."

"For what?"

"Many things, but let us begin with your accepting my invitation. I appreciate you making such a lengthy sojourn."

Pacella liked that word too. *Sojourn.* Pilgrimage. He still couldn't believe that publishers would reject somebody who knew such fancy words and used them all the goddamn time.

Pace said, "I didn't mind coming to Greece."

"Please sit." Kaltzas gestured to the chair directly across from him. He wanted to be close, face to face like gentlemen about to play a game of baccarat.

Pace sat, thinking, You come all this way ready for blood and butchery, prepared to die but aspiring to live, almost hopeful that the mysteries which bind you can be undone with the triumph over a labor. You come all this way expecting murder and instead you drink and dance.

He waited in his seat almost wishing someone would try to kill him. That he would, at long last, be able to accomplish something.

"Why did you invite us here?" he asked.

"I need you, Mr. Pacella. All of *you*. The many facets of you."

"Nobody needs all of me. Not even me."

The small man placed his arms against the armrests of the chair and smiled. "I needed to awaken what had been put to sleep in that institution with abundant amounts of medication. I own several pharmaceutical companies and asked a chief pharmacologist to give me an extensive report on your treatments. Perhaps your doctor was not aware of it, but if you continue with that mixture of medication for another year or so, you'll have complete renal and liver shutdown."

Laying it out like that, practically saying that Dr. Brandt was trying to murder Pace. Maybe it was true. You just couldn't tell with that lady.

"Why do you think you need me?" Pace asked. "The many facets of me?"

"To save my daughter," Kaltzas said. "To lift the curse upon her. To counteract what was originally done to her. What you, in fact, did to her."

"What did I do?"

"Infected her with your affliction."

Pace thought about that for a minute.

He said, "How do you know she didn't infect me?"

Kaltzas angled his chin. "Why do you say that?"

"My affliction, as you call it, began the day I saved your daughter's life from the fire that killed my wife."

Pace had a hard time saying *my wife*, talking about a woman he could hardly remember, but at the words Pacella chewed his tongue until his mouth filled with blood. He swallowed it and the taste made Jack throb.

Kaltzas's repose wavered for a second. His lips grew even more red until he looked like he'd bitten someone's throat. "My daughter...this illness...it may have originated with her?"

"I don't know. I'm not blaming anyone. It happened to me that day, I believe. In the fire. When I watched my wife burn to death."

"My daughter was always troubled, but it wasn't until after—"

"Why don't you say her name?" Pace asked.

"*Cassandra*," Kaltzas said, with so much emotion that it was like a hot wind in Pace's face. What did it mean, for a father to say his child's name like that?

Without turning in his seat, Kaltzas indicated the window behind him. It seemed like it might shatter at any minute and shred him to ribbons.

Kaltzas said, "This storm. It's yours, isn't it?"

"That sounds crazy."

"True. Nonetheless, it is yours."

"Yes," Pace admitted.

"As above so on earth. Heaven rages because your soul is not at peace." A strange, small sound fluttered from the man. It had almost nothing in common with laughter but Pace figured that's what it was supposed to be.

Pace said, "What the hell do you want with us?"

"My sole interest is in you." The steepled fingers returned to his beard.

"I see. Why?"

"As I said, because of my daughter, of course. Because we are blood now, you and I. Fate has seen to this."

"How so?"

"My daughter is pregnant with your child."

Pace stood. Maybe the knife was in his hand, maybe it wasn't. It felt like he'd just clutched it to his chest and stabbed himself. He had to look down to make sure the stacked micarta handle wasn't sticking out of him.

His mouth opened but he said nothing. His lips moved but framed no words.

"Yes, it's true, Mr. Pacella. As I said, we are now blood."

And then, for an instant, the man...*fluctuated*. His calm gone, his eyes suddenly filled with a swirling anxiety. Those eyes turned black and cold as quartz.

And Pace realized what was happening.

Faust had been right.

We're actually channeling these other individuals, entities, and beings. Drawing them from other dimensions, through time and space and across the cosmos. Gathering them to us. Them, and the souls of the departed. These others do not arrive organically, from within.

He wasn't talking to Alexander Kaltzas at all, not in the flesh.

They consume and subsume and, the worst of them, devour. We are simply the beacons. We are the vessels. We are the conduits. We are the possessed.

He stared at Kaltzas, into the man—trying to focus past the ghost to see the face of a dark-haired girl with sharp aquiline features beneath. A young woman of strength and independence, forged by heartache. With an expression that was, even now, undoubtedly reserved and remote. A girl who had buckled and broken, no worse than Pacella had, like Psyche driven down to the underworld by love.

Kaltzas remained before him, but Pace knew now, this was a girl with an affliction.

This was actually Cassandra.

A moment later, Alexander Kaltzas returned to his peaceful repose. He stood, extended his hand, shook with Pace, and said, "It has been a pleasure, my son. We shall talk again further." Kaltzas drew him forward, patted his back twice, added, "Welcome to my family," and walked out of the room.

twenty-eight

Pace stood there thinking, Christ, if she really is pregnant, the poor baby. With Pace as the father and Cassandra the mother, this kid was going to be born speaking ninety-seven languages, squealing, hissing, burrowing like a grub, gliding like a tree squirrel. Burning brighter than Apollo, red as Satan's sores. Reaching for mama's heavy breast, full of the murdered, the inhuman, and the insane.

That's my boy!

By the time he got out into the corridor Kaltzas was gone. Pace walked the hallway listening to the celebration still going on downstairs, Pia's laughter loud enough to rise above the music and other noise. The *bouzouki* band was really kicking into high gear, the crowd stomping in time with Pace's pulse.

His head swirled and he wasn't so sure that he liked being alive anymore, being the man in charge of the body. He was picking up a history in busted bits and pieces, gluing the shards together to form the mosaic of himself.

A shadow crossed his face and he spun, wondering who was coming after him now.

It was only another statue of an incomplete man standing on a pedestal, the spotlight rising from between his cracked legs, illuminating his missing hands, his marred face.

Sometimes you found your symbols, and sometimes your symbols found you.

He walked down the hall and, as he passed an open door of a dimly-lit room, someone called to him. "Will?"

You couldn't help thinking, Jesus Christ, now what?

He stepped inside the room, feeling the blade passing back and forth from one hand to other at incredible speed.

Dr. Maureen Brandt was seated before the window, a wretched expression writhing across her lovely face. You could take a lot, but this lady, your own doctor, she was just totally fucking disheartening.

"What are you doing here?" he asked.

"I failed you," she said.

"Not me. William Pacella maybe, but you and I are square."

"All of you. Pia, Hayden, Faust, even many of my other patients on the ward. I'm sorry."

"For what?"

The question seemed to stun her. "You're not cured."

She still didn't get it. If she cured him, she'd kill him. Reintegrating Will Pacella would squeeze out the In-between man. "We were in a mental hospital. There's not exactly a high rate of success in such places. It's a world where recidivism is on the rise."

"I don't think you should be so forgiving."

"It's my nature," he told her. It was the truth. "What are you doing here?"

"I had to come. To make certain you were safe."

"Vindi paid you and brought you here."

He stepped closer, willing her into his arms, but she remained seated. She still intoxicated him with her allure, perhaps more now than ever. Maybe he just needed someone from his past—his own past—to be here with him. He started to turn away but couldn't quite complete the motion.

He flashed again on the first time he'd seen her: waking up in the hyper-white cell room, strapped in the funky straitjacket tied to the stainless steel railings surrounding the bed. Dr. Brandt introducing herself by name while she flicked a fingernail against a syringe, sticking the needle into his neck. How could it not make an impression?

"I really wish you'd stop looking at me like that," she said.

"How?"

"You know how."

"Yeah, but I want to hear you say it."

"Like you want to fuck me."

There it was. He'd always known that, on some level, Dr. Brandt really hated her patients. They were, to an extent, infecting her with their troubles, putting different kinds of thoughts into her head.

"Maybe I love you," he said. "Maybe you're in love with me."

"That's ridiculous."

"Some people might call it crazy, but I'm glad you don't throw that word around so easily."

"No, I don't."

He remembered the final smile she'd given to him before he'd left the States, that condescension somehow mixed with bereavement. As if she'd almost managed to rescue the part of him worth redeeming, before he'd proven himself past all atonement.

"I need your help," she said, and moved in such a way that her breasts jutted, consciously or unconsciously luring Pace in to do her will.

"You need *my* help? To do what?"

"To save Cassandra Kaltzas."

It was acceptable to go mad with lust, but he didn't need the extra burden right now. "Kaltzas said the same thing. But what can I do?"

"I'm not certain, but you're a main part of her illness, and so you might be an aid in her treatment. Cassandra didn't have a breakdown in the accepted understanding of the word. She was...obsessive. Whereas you, Pia, Hayden, and Faust make each other more ill, I believe that you might actually be an aid to Cassandra, and help me draw out her primary personality again."

"Her father says she's afflicted. And that I'm the cause. She's pregnant with my child, he says."

Dr. Brandt's entire body tightened in the chair. Her brow furrowed and she shut her eyes, and he saw the muscles in her beautiful face working to no benefit. When she looked at him again she was nearly pouting. "At first I thought you were the impetus, the catalyst for shared mass hallucination. But you weren't merely seeing and interacting with the other patients' alternates. You were ingraining the ill with their fractured psyches. You were giving life to their additional personalities."

"That's not possible," he said. "You can't spread split personality disorder."

"Apparently you can. Perhaps with implanted suggestions. And with additional suggestions you can help seal the fractures and reverse the process."

"You know, lady, you're as nutty as any of us. And everybody knows it."

She gave him a sad smile there that made the center of his chest hurt. "We're breaking new ground here, Will. We're far and away from the usual psychoneurotic disorders."

How often did you hear that? *We're far and away from the usual psychoneurotic disorders*. She didn't even realize how ludicrous it sounded.

Dr. Brandt said, "That's why I know I'm responsible, in part, for your continuing illness. I should have turned your case over to psychiatrists whose skills exceeded my own. Or at least invited others to study your case and weigh-in with their professional opinions. But I was selfish. I was greedy. I wanted to keep you to myself. I guarded you jealously."

He didn't know how to take that. "But if you wanted to study me so badly, then why did you keep trying to shake me free from it? With such intense therapy? The medications? That fucking straitjacket?"

"I was...conflicted."

He let out a bark of laughter. "Yeah, I guess so, lady!"

"I've got to talk to him," she said.

Knowing exactly who she meant, but unable to say the name. "Who?"

"Jack."

"Why?"

"He's a part of this."

It made no sense. "He doesn't talk."

"Yes, he does. He spoke on the ward. Pia mentioned it in the car when we were leaving Manhattan."

"He doesn't talk to me or you. He just giggles."

She grinned with such sorrow that he took another half-step toward her. "There are ways to communicate with your alternates even without directly assuming their personas."

"He isn't an alternate."

"What is he then?"

"Something else."

"You might find you can speak to him directly, if you make the effort."

"I don't want to talk to him."

"No, but perhaps he wishes to speak to you."

Look at this. Two years at Garden Falls, maybe a thousand hours of group therapy and one-on-one psychoanalysis sessions, days and days in the straitjacket rig, all the pills, the months surrounded by Brutuses and Ernies, making ashtrays and pajamas, and she just brings up this new course of action now?

Two oceans away, in the heart of a hurricane, in the house of the enemy, who didn't even exist.

"Forget about that now," he said. "How did you get here? Did you come on Kaltzas's jet?"

"Yes."

"Were you on the helicopter?"

"Yes."

"But—"

She rose and slid into his arms, and kissed him with such passion that he actually moaned against her tongue. She tightened her embrace on him, urging him to crush her. Pace drew away and held her at arm's length as she struggled to reach him again. He stared into her eyes, thinking the last time he'd been this close to her, on the verge of touching her, the same storm had been breaking wide over them both. Maureen Brandt kissed him and he searched her face, hoping she wasn't going to stick a needle in his neck. The soft pressure of her body against his made his head swim, even a lunatic can enjoy a woman's love, and as she whimpered a name that wasn't his he felt—beneath the strata of concealing flesh—*oh Christ*—he felt the child within her womb.

He realized, Goddamn, this is Cassandra too.

twenty-nine

The hot breath of the Minotaur brushed against the back of Pace's neck, burning him once again.

He turned away from Dr. Brandt to see Vindi standing in the doorway, his expression as dark and dense as an outcropping of reef. When Pace looked back, Maureen Brandt was gone and Alexander Kaltzas was standing there with his red lips like crushed roses.

Pace walked out into the corridor and Vindi gently closed the door.

"You play a filthy game," Pace said.

"I am sorry."

"Toying with me the way you have. What happened to them? Kaltzas and Dr. Brandt. They're both dead."

Vindi's bullish face softened around the edges, and a touch of real respect and alarm worked through his features. It was about time. He swallowed heavily twice before he found his voice. "But how do you know that? How could you possibly know that?"

We are the possessed.

Even though the man claimed to be superstitious regardless of his education, having grown up in an ancient land full of custom and ritual and myth, and despite his fear of the strange things that had encompassed the Kaltzas family, he would never believe Pace.

"Don't you feel it?" Pace said. A surging tide of comprehension began to break inside him. "Can't you understand? We're getting to the end of it. This is almost over. I'm almost done. Then you'll have to deal with some other stupid son of a bitch who wears the same face."

Vindi was no longer the Minotaur at all, just a scared ugly man. "The end of what?"

"She's been making you jump through hoops and you have no idea why, do you?"

Pace's hands were so strong now that Vindi let out a small squeal of pain even before they touched him. And then Pace's fingers were digging into the bone and muscle of the once brutishly powerful arms, bending Vindi backward. Vindi's eyes flashed with terror and his tongue lolled, the flared nostrils becoming even wider as he gasped.

Pace said, "Tell me what happened to them."

"Alexander Kaltzas died of heart disease shortly after he had Cassandra returned to Greece."

"So he never had anything to do with this at all."

"No. He knew his daughter was ill. She had grown almost obsessed with you after you saved her life. And later, when you were brought in for questioning by the police, when you were suspected of those heinous crimes. He respected that. Taking matters into your own hands, it was what his father had done during the war. And then, when you committed yourself, and she did the same. At first he—and I as well—thought that the two of you in the same hospital might be beneficial to her in some way. She and Mr. Pacella."

"You finally understand that I'm not him. I'm not William Pacella."

"Yes." Vindi's Adam's apple bobbed and Pace leaned away, the hands calming down. "Alexander Kaltzas knew she was not raped. We all did. Even Dr. Brandt. You were in isolation, the girl free yet dominated by her adoration for you. Cassandra clearly found a way to get to you. But afterward, she was beaten. Scratched. Bruised by small hands. A woman's hands. It was then Dr. Brandt instigated an investigation. An investigation into *the rape of Cassandra*. Do you understand? It was then that I knew that this woman was greatly troubled. This doctor who selfishly studied you like a lab animal. Who tortured you. That her fear, or perhaps her love for you had begun to so negatively impact her. I believe she may have beaten the girl herself. In her own way, she was even more obsessed with you than Cassandra was."

Pace caught a fragment of his reflection in the window. He thought, Christ, Pacella, what have we done? Everyone we came in contact with has died or gone even more insane than we are.

"How did she die?"

"She slit her femoral artery in the house on Long Island where you stayed your last night in America. There were many knives in that house."

The blades, she did it with Jack's blades.

"You stayed behind," Pace said. "You were there. Watching the place, right? You saw us leave."

"I thought she might go with you. When I saw that she did not, I decided to speak to her. I believed she could still aid me in helping Cassandra. But when I arrived Dr. Brandt was dying. I tied a tourniquet about her leg and phoned for an ambulance, but the loss of blood was too great."

Jack was giggling like the maniac he was. The sound of it filled Pace's head and he pressed his hands over his ears and thought, Lunatics have been known to kill themselves in extremely bizarre ways. Men truly can hold their breaths until they die. The human will to destruction is one that cannot be defeated. He pressed harder and harder, knowing he could crush his own skull. His hands could do it.

He had his own love and hate and now he had his own sorrow and guilt.

Pace drew the knife and stuck it between his teeth and champed down, swallowing the laughter. It took a while for the noise to stop. When he was ready, he sheathed the blade and had to try a few times before the voice he spoke with was actually his.

"Did she say anything?" he asked.

Vindi's fetid breath blew a demon wind into Pace's face. "Only that she was sorry. She was not in any pain. She seemed quite...relieved. Quite happy, actually."

"Thank Christ for that."

All of this, and now you had to get away from it and talk about other, lesser, more futile things.

"You were in the helicopter."

"Yes," Vindi said. "The storm made travel very difficult. I spent two days circumventing it, only to have another descend on us here."

"It's the same one."

"No, that is not possible."

You couldn't make them accept the truth, you could only speak it and go on. "Cassandra was the one who made sure the electric lights in the caves didn't work. She lit the oil lamps."

"Yes, I believe so."

"You said there were monitors in the tunnels."

"Yes."

"Digital video cameras?"

"No, simple electric eyes at either opening, and others around the site perimeter."

"And there are no guards?"

"We had to take them off since Cassandra became ill. She would wander around the crypt at all hours of the night. She speaks in strange voices. Several times she was almost shot."

"And Cassandra's mother is entombed there? And her father?"

"No. The tomb is for an ancient, local magistrate named Terellicus who presided over the island three thousand years ago. Her parents are buried in Athens, near the university, as per their wishes."

"But she doesn't realize it."

"She doesn't want to. She wishes for them to be near at hand, in the place where her mother died, so she can do penance and suffer further."

Pace said, "I still don't remember everything."

"Do you recall her sitting with you—with William Pacella—ah, does he...?"

"Don't worry about getting the names right."

"She sat with you in the hospital while you recovered from your burns. She read your novel."

"She read the book?"

"And grew to love you even more. She could see the makings of Nightjack in you even before you began your vengeance against the Ganucci family. She talked of you constantly. She implored her father to pay your hospital expenses. That is when we first met, you and I. In the hospital, shortly after your wife's death. You could barely move because of your wounds but you were already toying with knives. Your silverware. Your ballpoint pens. We had to replace your hospital bed several times because you would stab and rip it to shreds. You tore open your wounds time and again. The skin grafts wouldn't take. Your scars are much worse than they should be because you would not rest. Later, after you were released, you refused any further assistance. After the destruction of the Ganucci syndicate, after you fulfilled your vengeance, she followed you into the psychiatric hospital."

"How could Kaltzas think that would help her? Why would he let her?"

"He didn't, at first. Her father would not even let her back on American soil. She was not allowed to leave the villa. But she grew sicker and weaker. As I said, we are a curious, superstitious people. We called in priests. We paid soothsayers from Crete to speak to the oracles. There were exorcisms. She spoke in strange tongues. Her obsession with you drove her. She needed you. In the end, that was all that mattered, all that might keep her alive. We admitted her to Garden Falls, and her health improved. I had—and still do have—a great admiration for you. A man who would pay off such an incredible blood debt, to avenge his wife. Your skill, your strength, is marvelous. Meritorious."

"There's a price."

"Yes, there always is. I now know the extent of yours."

Jack was actually starting to think about the baby. What it would be like to raise a child of his own, to have a son to teach all his methods and surgeries to, and place the scalpel into the tiny chubby hand even before the bottle. Jack's giggling petered out and he started imagining a cradle made from bones, how easy it would be to put the kid to use. Set him loose in the alleys where the whores would sweep him up in their arms and hug him to their diseased bellies. The boy finding the liver on the first stroke and cutting left, shearing it loose from the other organs. Jack trembled and Pace trembled.

"She apparently had—" Vindi smoothed his beard around his mouth, covering his lips, embarrassed by the words, "—*carnal relations* with you while you lay tied to the bed in solitary confinement as punishment for fighting with one of the guards."

"They told me there was no DNA sample. How can she be pregnant with my kid?"

"We believe Dr. Brandt bathed Cassandra and obliterated any evidence. After she had beaten her. And then proceeded with the investigation."

"Investigating a situation she herself was responsible for."

"Yes."

Pace stared at his hands for a while wondering what they were deciding to do. He raised his eyes and met Vindi's gaze. "You handled this thing really *really* badly, you know."

Vindi nodded. "Yes, I have. I have never had to deal with such bizarre circumstances before. I did what I could to control the varying degrees of subterfuge, illness, madness...this...this absurdity, but I failed."

He stood unmoving, no different than any of the other man-beasts on their pedestals in the gallery.

Pace heard someone shouting for him and turned back to the stairway. Hayden was running around downstairs calling, "Will! Will!" Pace moved to the gallery banister and shouted down to him. Hayden came rushing up the steps.

"Now what?" Pace said.

It took a minute for Hayden to catch his breath. He looked back and forth from Pace to Vindi. He was clearly drunk on metaxa but something had happened to start sobering him up fast. His clothes were wet and he was shivering. Pace had to put a hand on his shoulder before he became sturdy enough to speak.

"Ah, listen, I don't want to get in the way of anything, you know. You guys look like you're into something deep, but we've got a situation here."

"What is it?" Pace asked.

"It's Pia. She saw you and Cassandra kissing. It drove her wild."

Pace almost said, But I haven't kissed Cassandra, I haven't even *seen* her yet. It was the truth, or almost the truth. "Oh hell."

"She ran outside, man, into the storm. I chased after her for a while but I got lost, it's bad out there, I couldn't see anything. I don't know where she went. I think Faust went after her too. I saw him for a second and then he was gone. He hasn't come back yet."

"The village," Vindi said. "The guards at the south gate will stop her."

"No," Pace told him, knowing in his heart where she'd go, where he would go in his pain. To hide in the bowels of the underworld, where we are all driven down by love. "She's in the caves."

thirty

Blinding streaks of lightning clashed overhead, the thunder one long angry bellow. He rushed down the mountain path already calf-deep with the sweeping, rushing rainwater. His feet seemed to know where to go, how to maneuver the stony, rutted trail, and he just went along with them.

He got to the mouth of the cave and saw that the electric lights were already on. The oil lamp he had placed in the niche of rock had been taken away. He sprinted into the narrow tunnels and wove his way through them, thinking that, somehow, his own redemption was tied to the others, and he couldn't break his promise to Pia.

The long-dead architects of the tomb of magistrate Terellicus must've built in a water-runoff system this close to the ocean. He heard the staccato pounding of the storm beating against the cavern from above, but there was hardly any leakage into the catacombs.

He called Pia's name and his voice and many other voices circled around the stone rooms. He shouted for Faust and Daedalus, who had built the labyrinth and would know how to escape it.

It took ten minutes before he caught up with Pia close to the *heroon* shrine in the middle of the central cavern. The pyre was lit for Cassandra's parents, whose graves weren't even on Pythos. In the cold glare of the electric lights the temple had lost its romanticism and sat in a thirty-centuries-old heap of indifference.

There was no more history here than in the graveyard where your old man was buried. The stone no more important than the gravel driveway of William Pacella's house.

Pia lay slumped over the corner of the tomb, like she wanted to join with it. All the happiness he had seen in her today while she danced and sang, while she laughed and wooed the boys, was gone. Its loss left her reduced and deflated, the blackness beneath her eyes much darker than ever before. Pace finally understood that she didn't just want to die, she was already dying.

"So, you love her," Pia said.

"No," he said.

"Now you'll stay here with her and her father and you'll be the new master of the island, the mad king of Pythos."

"Her father is dead."

"Then there'll be no one to come between the two of you."

"Get up, Pia, we're leaving."

"There's nowhere left for me to go." Her eyes welled even as a cruel grin spread across her face. Here she was, the girl next door you wanted to cuddle with so badly, who would always take care of you while your fevers ran their course. Here she was, almost dead, and you couldn't figure out a way to save her. Jack's stomach fluttered.

"You still want to know what I did to her?" she asked.

"Yes," he said.

"After you made love to her—after she fucked you that night—I told Dr. Brandt. I told her and I watched her beat the hell out of Cassandra. I watched her drag her into the showers and try to wash your seed right out of her womb. I thought she might get pregnant with your child and I wanted it dead too. You hear me, I wanted your baby dead!"

"Why?"

Her tears ran and hung in the hollows of her cheeks. "What?"

"I asked you why."

"Because I'm crazy, you idiot!"

"That's not the reason, Pia."

"Because I love you! I love you and need you to love only me!"

"Why?"

"So you'll kill me!"

He said, "That's not what love is, Pia."

She held her face up and presented her throat. "Don't you understand? It is to *me*! That's what love is to me!" She closed her eyes tightly and begged. "*Jack*! *Jack, please*! I'm the whore that got away!"

Jack wanted out. Jack wanted this little bitch once and for all.

"It's not going to happen," Pace hissed.

His hands were ahead of him again though. They moved. His feet moved him. The knife was there and he bent forward and angled it close to Pia's jugular, and Jack showed his teeth and his mouth watered with the hope of dissecting her later.

Pace said, "No."

Jack exerted himself, under wraps for too long. The laughter broke free from Pace's throat and his breath blew stray hairs back and forth on Pia's forehead. The hand grew uncertain of its purpose. The laughter grew frenzied and much more horrible, and Pia's smile grew even more ugly.

"Yes, that's it, Jack," she said with the huskiness of an impassioned lover. She kneeled before him and panted. "Give it to me, baby."

"No," Pace said, louder. He might only be the In-between man but he had made his own oaths. Even if he wasn't here tomorrow—even if some new aspect of Pacella arose in the night—his promises mattered. They had weight. They held power that would continue on without him.

Jack roared and grabbed Pia by the hair and pulled her closer. She crawled on her knees, sobbing but with her mouth curved in a smile. She pressed her face into Jack's crotch, the way the prostitutes in Whitechapel had more than a century ago. The things you could do to a woman when you had the time and the proper tools, and this one was even willing. Jack felt a twinge of real adoration for her within his consuming hate.

"Don't do this," Pace said, but his voice was the voice of another man. Maybe Pacella, maybe another him—all the other *hims* that hadn't turned up yet, hadn't gotten their chance in the flesh. "Don't let Nightjack out."

His mind chimed with names. Nipple Jones. Where had he heard that before? Freddie "Double Tap" Freeman. Caramel Skankie. Katie. Duchess Crotch Stink.

Katie. Katie, that was it.

He said Pia's sister's name as gently as he could. "Katie."

"You know you want me," Pia said. "You know you've always wanted to drive it in. To feel my blood beneath your touch. To flay me and fuck me to death."

The blade froze at her throat.

"I'd like to talk to you, Katie."

The dead will follow.

We are the vessels. We are the conduits. We are the possessed.

"Katie, please talk to me."

Pace felt an odd surge of confidence because Jack, like all men, wanted to extend the moment, prolong the climax. Jack's eyes rolled up in his head and his giggle echoed in the cavern, back thousands of years through time.

Pia's sister, with the same heart-shaped face, the same warm pale-eyed stare that made you want to curl up beside her, was down on her knees before him. She looked up and said, "It's my fault. She wants to be like me. She wants to be dead, murdered by someone she loves."

"How do we save her?" he asked.

"You can't, you can only give her what she wants. You have to kill her."

"I promised that I...would...save her."

Jack's cackle grew louder, the blade starting to move, a fraction of an inch closer, cutting Pia's cheek, and a spurt of blood arched over the knife handle to splash on the back of Pace's hand.

Pia didn't really want Jack to kill her anyway. She wanted her father to do it.

Pace shouted, "Faust! Where the fuck are you! I need help!"

Fighting himself—battling Jack—Pace managed to turn his chin aside and focus on the dim stone recesses of the cave. He pressed his affliction forward into the darkness until the man came dancing out of the shadows.

Pia's father spun and did the bump, then slowly came to a stop beside her. Beneath his maroon suit jacket he had the piano wire tied around his waist.

She said, "Daddy—"

"Shh, baby, don't you worry about anything. I'm here now, I'll take care of you."

"Yes, Daddy, please...finish it..."

He undid the piano wire and slipped it over her neck and pulled it tight from behind. Pia's face lit with a smile so incandescent that Pace had to narrow his eyes to slits.

Jack wanted more blood. He always did, it was his natural state of being. He drew out all kinds of surgeon's tools from his little black bag. He wanted to make this last a long while, really get in there and start snipping away, pull out bones and sacs and tissue, but leave the heart beating.

Pia was choking to death, her face turning an awful indigo as her father continued to tighten the wire. The blood vessels in her eyes were purple and ready to burst. Jack thought it was a waste, having the girl die this way, but he didn't really mind. He could have just as much fun afterward with the body, scooping and flinging.

With the details so lovely and vivid in his mind, Jack stepped away to relish them, hugging himself. Pace felt a little stronger and managed to work the tip of the Trident with its Bowie-style blade between the wire and Pia's throat. It was sharp enough to cut through damn near anything.

The wire snapped from around her neck. Pia's father dropped away with an expression of indignation. Jack turned back and wore the same shocked expression, like he'd made a foolish mistake and couldn't believe he'd done so. He licked his lips and cocked his head in a rage, the way your father did when you didn't put out the trash.

Pia took a deep breath and fell into Pace's arms, sobbing against his chest.

She went completely slack and they both dropped to the dirt. Her father and sister wandered around for another moment, confused and at a loss, their chins slack and hands open. They brushed against Pace and he shuddered at their touch, his flesh going cold where they passed through him. Pia's eyes were black and lidless like a shark's and then he saw them become beautiful and blue and wet and pained again. He held her and felt the human heat of her body against him, warming him.

With the quiet strength and mewling of a lover in need, she kissed him. Pace held the kiss, their tongues touching coyly, almost shyly, afraid of the intention or where it might lead.

Then he began to draw from her the venom, the poisons, toxins, repressions, and subjugations. The children started dancing with Pia's father. They welcomed her sister, calling her Nipple Jones, Siobhan, Yokahama Yolanda, Pookie. If Pia was going to have a chance, it had to be this way.

She tried to break their kiss and struggled to get free of him, but he held on, drinking her in deeper and deeper. She squealed beneath his lips and scratched at his chest until it was finally over.

Then she slapped him so hard that he tasted blood.

"I didn't want an exorcism," she said.

"I know that."

"You had no right!"

"I told you I would save you."

"God damn you," she moaned, and then went slack in his arms and began to sob.

As he kneeled there with her, hushing and patting her back, blood on his tongue, he watched a shadow thrash along one of the alcove walls. It squirmed beneath flame. As Pace kissed Pia's brow he held up his fist.

He opened his hand and read the message there, and realized then that in the end maybe he would have to kill somebody after all.

thirty-one

He pulled her to her feet and gently began to press her away.

"No," she said. "I want to stay with you."

"You can't."

"Why?"

"I need to be alone for this. As alone as I can be."

"For what? What are you doing?"

"Completing a very vicious circle. Stay here if you want and wait for me, but don't follow."

He could tell she wanted to argue, to continue the fight she'd been fighting all her life, but there was no reason for it now. She seemed stunned as she turned and didn't find her father behind her.

She wiped the back of her hand across her dripping nose and said, "All right."

Pace spun toward the alcove where one of the ancient lamps threw light against the dark rock mottled with minerals. He followed the shadows, like the contours of a nightmare, through the small stone rooms until they led him to Faust.

"There you are," he said.

Faust was crouched before the burner. "The old gods die, and new ones are built on the bones of them," he intoned, repeating what he'd said the first time they'd come through the cavern. "The same as men."

"What did you do in the world, Faust?" Pace asked.

"I don't know."

"Think about it."

"That hurts too much."

"Try."

Faust looked at the friezes as if trying to spot himself in their scenery and stories. Himself or someone like him. "I was an insurance salesman.

Yes, I believe that's it. I sold insurance and enjoyed helping those hurt in accidents, providing comfort for the downtrodden. I went to houses and they gave me money and I protected them from termites, floods, earthquakes, and other acts of God. That's what I did, I'm pretty sure of it. Almost certain, in fact. Yes, that was it."

"I don't think so," Pace said.

"Why? Why do you say that, Will?"

"What kind of man were you, Faust? Do you remember?"

"I told you—"

"What's the long green spinach?"

"I don't know. And I'm a little offended you aren't taking my word for it."

"Why are staring into the lamp?"

"Because. Well, maybe you've heard this already, but you see, my wife, she died in a restaurant fire—"

"No," Pace said. "That wasn't your wife. What did you do before?"

"Stop asking me that."

"It's important."

"Is it?"

"What did you do on Park Avenue? The Gold Mile?"

"Stop hammering at me, Will. It's very rude. Yes, very rude, coarse, and disrespectful of you. Let's have no more of that."

"Philly's Main Line. Malibu. Beverly Hills. You said you did a lot of work in L.A. What did you do?"

The storm swept down over the mountain, beating against the earth so that, in the underworld, the force of heaven rang like a death knell. Pace felt the atmosphere changing. Faust's beard and hair danced in the air. Pace felt a powerful draw at his back and realized it was the knife being pulled as if by a magnetic wave. He wondered if lightning were striking directly over the cave, if the *heroon*, the tomb itself, was calling down the gods.

"I remember now!" Faust screamed. "The long green spinach. That's big money. I got paid the big green!"

"For what?" Pace asked.

He looked to his left and saw Rimmon, governor of the first order of seraphim, angel of lightning and fire, whose sword set fire to the bush that brought clarity to Moses, who must have written with a fiery finger across Pace's palm. He opened his fist. There was no paper in his hand, the note was cut directly on his calloused flesh in a shaky scrawl that extended across each of his fingers:

> **Faust is the torcher. You're the one who gave him the scar on his forehead. Murder him.**

"For setting fires," Faust said. The scar was as red as the womb. "And you, you son of a bitch, I remember now, you, you stabbed me in the head!" he shouted, and hurled the burning lamp oil at Pace's face.

Pace managed to duck and get the knife out of its sheath and up in front of his face to take most of the flaming oil. The rest splashed across the back of his hand and swept against his chest, instantly burning through his shirt and chewing into his flesh, scorching the thick scar tissue.

He cried out in agony and threw himself down on the cave floor, tearing at his blazing shirt, rolling.

There are no coincidences. The world will only have so much to do with you before it starts repeating incidents. We live to repeat the past. We wouldn't know how to move forward even if we could.

Always on fire, always rolling.

His mind rang with Jane's name though he didn't call out for her. The skin of his face tightened and dust circled him, sweeping along as he thrashed.

He remembered the night of the restaurant fire, how Pacella's hand shot forward and brushed against some silverware lying in the busser tub.

His hand was open and a steak knife leapt into it. The mad rush of gratitude for the blade and *to* the blade.

Pacella went after the torcher. There had been a great sense of speed and capability as he was ferried by the crowd in his head, people appearing around him and pressing him onward. Pacella had lunged and the guy sidestepped but not fast enough. Pacella had felt the blade scrape bone.

He had stabbed Faust in the forehead.

You went mad by fractions. The scream was still there rebounding inside his skull. It had been joined by many other voices also shrieking.

You went mad by trying to decide your next step.

You went mad with the wonder of Why.

Pace opened his mouth and a hundred tongues fell out. Disgusted, Faust drew away from them as they crept across the cave floor toward him.

The fire was out but Pace's skin still hissed and bubbled, the centuries-old dust clinging to his wounds, the popping blisters turning it to mud. Pace dove at Faust's legs and knocked him down.

He dragged himself forward until he had the knife at Faust's throat.

Jack moaned through clenched teeth, wanting to feast on cooked entrails. Frying them in the same way the Greeks did before their oracles, to learn their fortunes.

Pace's mouth watered so badly that he had to spit several times before he could speak.

Faust screamed, "Just do it. Kill me."

"No...I want answers."

"That's not how Jack plays!"

"I'm not Jack. Tell me...what happened."

"I don't remember! Finish me. I can't take it anymore!"

"I told you, nobody's going to die."

"You...you son of a bitch, you stuck a knife in my head! I killed your wife!"

Pace gasped, fighting back the pain. His flesh sang in agony. "That was Jane Pacella. She wasn't my wife." Pace gritted his teeth. These would be his scars, and nobody else's. Nobody else's, until the next guy got them. "Talk to me."

Faust swallowed and gagged as the stink of Pace's steaming flesh streamed into his nostrils. The torcher inside him came out and spoke quickly in a monotone, as if reciting. The words had gone around inside his head for so long, trapped there circling, that he knew them by rote.

"The consigliere got in touch with me about burning down *Emilio's*. It was easy money, a simple job. Restaurants always are. The fire marshals can't bitch about arson if you blow the gas main. The trick is to not go up with the place. The building was supposed to be empty. But there were still people there, in the back, scurrying like rats in the kitchen. I should've walked away from the job, but it was already inside me...the need to let the fire out, get it? The flames had already been stoked. I had to go through with it. I didn't even carry a gun. I just walked in and socked the help still in the kitchen. I'd never even *punched* anybody before. I knocked them down and tied them up. It was the fire's fault. It's always the fire's fault."

The muscles in Faust's face twitched but the voice was calm and level and barren. "I never killed anybody before in my life. Never even thought of it. I'm not like that. They don't pay extra for that. But they were there...

these people, these two Mexicans and the Greek girl, they were right there on the floor, and the more the fire spread, the more I wanted to watch somebody burn. I spritzed the accelerant around, watched them jump around. I was going to start tossing the kitchen staff in when your wife ran out covered in flame. It was beautiful."

"Faust—"

"Do it, Will. Do it with the knife or I swear I'll burn you again. I won't stop until I burn you alive. Our father who art inferno!"

Pace eased his own forehead against Faust's.

The scar pulsed, excited, and beat to its own rhythm. Pace felt all the struggling aspects, facets, beings, and beliefs in there, so much like his own. Faust's mouth opened and he let out a keening wail. His fists came up and he beat weakly at Pace's stomach and chest, the scorched blackened skin coming off in strips, until finally Pace moved his mouth over Faust's scar and licked at it, savoring the different histories like seasoning.

"Don't do that!" Faust screamed. "It's mine!"

"No, it's not," Pace said. "I gave it to you. It's mine. I gave you my affliction."

He pressed his lips to Faust's damage, feeling the pressure inside. Faust's alternates slipped out from beneath the ruined brain tissue and slid over Pace's teeth. Faust strained and went into a seizure and finally relaxed in Pace's arms.

Pace could taste the answers to his questions about what happened after that day at *Emilio's*.

Faust with a head wound, a four-inch-deep incision in his temporal lobe. Stumbling through the city at night as his personality leaked out behind him, step by step. He'd been paid twelve grand in cash for the restaurant torch job. The money was still on him, in his coat pockets, but he no longer knew what it meant or how to use it. Under six different names he had bank accounts in twenty cities across America, totaling four million bucks. The long green, the big spinach. But he couldn't remember any of the names, and now he had a head full of different people.

Faust had wandered the streets of New York until he passed out from exhaustion. He lived in the alleyways eating scraps out of garbage cans for months, with twelve thousand bucks on him, until he was rolled by a couple of upscale teenagers from the suburbs who liked to come into the city to beat the crap out of the homeless. He managed to survive while the people in his head tried to scratch their way out.

Eventually he got on the nerves of the corner grocery store owner who felt Faust's presence in the alley outside was driving off business. The cops rounded him up along with a dozen meth-fiends and schizophrenic homeless folks. They all took a van ride up to Garden Falls and wound up in group therapy together.

A year later he was the last one left from his original cluster of city jetsam. Sitting in his chair waiting for something to happen when Pace voluntarily committed himself and took the seat between Faust and Pia, across from Hayden, and said, "Hello, does Dr. Brandt stick needles in your necks too?"

thirty-two

Pace carried Faust back to the tomb, where Pia lay nearly unconscious draped over the polished stone.

Hayden came limping down the tunnel, totally drenched. He took a quick look around, and said, "Jesus, what happened. What's that smell?" Sniffing like a dog. "What'd you do, man? Is he dead? Is she dead?"

"No."

"They look dead. Sorry it took me so long to get here, but there was lightning all over the place. How did you run down the mountain? I couldn't do that. Nobody else could ever do that. I think I broke my ankle."

Pace stared at Hayden and asked, "What do I need to do with you?"

"What?"

"Tell me. You got some grievance with me?"

"Are you eating paste?"

"No."

"Don't eat paste!"

"I won't."

"What the hell happened to you? You're all burned up again, man!"

Faust began to come around. Pace set him down and Pia worked her fingers through Faust's hair, soothing him like a child. She caught Pace's eye and gestured to Hayden.

She said, "Go on. Go do it, Will. It's not for us, you know, that's not why you're doing it. It's for you."

Hayden said, "Oh no, oh no, what is this? You're not going to hurt me, are you, man? We both hate tuna. We are brother tuna-haters! You can't hurt one of your own!"

Pace didn't need to hug him or make any contact with him at all. He reached down and took Hayden's endless letter to his mother—the paper soggy and pulped together, the ink washed away—and again felt the sense of other people entering into him, leaking from the pages, the will behind all that writing, Hayden's flesh, through his cells, and across Pace's body, being absorbed into his skin. Crumble danced in circles, moving closer and closer to Pace's leg. Sister Lurteen took her Bible and the broken pieces of her yardstick and followed.

Hayden was holding out his arms to them, going, "Wait...hold it... wait! Don't! Don't go! What's happening here? This...this can't...what's happening? I don't want to be lonely!"

"You won't be," Pace said. "You're going to go out into the world and find a job, rent an apartment, and get yourself a girlfriend."

"Oh Christ, oh Christ no!"

"I'm sorry, Hayden."

"No!"

Too full of sorrow to even cry, Hayden's knees gave out and Pace caught him before he fell. He knew the feeling—the fear of becoming a whole person, of living only a single life. All three of them in the dirt were looking up at Pace, who stood above them carrying all the many wraiths of their stolen histories.

Pace led them single file through the tunnels. The three of them staggered after him, Pia occasionally calling for her father, Hayden for his mother, Faust stuffing his finger into his scar trying to push something back into his skull.

When they came up out of the underworld, the storm had broken. The black smooth night, heavy with promise and charged with possibility, seemed endlessly wide and empty around them, through which their small and forlorn passage meant everything and nothing.

In the morning, Pace sat on the beach and thought about going to look for the pit that Stavros...the second Stavros...had told him about. You dive in and go straight through the island and you don't stop.

Are you cured?

It was a trick question.

Was anybody, ever?

He would not give up his place. As ugly and ridiculous as it might seem, even to himself—to all the many *hims*—Pace simply enjoyed life too much.

Eventually Cassandra came down to the sand.

He wasn't sure if he could cure her of the affliction. He didn't know if he'd infected her or if she'd infected him, or if it mattered at all.

She stood over him and said, "The others are leaving. They don't want to see you."

"All right," he told her.

"One of the pilots will fly them to Voros in the helicopter. I've given them each one hundred thousand dollars."

"That was nice of you."

"No, it wasn't."

Pace asked, "Why wouldn't you take your father's money, Cassandra? When you came to the States?"

"Because I wanted to prove myself. That I could stand on my own and be my own person."

Pace turned away and stared at the sea again.

She said, "They wish to return to Garden Falls, but Vindi, our attorneys, and the accountants believe we can force the state to shut it down, so we can buy the land. I want it closed. I want the others to leave and go somewhere else, anywhere else. I want it *ended*."

He didn't have the heart to tell her, It will never end.

"Why did you steal pocket change from *Emilio's*?"

"To show that I was independent. That I could pay my tuition by myself." She tried to take his hand but it was like trying to grasp rock. "Please, let us go up to the house."

"I'd rather sit here a while."

"I want you to see the baby's room."

"I'm sure it's beautiful," he told her.

"You shouldn't look so sad, you're one of the richest men in the world now."

"That doesn't mean anything to me," he admitted.

"It will one day."

"I don't think so."

"Anything you want is already yours."

"I don't want anything."

The knife moved between his hands. He stopped it, grabbed the blade between two fingers, and threw it in the ocean.

"You're still holding it," she said. "You pretended to throw it away, but you've still got it in your hand."

Pace looked and there it was, in his fist. He sheathed the knife and wondered if he'd ever be rid of it. Or it of him.

"We must take care of your burns."

"I'm all right."

A hint of impatience tightened her voice. "You'll learn to love me."

"Maybe," he said.

She left and he sat and watched the waves curling, crashing, and receding. His father said, Thanks for taking out the garbage, son. But you forgot to put the rock over the can and the raccoons got in again, there's shit strewn all over the place, you think I got nothing better to do on my day off than run around the yard picking up old tuna cans?

Always with the tuna cans.

Robbie came by and sat in the sand. Pace asked, Hey, where's all the chicks? Robbie's chest opened and a martini and a lit cigarette popped out. He said, The chicks, sport, they're way too much, the chicks will drive you crazy.

The others followed and filled the beach, one by one. Jimmy Boyd, Smoker, all the kids building sand castles, making little moats, digging holes deep as graves. Jack stood at the shore wearing his leather apron, washing his red hands in the ocean. The tide grew bloody.

Pace thought he heard the baby who would be born in a few months, trying to tell him something important. Pace turned his ear and listened, but the whispers of the child were lost in the churning of the ocean. Jack cocked an ear too. He wanted a son badly and would fight to be the father.

Out there, in the red waters, Princess Eirrin watched him as the ghosts of drowned sailors swam about her.

William Pacella tried to rise to the surface one final time, but the guy was too weak and Pace resisted. There was a brief animal mewl of anguish, a breath heavy with tobacco and chocolate, and then nothing more.

Crumble ran by and the kids threw down their shovels and chased after him. Daedalus circled far above, catching a warm air draft as he sailed above the limestone caves in the cliffs. His tears fell like rain across the harbor. Thaddeus, friend and companion to St. Paul, was still spreading the word of Christ across a troubled world, going person to person along the beach, holding Paul's head out before him.

He whispered in Pace's ear and told him that Armageddon approached.

Pace didn't argue.

A moment later, Sariel and Rimmon sat beside him, waiting for the end times.

Rimmon, who grants success and good fortune, governor of the first order of seraphim, angel of lightning and fire, commanding 29,000 legions of burning choirs, stared into the horizon with a playful smile decaying on his lips. His sword was half-drawn, prepared to point at the sun.

Sariel, issuer of new bodies to the dead, chief of the repentants, possessor of the four keys to the four corners of the earth, and who will, when instructed by God, re-open the gates of Eden locked after the fall of humanity and guarded by the damned, reached out and offered Pace the keys.

Pace took them, raised them to his ear and gave them a little shake. The gentle ringing lifted the red waves higher and brought the moon closer. He still wasn't sure if he was the guy who was supposed to build the ark this time or the one who just makes it keep raining.

You've come a long way since sewing the pajamas in the Work Activities center. He wanted another shot at making an ashtray. This was the place where all our psyches have been driven down by love. Eros is the god behind vulnerability, who exposes all of mankind, through love, betrayal, and cruelty to the inseparable blend of pain and pleasure. Pace was prepared for the place beyond love and hate.

He opened his fist. There was another torn, curled slip of paper in it. He refused to read it, for now.

He sat at his post, guarding the oblivious and ongoing sleeping world around him, awaiting the next call from the Lord to put everything down again.

about the author

Tom Piccirilli is an American novelist and short story writer. He has sold over 150 stories in the mystery, thriller, horror, erotica, and science fiction fields. Piccirilli is a two-time winner of the International Thriller Writers Award for "Best Paperback Original" (2008, 2010). He is a four-time winner of the Bram Stoker Award. He was also a finalist for the 2009 Edgar Allan Poe Award given by the Mystery Writers of America, a final nominee for the Fantasy Award, and he won the first Bram Stoker Award given in the category of "Best Poetry Collection."

www.ingramcontent.com/pod-product-compliance
Lightning Source LLC
Chambersburg PA
CBHW060607310726
48982CB00008B/1268/J

* 9 7 8 1 9 3 7 5 3 0 2 8 0 *